A
White Christmas

IN WEBSTER COUNTY

LAURA V.
HILTON

WHITAKER
HOUSE

Publisher's Note:
This novel is a work of fiction. References to real events, organizations, or
places are used in a fictional context. Any resemblances to actual persons,
living or dead, are entirely coincidental.

All Scripture quotations are taken from the King James Version of the
Holy Bible.

A WHITE CHRISTMAS IN WEBSTER COUNTY
A Novel

Laura V. Hilton
http://lighthouse-academy.blogspot.com

ISBN: 978-1-62911-178-0
eBook ISBN: 978-1-62911-179-7
Printed in the United States of America
© 2014 by Laura V. Hilton

Whitaker House
1030 Hunt Valley Circle
New Kensington, PA 15068
www.whitakerhouse.com

Library of Congress Cataloging-in-Publication Data

Hilton, Laura V., 1963–
  A white Christmas in Webster County / Laura V. Hilton.
    pages cm
  Summary: "Mercy Lapp and Abner Hilty weren't looking for romance, but
anything can happen when a rare snowstorm strikes and tidings of joy are in
the air"—Provided by publisher.
  ISBN 978-1-62911-178-0 (alk. paper)
  1. Amish—Illinois—Fiction. 2. Christmas stories. I. Title.
  PS3608.I4665W58 2014
  813'.6—dc23
                          2014021370

1 2 3 4 5 6 7 8 9 10 11 **W** 21 20 19 18 17 16 15 14

Dedication

To all the readers who asked for a Christmas story, and to
Whitaker House for listening.

To my family, for picking up the slack despite all the chaos.

And as always, to God, who has, for now, blessed me with these.

Acknowledgments

No writer can do it alone. Thanks to Courtney, for her expert editing, and to my critique partners (you know who you are), especially the ones who really tear my work apart and ask questions that force me to take the story deeper.

Thank you to Steve, for doing most of the shopping; my children Michael and Kristin, for doing most of the cooking; and to everyone, for all your help in other areas.

Thanks to my church, Foothills Baptist Church, for praying me through, and for my horse-and-buggy team members and critique group who prayed when I didn't have a clue where the story was going or how to get there. God answered in a big way.

Glossary of Amish Terms and Phrases

ach	oh
aent(i)	aunt(ie)
"Ain't so?"	a phrase commonly used at the end of a sentence to invite agreement
boppli	baby or babies
bu	boy
bundling	a traditional courtship practice that involves spending the night side by side in bed (often in separate blankets or sacks), talking and getting to know each other, without actual intimacy
buwe	boys
daed	dad
danki	thank you
der Herr	the Lord
dochter	daughter
dummchen	a ninny; a silly person
ehemann	husband
Englisch	non-Amish
Englischer	a non-Amish person
frau	wife
Gott	God
grossdaedi	grandfather
gross-dochter	granddaughter
grosskinner	grandchildren
grossmammi	grandmother
gross-sohn	grandson
gut	good
"Gut morgen"	"Good morning"
"Gut nacht"	"Good night"
hallo	hello
haus	house

"Ich liebe dich"	"I love you"
jah	yes
kapp	prayer covering or cap
kinner	children
kum	come
maidal	an unmarried woman
mamm	mom
mann	husband
maud	maid/housekeeper
morgen	morning
nacht	night
nein	no
onkel	uncle
Ordnung	the rules by which an Amish community lives
rumschpringe	"running around time," a period of adolescence after which Amish teens choose either to be baptized in the Amish church or to leave the community
schön	beautiful
ser gut	very good
sohn	son
to-nacht	tonight
unwelkum	unwelcome
verboden	forbidden
"Was ist letz?"	"What is it?"
welkum	welcome
wunderbaar	wonderful

Chapter 1

"Would you kiss me?"

Mercy Lapp stumbled to a halt. She looked up from the list she'd been perusing and into a pair of beautiful, twinkling blue eyes. They belonged to a clean-shaven Amish man who held out a pair of plastic vampire teeth from a Halloween clearance rack. They were brown, crooked, and ugly. He moved them closer to her.

Her stomach lurched. "Ewww. Nein!"

He chuckled, then glanced around.

She followed his gaze. They were alone in the aisle. She turned her attention back to him, surprised to find him falling to his knees in front of her, his hands clasped together as if in prayer, the package of teeth dangling from his fingertips.

"Have mercy!" He puckered up in an exaggerated kiss.

She blinked. None of the Amish men back home acted like this. So bold. So...tempting.

"Please? I'll never get kissed by a pretty girl if I have teeth like these." He lifted his hand and shook the package.

She wrinkled her nose. "Enough already, jah?" She tried to look away from those yucky teeth but got distracted by a dimple in the bu's cheek.

He reached forward and fingered the hem of her dress—a bold move—then gazed up at her with an inquisitive expression as she stepped away. "An Amish-style dress. Pink. Camouflage. You aren't from around here, are you?"

Mercy's face heated. "Uh, nein. But...well, I just got here. I took a job advertised in *The Budget* for a mother's helper, and I haven't had time to make any new dresses. And Shanna, the woman I'm staying with, just laughed and said it'd probably be a gut thing to add some color around here anyway. I'm from Shipshewana." Her words tumbled out in a rush.

9

He slowly straightened to his full height, and she had to tilt her head back to see his face. "Shipshewana, really? Me, too. I'm here visiting my twin brother, Abram." He licked his lips as he returned the unopened package of false teeth to the display of clearance items. "I'm Abner Hilty."

Abner Hilty? She hadn't grown up in his district, but she vaguely remembered seeing him and his twin brother at various frolics. She never would've recognized him if he hadn't introduced himself. He'd filled out. Broader shoulders than she recalled. She eyed his upper arms. She couldn't tell much about his muscles, given his casual stance and his long shirtsleeves. Not that she should think about such things.

"I see a spark of recognition in your pretty hazel eyes." He leaned closer, studying her. "And you look familiar. I've seen you before."

"I'm M—"

"Don't tell me—I've got it," he said. "It's…Mary? Martha? Marianna?" He shuddered. "Nein, not her. Miriam? Melinda? Melissa? Mercy? Jah, Mercy! Mercy Lapp."

"I'm impressed." She smiled, flattered, even though he'd had to run through a list of names before guessing hers.

Abner chuckled. "Don't be. Your eyes lit up when I said it."

"Still impressed." Mercy backed up a step. "I need to buy the items Shanna needs and go to the grocery store. Her ehemann, Matthew, is running other errands in town, and I don't want to keep him waiting."

Abner grinned. "Happy Thanksgiving, Mercy. Maybe I'll see you around."

She doubted it. An unexpected flicker of disappointment shot through her. She squashed it. She wasn't here for a relationship. "Maybe." She looked at her list again. Primarily supplies to make homemade laundry soap: Borax, Fels-Naptha or Ivory bar soap, Arm & Hammer Super Washing Soda….

Abner's fingers grazed hers. Sparks shot up her arm. She jerked away in surprise.

"Hey, I mean it. McDonald's sometime? I'll treat you to a…a pumpkin spice milk shake, if they're still available. If not, then an eggnog one."

The invitation evoked mixed feelings. She and Paul used to order pumpkin spice milk shakes, but never eggnog. Paul didn't care for the taste. Mercy did.

She nodded. "Jah. Jah, fine." She'd like the treat, but she was still settling into her new job and doubted she'd have enough free time.

"You want a firm date? I see doubt in your eyes. Very expressive, they are. How about Friday? I'll pick you up. Give me directions."

She forced a smile and backed up another step. "Maybe some other time. Danki, though." She took a deep breath, moved to the side, and hurried down the aisle.

"I'd really like to see you again."

"I have to clear it with Matthew and Shanna," she said over her shoulder. Not that she would. She was here to escape the memories, not relive them. "See you." She waved and then turned at the endcap.

❧

Abner watched her go with the unfamiliar sensation that his heart had just disappeared around the corner with her. He looked back at the discarded teeth on the shelf beside a plastic ghost. "Not my best pick-up line, ain't so?"

The teeth didn't answer. But then, he would've run screaming from the store if they had.

He hadn't had enough time to think of a better line. Picking up girls wasn't something he did on a regular basis. But when he'd seen the pretty blonde walking down the aisle, he'd had to say something—anything—to get her attention. It was as if a fancy neon light had flashed the words, "Here she is. She's the one."

Maybe he should've taken notes when his friends or his brothers had asked girls out.

He swallowed an unwelkum lump in his throat and turned away from the clearance shelf. His twin brother's new bride, Katie, had sent him in here for one thing, and one thing only, and he had gotten sidetracked. She wanted a couple of pumpkin- or spice-scented candles for the dining-room table. Not that they were needed. She and her mamm, Mose Detweiler's Ruthie, had been baking up a storm since Abner's arrival, making apple pies, pumpkin pies, mincemeat pies, and who knew what else. The haus already smelled mouth-wateringly delicious. Katie's biological sister and brother, who were Englisch, and their significant others would also be joining Katie's family for Thanksgiving.

With real sweets tempting the senses, why did she want to add food-scented candles? Women baffled him. Abner, Abram, and Abram's father-in-law, Mose, had enough trouble staying away from the treats. With three days to go until Thanksgiving, their stomachs would be making a perpetual rumble.

Katie and her mamm had gone to the grocery store to start purchasing ingredients for Thanksgiving dinner. Big bags of flour and sugar were on the list, as they had even more baking to do before Thursday. More! Why'd they need more? But then again, that meant there'd be more gut food for Abner to eat.

His stomach growled at the thought.

Mose and Abram were busy with something at the farm, so Abner had been recruited to take the women to the store. And sent, alone, for the candles.

He found the display and picked out two, then headed for the checkout line, trying to ignore the prominent display of candy bars.

Mercy was three people ahead of him in line. Most of her purchases looked like soap-making supplies. Abner recognized them from the countless times his mamm had made soap. Mercy paid the Englisch clerk, carried her purchases out of the store, then disappeared around the corner. Gone, with nein chance for him to talk more with her. He wished he'd found out how to contact her.

Wait. He smiled.

Hadn't Mercy said she was going to the grocery store?

Once more, Mercy studied the grocery list Shanna had given her. She wasn't familiar with this particular store. After all, it was the first time she'd been here. But most stores seemed to be laid out generally the same. Mamm always shopped the perimeter of the store for meats and cheeses and the few vegetables they didn't raise in their garden, and Shanna's list seemed to indicate that she did pretty much the same thing. There was neinmeat on the shopping list, since Matthew raised a few chickens, turkeys, hogs, and beef cattle. But she did need to pick up walnuts, cranberries, carrots, and celery, as well as bags of apples and oranges. She'd start in the produce section.

She bagged several scoops of mixed nuts, still in the shell, tied the bag shut, then added it to the cart. Nuts weren't on Shanna's list, but Mercy's family always used a bowl of them as a Thanksgiving centerpiece. And after dinner, they sat around, cracking nuts, drinking hot cocoa, and—

"So, we meet again." A male voice intruded.

She looked up from the cart. Her gaze traveled up a broad chest, trailed past a firm chin, and met a pair of familiar blue eyes. A foreign flutter filled her stomach. She gulped. Was he following her?

Abner winked and held out a ragged-edged piece of paper. "Shopping. I got part of a list from my sister-in-law, Katie. Told her we should divide and conquer." He pushed his cart alongside Mercy's. "Those nuts look gut." He glanced down at his paper. "Not on the list, though. She wrote 'some ingredients for saltwater taffy.' What does that mean? How do women shop like this?" He scratched his head.

Mercy giggled. Mamm wrote her lists the same way. It felt gut to laugh. It'd been a long time. "For saltwater taffy, you'll need salt, butter, flavoring, food color, sugar, cornstarch, light corn syrup—"

"But how do I know which of those are included in 'some'?"

"Why don't you go ask her? She's here, ain't so?"

Abner nodded. "But—"

"The other option is to assemble them all and then put back whatever she doesn't need."

He wrinkled his nose. "Involves backtracking. I'll ask. Better yet, I'll just give the list back to her and follow you around instead."

Mercy blinked. "Follow me? Why?" Though it made some sense that a man who'd both asked her to kiss him and invited her on a date within five minutes of meeting her might also be forward enough to trail her around a store. For a second, she basked in the flattery, but then she put up a wall of defense. She had nein right to enjoy his company. Not when—

"Why not?" Abner shrugged. "You're pretty and single, and I like you. I'd feel weird following my sister-in-law and her mamm around. Besides, they know there's a girl involved." He nodded at two Amish women staring at them from a couple rows over. "Kum meet them."

"What? Why?" Mercy picked up a bag of celery, hoping to distance herself. Then she winced. *Celery. Weddings.* Something that wouldn't be happening for her. Not this fall. *Not ever.* Her eyes burned. Still, Abner's warmth beside her, and his deep voice teasing her from above, brought back welkum memories. What was the chance that this feeling would last? She shook her head.

"Katie's really shy," Abner whispered. "I think she'd like to have a chance to get to know her future sister-in-law before we marry."

Mercy's mouth dropped open, and she stared up at him as the celery slipped from her hand and hit the floor.

His eyes widened, as if he'd just realized what he'd said. A dull red crept up his neck, and he bent to pick up the celery. "Kum on." His hand grasped her elbow. Sparks flared as he tugged her toward the two women. "Katie, Ruthie, this is Mercy. Mercy, meet my sister-in-law, Katie, and her mamm, Ruthie." He handed Katie his part of the grocery list. "I want to invite Mercy to the taffy pull."

"Sure, you're invited." Katie's face turned a bright pink, and her smile faded, her expression turning almost sympathetic as she studied Mercy. "I guess all the Hilty brothers move relationships along at dizzying speeds. Four months ago, I didn't even know Abram. And now we're married. Hang on for the ride, Mercy."

Four months? Married? Mercy reared back. "Actually, this is scaring me. And I see Matthew." Not really, but he would be there soon. "Nice meeting you." She managed what she hoped was a polite smile and tried to keep from racing back to her cart to finish shopping.

Abner Hilty was scary. Very scary.

But also gut-looking. Outgoing. And apparently interested.

She glanced back at him.

He'd turned and started walking away, as if her public rejection meant nothing.

Disappointment ate at her.

Maybe he wasn't interested, after all. Maybe he was just…scary.

Either way, she would be keeping her distance.

Any other girl would be running into his arms, but Mercy's heart couldn't take being pulled around like taffy.

Chapter 2

*A*bner heaved a pitchfork of hay into a stall, then paused to rub his grumbling stomach. At least out here in the barn, he couldn't smell the meal being prepared. He looked at Abram and Mose working nearby. Both of them stole frequent glances at the haus, too. Maybe it was best to stay busy to keep his mind off his hunger. His stomach kept up its complaints, and he feared he'd flat out starve if he didn't eat soon.

He wouldn't get any sympathy, though. When he and Abram had tried to snatch a couple of cookies earlier that morgen, Ruthie had slapped their hands. And when he'd attempted to lift a biscuit, Katie had scolded him. Ach, to be a child again. Adults fasted during the morgen on Thanksgiving, giving thanks to Gott. Supposedly. Mostly, they visited. Kinner were allowed to eat, but there weren't any here this year. Next year, possibly.

A pang of envy shot through him. He probably shouldn't be jealous of his twin brother, but he wanted what Abram had. Well, not Katie, specifically, though she was cute. But a frau…Mercy. Just as Abram had once said about Katie, there was something about her his heart had recognized.

A little later, two cars pulled into the driveway: one pink—Really? Abner thought—and the other a bluish-green color. He watched as the man driving the pink car carried a casserole dish to the haus, then came back to assist a thin, dark-haired woman wearing tight blue jeans up the stairs and inside. The man from the other car looked around, briefly met Abner's gaze, and then headed for the barn, leaving his frau to go inside alone with two more casserole dishes. Abner couldn't imagine that any more food was necessary, considering the abundance of dishes and desserts Katie and Ruthie had prepared.

At least there would be plenty of leftovers.

His stomach rumbled. Again. He glanced at his pocket watch. Only ten. Jah, he'd starve in the two hours remaining before they could eat.

The Englisch man approached him. "Whew. Some interesting smells in here." He wrinkled his nose.

Abner shrugged. It smelled like any other barn, with a hint of something soapy, probably from the supplies used to make soap. Which made him think of Mercy…again. He forced his mind back to the present.

The Englisch man wore black pants, a black belt, and a light blue button-up shirt with a multicolored tie. He resembled some of the businessmen Abner had seen around Shipshewana. He held out his hand. "I'm Wesley, Katie's biological brother. We met at the wedding, but I'm sure you were too busy looking at your bride—"

Abner shook his head as he took Wesley's hand. "That'd be Abram. He's back there." He nodded toward the other end of the barn. "I'm his twin brother, Abner." Abner hadn't been at the wedding. He hadn't found out about it in time. Instead, he'd scheduled a visit for November. After they'd been married almost a month. *Still newlyweds.* His face heated.

"Nice to meet you, Abner. I'll go find Abram and let him know I'm here, then find my wife." Wesley smiled politely before turning away.

Wife. Another pang. Everyone would be paired up. He'd be the lone man out.

He really had to get over this. Maybe he could hitch up a buggy and go get Mercy. But he didn't have any idea where she lived. When he'd asked Abram if he knew where he might find her, his brother had just given him a blank stare. He didn't dare ask Katie, not after she'd teased him about being smitten with a girl at the store.

Smitten. Jah, that pretty much described it.

Hopefully, he'd see Mercy again. Maybe she'd kum to the taffy pull Saturday nacht. Katie had told him it was open to everyone, but that wasn't really true. It was for all the singles in their rumschpringe. Ruthie had hosted it every year and wasn't prepared to give it up yet. Now, Katie would be a chaperone instead of an attendee.

How would Mercy know where it was being held unless she lived in the same district? And she didn't. At least, Abner hadn't seen her at church on Sunday.

He sighed. He doubted Mercy would be there, especially after her parting words: *"Actually, this is scaring me."* He pulled in a breath. Scaring her hadn't been his intention.

The plastic teeth he'd teased her with had been rather gross, but the rest of him was an attractive package, at least according to the giggly girls back home. He probably shouldn't have stalked her from store to store. That had probably scared her more than the teeth.

There hadn't been any teeth on display at the grocery store. Nein, there'd just been a declaration of his intent to marry, made over a bag of celery. His face warmed.

Mose stepped over to Abner, who'd been leaning against the barn door, staring out into the fields. Slacking. Mose stood in silence, gazing out at the same landscape. The sky was gray, as if it might rain. The remnants of the heavy morgen fog still lingered in spots. Some trees still held dead leaves, waiting for a hard rain and strong wind to bring them down. The horses and cows were grazing—

"Who is she?"

Abner about jumped out of his skin. His heart pounded as he spun around to look at Mose. "Who?"

"The girl you're interested in."

Flames of embarrassment licked at his cheeks. *Interested in.* Such a mild phrase. He smiled, remembering the sparks he'd felt during the too-brief time he'd touched her. "Ach, Mercy Lapp. She's…she answered an ad in *The Budget* to work as a mother's helper for Matthew's Shanna." He didn't know their last name, but Shanna wasn't a common name among the Amish. Hope flared. Maybe Mercy wouldn't be all that hard to find.

Mose raised his hand and pointed north. "A couple of districts over. I'll draw a map later. After we eat. Don't want you racing there now." A smile quirked his mouth.

Abner scrunched his nose, trying to stay calm. Inside, he was jumping up and down as if it were Christmas morgen and a coveted pair of ice skates waited on the wood box. "What makes you think I would do that?"

"I've seen your brother in action." Mose leveled a gaze at him. "The girl's not going to have a chance. I'm feeling the urge to write her daed and warn him about you."

Abner looked away. "I'm not going to cause any trouble."

Mose snorted. "Right. I'll believe that when I see it."

Jah. So would Abner.

                              ❧

"Make mine chocolate."

Nodding, Mercy filled two glasses with milk, stirred some chocolate powder into them, and situated herself across from Shanna at the kitchen table. Shanna took a straw from the colorful bouquet in the glass jar in the center of the table, stuck it in her glass, and took a sip. "Mmmm. Awesome." She rubbed her very pregnant belly. "As much as my back aches today, I wonder if I'll last another month."

Mercy glanced at the wall calendar, a year's worth of peaceful pasture scenes with Scripture verses in Englisch. This month's verse was Psalm 61:2: *"From the end of the earth will I cry unto thee, when my heart is overwhelmed: lead me to the rock that is higher than I."*

Appropriate, especially considering she'd kum here because of her overwhelmed heart. She swallowed the sudden lump that had formed in her throat. "I thought Englisch verses were frowned upon." In her district, only German Bibles were allowed.

Shanna looked at the calendar as if she'd never seen it before, then shrugged, the same way she'd done when she'd seen Mercy's pink camouflage dress. "Easier to understand, ain't so?" She kept her gaze on the picture, or maybe the numbers. "My due date is Christmas, but a boppli tends to kum when it wants, not according to a calendar. I'm more than ready for this little bu to arrive."

"A bu?"

Shanna shrugged. "Maybe. According to old wives' tales, you can tell based on the heart rate. It's fairly accurate. A mamm usually knows."

Mercy glanced down at Shanna's little girl, eleven-month-old Serena, who made a gurgling sound and pulled herself up on the edge of Mercy's chair to stand, wobbling slightly.

"I'm exhausted, but Matthew wants to go for a walk before bed." Shanna's smile was soft. "He's not ready to give up our walks. I hope he never is. I enjoy our time together. But, wow. Even with you here doing the bulk of the work, preparing Thanksgiving dinner for my whole family exhausted me. I didn't know Mamm put so much effort into it." She laughed and set down her empty glass. "I never should've volunteered to host. I didn't know I would be expecting another wee one so soon."

The door opened, and Matthew peeked in. "Ready, Shanna? Would you like to join us, Mercy?"

"Dada dada da," Serena squealed, falling on her bottom with a thump.

Grinning, Matthew wiped his shoes on the mat, strode across the room, and scooped up Serena in his arms, holding her to his chest. She squealed again, splaying her tiny fingers in his short beard.

Shanna pushed to her feet. "Jah. Let me get my shoes. Feel free to join us, Mercy."

"Danki, but I think I'll stay here and read." She didn't want to intrude on their date. "Let me check her diaper before you go." She stood and reached for Serena.

The boppli snuggled against Matthew's chest. "Dada dada dada."

Matthew chuckled. "I'll take care of it this time, Mercy. But danki." He raised his daughter higher and blew noisily against her belly. She squealed again as they disappeared down the hall.

Shanna picked up her glass, carried it over to the sink, and rinsed it out. "What are you reading?"

"A historical about a logging camp in Michigan. I haven't started it yet, but the librarian recommended it. She said it was about common people, and I'd probably find it more to my liking than one about the Gilded Age. Whatever that is."

Shanna laughed as Matthew reappeared. He caught her hand in his and opened the kitchen door.

Mercy sighed. Someday, maybe someone would love her like Matthew did his frau. Someday, she'd ride in a buggy after dark with her beau. And take long walks. And...*nein*. She shook her head.

"See you in a little while." Shanna stepped outside, then squeaked.

"Hallo," said Matthew. "May I help you?"

"I hope so," said a male voice. "I'm looking for Mercy Lapp."

Mercy's eyes widened. *Abner?* He *was* scary. How had he managed to find her? But her traitorous heart jumped in anticipation. Spending time with a bu, instead of being left alone trying to escape her thoughts, memories of—

Matthew glanced over his shoulder and raised an eyebrow at Mercy. Nein doubt he would question her upon his return from the walk. *Only a week into your stay, and already buwe are coming around? And I thought you said you weren't interested in a new relationship.*

But with Abner? Her heart jumped again. *Tell him I'm not here,* she willed. But Matthew wouldn't lie. *Tell him to go away.* Even though it'd been a year, she wasn't ready.

Matthew took a step forward. "Mercy will be right out. Have a seat on the swing."

Mental telepathy hadn't worked. She had nein choice but to join Abner. Her disloyal heart leapt again. Although…she could be rude and go upstairs to read, pretending she didn't know he was here.

A shiver worked its way up her spine.

Would he hesitate to kum inside and look for her?

⌒⌒⌒

Abner adjusted his suspenders a little, then sat on the swing and set it in motion, eyeing the front door in anticipation. In mere minutes, he'd be with Mercy. Maybe he'd get to touch her hand again. He wiped his sweaty palms on his pant legs. He could hope. But, probably not. They weren't courting. And judging by the way she'd jerked away when he'd touched her elbow at the store a couple of days ago, the gesture wouldn't be welkum.

He sighed. He *had* to be attracted to a woman who didn't like him. Who thought he was scary. Unless she'd been referring to the taffy pull, but those weren't scary. They were fun. Sometimes, couples leaned across the table to steal a kiss while they worked.

And there he went again, fantasizing about having a girl to call his own. Funny how it hadn't bothered him until he'd met Mercy. Now, he wasn't content to wait for a relationship. He wanted it now.

Daed would have something to say about patience being a virtue.

Long minutes crawled by as Abner waited in the gathering dusk, listening to the katydids, the sounds of other unidentified insects, and the honks of the Canada geese stopping along their southward migration to spend the nacht at a nearby pond.

Mercy wasn't going to join him. She must've been standing in the kitchen when Matthew had turned back. Must've heard. And she'd decided to ignore him? That hurt. Abner stood, staring at the shut door. Willing her to appear.

Nothing.

His shoulders slumped as he turned to go. She couldn't have made her disinterest clearer if she'd handwritten it on paper in bold black marker. Had she heard something about him from back home that had made her wary? Had she found out he wasn't the perfect Amish bu he'd long pretended to be?

He grimaced and shook his head. He wouldn't think of that. Besides, she couldn't know. Nobody knew.

He growled.

Something creaked behind him, and he turned. The door opened, and Mercy appeared. Abner sucked in a breath. If he'd thought she was gorgeous in pink camouflage, she was even more appealing in dark green—a shade that reminded him of the pine trees back home.

"Wow. You're beautiful."

Her cheeks flamed red.

Why did he have to blurt out what he was thinking? He'd have to watch it, or he'd scare her more, spilling his hopes, dreams, and desires before she had a chance to decide if she liked him.

"How'd you find me?" she asked.

He blinked. "I asked Mose Detweiler. He drew me a map." He reached into his pocket and pulled out the crumpled piece of paper.

She gave it a cursory glance. "Would you like something to drink? A slice of pie?"

"Ach, nein on the pie, danki. I'm stuffed. But a drink would be gut." Stressing on the way to see a girl and then sweating it out on a porch swing was thirsty work, in spite of the cool autumn temperatures.

"What would you like? I can make koffee or tea, or we have some cider that Matthew made."

"Cider would be gut."

She indicated the swing. "Be right back."

He glanced in that direction, then again at her, watching the sway of her skirt as she hurried inside.

He bit his lower lip, wiped his palms again, and sat. He bounced his knee while he waited, and when the door opened again, he pressed his fist down to try to still it. Or maybe it was okay for her to see his nervousness.

She carried only one mug, which she handed to him, and then she took a seat on a chair as far from him as she could get without picking it up and moving it to the opposite side of the porch.

So much for holding her hand.

"So, how was your Thanksgiving?" she inquired politely. "You were with your brother and his family, jah?"

He knew he had to start somewhere to earn her trust, but he didn't want to rehash the day he'd spent with Englisch strangers. They were relatives of Katie's, and she was still in the process of becoming acquainted with them. Extremely awkward, especially when the one Englisch man, Tyler, had looked at Abner and then at his brother before muttering, "Thing One and Thing Two." Abram had looked as confused as Abner still felt.

But he didn't know what else to talk about. All the wunderbaar topics he'd dreamed up on the way over had fallen off the buggy as he'd pulled into the drive, leaving him befuddled. Like a dummchen. Just how he wanted to appear. Not.

He blew out a sigh of frustration and shrugged. "Fine. Yours?" He took a sip of the cider. It was gut. She'd added a touch of cinnamon.

She gave him an odd look, as if to say, *"You went to all the trouble of tracking me down, and all you can say is 'Fine'?"*

He grimaced. She'd spent the day with strangers, too.

A look of discomfort crossed her face, and she glanced toward the road, as if searching for a distraction.

She probably was, so she could send him on his way.

"Gut. It was gut." She looked back at him.

"Can I kum by to get you for the taffy pull next weekend?" he asked. "There'll be others there. A frolic. It'll introduce you to some of the other young people in the area. Please?" His knee started jiggling again. Nerves. A habit he'd thought he'd broken.

She didn't seem to notice his tap-dancing leg. Instead, she shook her head as an expression akin to fear crossed her face. She folded her arms protectively over her chest, seeming to physically retreat. Why would she fear taffy pulls? That didn't make sense.

"I can't. I was hired to be a mother's helper, not to attend frolics. And besides, I—" She pressed her lips together.

"What? Besides what?"

Moisture gathered on her eyelashes. She shook her head, then stood and fled.

Abner jumped to his feet as the kitchen door slammed behind her.

Matthew rounded the corner of the haus. Alone.

Chapter 3

*M*ercy jumped over the ruins of a fallen toy tower in the kitchen, then skidded to a stop, halting her dash through the haus. Serena likely would have fallen asleep by the time Shanna and Matthew returned from their walk, and they wouldn't wake her to clean up her toys.

Mercy turned and scooped up the colorful wooden alphabet blocks, dumping them into the wicker basket that had been handmade by someone in the community. Shanna had mentioned the person's name, but Mercy couldn't remember it. At the time, it hadn't meant anything to her. Right now, she wondered. It beat thinking about the man she'd left sitting outside.

The man who wanted to court her.

Well, maybe not *court*. Taking someone to a taffy pull didn't require a lifetime commitment. It was simply a chance to get to know each other. As friends. And a chance to—what had he said? Meet other young people in the area?

He certainly hadn't said anything about making her fall in love with him, only to leave her struggling with a shattered heart.

He couldn't know that her heart had been broken beyond repair. That she was still picking up the tiny shards.

Mercy sighed. She'd overreacted. Was he still outside? She should go apologize. He wasn't suggesting they get married or anything.

Wait. He had said something about marriage.

Scary.

And not worth any more thought. He'd change his mind fast enough when she kept refusing to have anything to do with him. He would never win her over. Especially after what she'd been through.

She picked up the basket of blocks and started for the living room, almost plowing into Shanna.

"Whoa! What's your hurry?" Shanna grasped her shoulders. "Slow down. That bu didn't try anything inappropriate, did he?"

"Jah, he invited me to a taffy pull." Mercy's voice shook, then broke. She pulled out of Shanna's grasp.

Shanna tilted her head. "And that's so terrible…how? Sounds fun to me. I haven't been to one in ages."

"I'm not here to court. I'm here to work, and I told him so." Mercy straightened her shoulders.

Shanna shrugged. "We never expected you not to socialize. Go. Have fun. I can manage for a few hours here and there, ain't so? Tell him you changed your mind and you'll go. Unless you don't like him. But even then, there'll be other buwe there."

Ach, she liked him fine. At least, what she knew of him. Except the scariness factor. And that might have more to do with fearing for the safety of her heart than of actually being afraid of him. But…. "My fiancé drowned a year ago, remember? I'm not ready." Tears burned her eyes.

Shanna blinked. "I know grief sets its own schedule, but you need to start living again, and a taffy pull will be just the thing. Kum on."

Mercy shook her head and peered past Shanna at the stroller, where Serena lay sleeping. "I'll put her to bed."

Shanna frowned, opened her mouth as if to argue, then shut it. "Danki." She moved past Mercy and opened the back door. A few seconds later, the latch clicked.

Mercy carried Serena upstairs and gently laid her in her crib. She hadn't expected Shanna to give in to her wishes, but she had, easily enough.

A blessing, to be sure.

Still, disappointment ate at her. It might've been fun to attend a frolic with others her age. To make friends. But she didn't want to be part of a couple. Or maybe she did. She wanted to be loved. And to be in love. But without Paul….

She'd vowed to love him forever. Then he'd left on that horrible rumschpringe trip, fishing on Lake Michigan. It must've been some storm that had blown in, because only one of the buwe had returned. The rest were presumed dead, even though nein bodies had been recovered. The Coast Guard officer had told her the lake didn't always give up its dead.

Hot tears burned her eyes, and her shoulders slumped. After a year, she barely remembered Paul's face. The sound of his voice. But she couldn't risk heartbreak again. Couldn't. She'd promised.

⤜⤏

"You need to respect her wishes. If she doesn't want to see you, then stay far away." Matthew's voice was stern, as if he expected Abner to nod his agreement and then make his exit.

Abner hung his head, his fists clenched at his sides. He wanted to argue. Instead, he clamped his lips together. Maybe he would leave.

He could do that much, at least. Abner started down the steps, his heart aching.

How could he stay away from the one girl who'd caught his attention? How would he convince her that he was *the one* if she wouldn't have anything to do with him?

Abner had just reached the bottom step when the door swung open again. "She'll go," said a slightly husky female voice.

What? Hope flooded his heart, and he turned around. *She will?*

"Shanna…." There was a buggy-full of warning in Matthew's voice.

"What?" Shanna raised her eyebrows. "He invited her to a taffy pull, and she didn't think we'd let her go." Her attention shifted to Abner. "You'll be nice, jah?"

Of course. He nodded.

"Shanna…." Matthew said again. He exhaled, then shook his head. "You shouldn't interfere. I mentioned—"

"She *might* be a little worried that's it's too soon after the death of her fiancé. But it's been a year. I don't care if she's ready or not. It's time."

Matthew shook his head but remained mute.

Dead fiancé? Abner's mouth worked, but nothing came out. Though, he could sympathize. Hadn't he felt the same way when his closest friends had all been murdered, and he'd fled to a faraway state?

"I still leave men speechless. Love that. Especially when Bishop Sol is left without words." Shanna laughed, then glanced at Abner. "She'll be there," she assured him, then turned and went inside.

Abner glanced at Matthew and shrugged. "Danki." He'd found his voice, but it quavered—whether with thanksgiving and relief that she would kum after all, or with empathy and pain, he didn't know. Maybe a combination of both. "I'll be nice, I promise. And I'll bring her home aft—"

"One shouldn't interfere with matters of the heart," Matthew muttered before going inside.

Abner's shoulders slumped as he trudged to the waiting horse and buggy. Mercy had run away, and someone else had pushed her to go with him. Before him loomed a big battle to win her broken heart. He grimaced. Her pain reminded him of the hurt he was still trying to forget.

He untied the horse's reins, then climbed inside the buggy, glancing up at the lit window on the second floor. She stood there, gazing down at him.

He found a smile and waved.

She raised her hand, a soft smile beginning. Then it faded. She spun away and disappeared.

His heart hurt as he stared at the empty window. She'd been engaged to another man. He didn't want her on the rebound.

But he wanted her. Wanted to spend time with her. Wanted more than he had the right to want at this point.

Would she really kum?

Mercy fidgeted on the buggy seat next to Matthew. His mouth was set in a firm line, making her uneasy. Shanna had been called away to assist with a childbirth, so Matthew had stopped by her parents' haus long enough to leave Serena with her grossmammi, then continued on with Mercy by his side.

Destination unknown.

At least, Mercy didn't know where they were headed. She just did as she was told. Matthew had said "Kum," and she'd gone, trying to remember where she needed to go and why. Maybe to pick up more of those disposable diapers Shanna used on the boppli at nacht. The supply was getting low. Or was there another reason? Maybe she'd remember by the time they reached wherever they were going. If not, she'd ask.

The sky was gray and overcast. The colorful leaves that remained on the trees were upside-down, as if expecting rain, and a slight breeze stirred the topmost branches. The horse clip-clopped down the dirt road, going past small Amish farms that vaguely reminded Mercy of home. Laundry hung limply on clotheslines. They passed a young bu leading a horse down the road. The scene beckoned with peace and dreams of the future that her heart longed for. If only Paul hadn't gone on that trip....

Matthew pulled into a yard where plenty of other buggies were already parked. The haus was big, with a long porch and a roof overhanging it. An inviting swing hung there, too. He maneuvered the buggy around the circular drive and stopped by the front steps. "Here you go."

Laughter spilled out the open door.

Mercy blinked and turned to look at Matthew. "Where are we?"

His Adam's apple bobbed. His brow furrowed. "Shanna didn't tell you?"

"Nein." She'd said nothing. And Matthew had just told her to "kum."

Matthew glanced over her shoulder. Behind her, footsteps sounded.

Her stomach churned as the *who*, *what*, and *where* suddenly dawned. "Nein—"

"Mercy, you came!"

She heard a smile in Abner's voice. Her stomach came alive, as if filled with zillions of tiny butterflies fluttering their wings at once. Her heart jumped. But....

Nein. Nein. Nein. She stared at Matthew, speechless.

Abner's fingers grazed her waist. Sparks shot through her.

"May I help you out?"

She sucked in a deep breath, found her courage, as well as some semblance of a smile, and turned—into his arms. He lifted her out of the buggy and held her a second while she found her footing. "Danki." Her voice shook with the effort to pretend to be happy and polite, like Mamm had taught her. Might as well make the best of it.

A smile lit his face. "Kum on. I'll introduce you to everyone." He led her up the stairs and into the kitchen, where a long table was set up, with buwe on one side, maidals on the other. Abner rattled out a steady stream of names. They all floated past her, not registering. All she saw was a sea of unfamiliar faces.

Except for Katie. She remembered her. And a man who must be Abner's twin brother. She could see the resemblance beneath the beginnings of a beard. But she couldn't recall his name.

"Let me take your purse and bonnet." Katie approached and waited until Mercy handed them to her. "You can wash your hands over there." She nodded toward the sink, where Abner already stood, rinsing off soap suds.

Mercy did as instructed, returning the friendly greetings of the other youth as she passed. The whole experience brought back memories of home and the last taffy pull she had attended—with Paul. She forced her smile to stay put. The scent of the cooking candy made her mouth water.

"Sit here." Abner pulled out a chair next to another girl and held it while Mercy slid in. His fingers brushed her upper back as he gripped the chair and pushed it in. Then he hurried around the table, a bounce in his step, a grin on his face. He dropped into the empty seat across from her.

Katie's mamm placed some candy between them. "Be sure to oil your hands. And be careful. The candy feels cool enough to touch, but it might still be hot underneath."

As Mercy oiled her hands, Abner lifted the chocolate taffy from the pan with an oiled spatula and formed it into a cylindrical shape. Mercy reached across the table and took one end, pulling it toward her. It sagged in the middle.

Abner grinned at her as they began working together, pulling and twisting, mixing in the syrup, until the taffy finally began to hold its shape.

The girl next to her leaned closer. "I'm Natalie Wagler. And that's Abner's cousin Micah Graber." She nodded at the man across from her. They were pulling glossy, pearly yellowish taffy. Butterscotch, maybe. It looked done.

"Nice to meet you both," Mercy said. "I'm Mercy Lapp." She glanced pointedly at their candy. "I didn't realize I was late."

"Just a little." Micah set down his end of the taffy and wiped his fingers on a towel as Natalie raised her hand, indicating they'd finished. Micah pulled a persimmon from his pocket, as well as a pocketknife. *Odd.*

A new experience in a new location.

"At least you're here. That's all that matters." Abner moved his sock-covered foot so that it bumped Mercy's. She pulled back, not prepared to deal with the sparks or the memories. She didn't want to encourage him. While she had kum here with him, it didn't necessarily mean she would do things with him in the future.

"Ach, don't worry about being late," Natalie told her. "We've plenty to do. We all get to take some taffy home. Getting a start on the holiday candy-making. Want to kum to my haus two weekends from now and help make fudge?"

Making friends here—friends who hadn't known Paul and therefore wouldn't mention him—was a definite benefit.

"Sounds fun, but I'll have to ask permission."

"I hope you can. I can't wait to get to know you."

"Me, neither," Abner said.

Micah removed the seed from the persimmon. "Grossdaedi heard there was a shovel in the seed. I want to see." He split the seed in two, then held up the halves. A little white spade shape appeared. "That means we're supposed to have a snowy winter."

"That'd be nice." Natalie glanced at Mercy. "We don't get much snow in southern Missouri." She looked at Abner. "Not like Indiana."

Abner chuckled. "I probably won't need as big a snow shovel as I used in Montana."

Montana? What about Shipshewana?

At any rate, it would be fun to play in the snow…maybe with a man by her side. Strolling with her mittened hand held firmly by his larger, stronger one….

Her cheeks warmed. She glanced at Abner. He met her gaze and winked, slowly, deliberately. Almost as if he had read her thoughts.

Her heart thudded in response.

Maybe, just maybe, it'd be okay to get to know Abner. As a friend.

But as she gazed into his twinkling blue eyes while they worked together, twisting and pulling the chocolate taffy, something shifted.

Friendship wouldn't be enough. Not as attracted as she was.

Yet it would have to suffice.

She'd have to be careful to guard her heart. There was nein way she was going to fall in love.

Chapter 4

*A*bner had told Matthew Yoder that he would bring Mercy home after the taffy pull, but uncertainty filled him due to the mixed signals he'd been picking up from her during the frolic. He didn't want to scare her off.

He bounced on his heels as he stood in line to get something to drink. He wasn't sure what Katie had prepared. Something with fresh strawberries, pineapple, Sprite, and ice cream, served in a big glass bowl with a ladle. He remembered those ingredients because she'd threatened him if he so much as thought about getting into them beforehand.

Gut thing she couldn't read his mind.

Tell a man he couldn't eat something, and his stomach remembered it. And asked for it. Repeatedly.

Kind of like a girl. He wanted Mercy, especially now that it seemed he couldn't have her. At least there was something to be said about the thrill of the chase. He glanced at her, standing stiffly beside him, as if afraid that the slightest movement would cause her to brush against him.

Would that be so bad?

Not as far as he was concerned.

But then, she'd called him *scary*. He needed to take it slow. "Can I take you home afterward?" he risked asking.

Mercy glanced out the window at the heavy gray clouds. "I don't know. Matthew…." She nibbled her lower lip.

He could think of more pleasant things to do with that soft-looking lip.

But he shouldn't follow that train of thought. Not so early in the relationship.

"Did Matthew say he would pick you up?" *Say nein.* Besides, he'd told Matthew he'd bring her home.

But Matthew might've decided to kum for her anyway, especially after his warning about messing with matters of the heart.

Her wide eyes met his. "Nein."

Abner grinned. Maybe something would go his way. "Then I'll take you home. I borrowed Micah's old horse, Savvy, and the buggy Abram used when he first moved here. I'd get my own, but...." He shook his head. Nein point in telling her he planned to return to Montana after Christmas.

Or maybe there was. She might be more apt to open up to him and let him start a *friendship* if she thought he wasn't a risk.

Shanna's comments replayed in his mind. *Dead fiancé...not ready....*

So many questions had been generated by just those few words.

Mercy looked toward the door again, as if willing Matthew to appear.

Abner slid closer to her, near enough to smell the powder she must've patted over the boppli's skin before she left the haus. Probably the same chubby-cheeked tot who'd been in Matthew's arms on Thanksgiving.

If only someone like Mercy had worked as a mother's helper for Mamm when she'd been laid up with a broken leg at the beginning of the year. Instead of a fresh-faced, pretty maidal, they'd gotten a sour, gray-haired old maud who seemed to hold a grudge against anything and everything male. The same woman had kum when Mamm had given birth to his brother Adam, born while Abram had been in the hospital after someone had made an attempt on his life. Adam had been a change-of-life boppli, Mamm had said, since he'd followed so far behind his next-oldest sibling, Amos. Boppli number six, coming so far behind the other five. Abner still hadn't met him. He should go home at least long enough to meet his brother before heading back to Montana.

Abner forced down a pang of homesickness. He did miss his family. But, that aside, Daed had probably known what he was doing, hiring a grumpy old maud instead of a pretty maidal to kum live with a predominantly male family. Hopefully, she would go back home before he visited.

Katie handed him a cup of the strawberry-pineapple-Sprite-ice cream concoction. Abner took a sip of the tangy drink and wrinkled his nose. It was tasty, but any of the ingredients on its own would've been just as gut, if not better. He glanced at Mercy. "Kum on. I see a place to sit over there. We can eat, and then I'll take you home after we get our share of the taffy." Not that he would get to enjoy his share. Katie and Ruthie would confiscate it and limit his rations, and he'd get his fingers rapped if he tried to take some too close to mealtime. Ruthie Detweiler wielded a mean wooden spoon, and she seemed to use it with glee. Smiling while inflicting pain. Amazing how such a calm smile could mask such a cruel streak. But it reminded him of the way Mamm handled her buwe.

Abram had once said Ruthie missed having a bu around the haus.

Seemed she'd be over the moon to have two, then; but if so, she didn't show it.

Abner shook his head to remove the thoughts and focused instead on his destination. The only available seat was on the couch, one cushion, but he and Mercy could squeeze together. He'd try to pretend not to enjoy it too much. He grinned and headed that way. But when he glanced back, she wasn't behind him. She'd gone to stand over by the stairs with Micah and Natalie.

So much for cuddling with her.

Mercy struggled to control a grin as a look of something akin to disappointment crossed Abner's face. He masked it with a bright smile, then turned and started toward her. She hadn't been quite ready for snuggling next to a bu on a narrow cushion. She would be alone with him soon enough on the ride home. That was enough to send shivers—of terror? anticipation?—down her spine.

"Seems I lost you somewhere." Abner balanced his cup on his plate and reached for her, but his drink wobbled in its precarious position, and he pulled back before making contact.

Micah chuckled but didn't say anything to Abner. He'd probably tease him later. Mercy didn't know the details of the relationship between the two cousins, but they seemed to get along well enough.

Natalie touched Mercy's arm. "I can't believe you and Abner are both willingly so far from home during the holidays. It must be hard being away from your families. What brought you here, Mercy?"

She swallowed a sudden lump in her throat and frowned. Abner's gaze shot to her, curious. She forced a casual shrug. "Ach, I saw an ad in *The Budget* for a mother's helper." Following in the footsteps of her sister Joy, a caregiver to an older woman in Wisconsin.

"Jah, but doesn't your family miss you?" Natalie asked.

"Probably, but I needed to get away." Because she would've been getting married to Paul a week before Thanksgiving if he hadn't gone on that ill-fated fishing trip last year. The death of a fiancé had a way of putting wedding plans on hold—permanently. Not that too many people knew about her engagement to Paul, since the two of them hadn't been published; but all her friends were either married, promised to a bu, or on their way there, and the pitying looks were hard to take.

Not to mention, the other buwe back home kept their distance, giving her space to mourn. Probably wise, since she didn't want to get involved in a relationship on the rebound. But in another way, it hurt. She felt very alone.

She glanced at Abner. He tilted his head and raised an eyebrow.

She also didn't know how to respond to his open interest. Paul had never been so bold in his pursuit. His approach had been reserved. Steady. Methodical. Like him.

She shook her head. She wouldn't think about him. Maybe she should just enjoy the moment.

But it'd been so long. She didn't know how to act, what to think. She touched her cheek, where Paul had kissed her right before he left, trying to imagine another man—Abner—kissing her.

Abner's gaze turned sympathetic. And sympathy was the last thing she wanted. Did he know something about her relationship with Paul? *Nein.* How could he? She hadn't told anyone here, except for Shanna.

The same scheming Shanna who was apparently responsible for orchestrating her presence here with Abner. She'd need to set that record straight as soon as possible.

"I'm planning a trip home after Christmas to see my new boppli brother," Abner said to Natalie. "He was born in September when Abram was in the hospital, and I haven't met him yet."

"Are you the oldest?" Natalie asked him.

"Nein. Anna is married with a boppli, and Aaron married his girl a couple weeks before Abram married Katie. We have a younger brother, Amos, and, of course, the boppli, Adam. Everyone lives around there, except me and Abram." He hesitated, then glanced at Mercy. "I'm going back to Montana." His announcement was punctuated with a shrug. As if he weren't quite sure. Or maybe he was apologizing.

"What's in Montana? And how'd you end up there?" Mercy blurted out, then cringed. She shouldn't have asked. "I'm sorry. It's none of my business."

Abner shrugged again. "Hey, my life's an open book. I went to Montana because I got a job on a ranch to establish residency so I could go big-game hunting." But he glanced away, as if what he'd said hadn't been the whole truth.

And, judging from the expression on Micah and Natalie's faces, whatever he'd decided to hide from her was known to them.

She didn't want a man who lied. That much was certain.

She took a sip of her punch and watched as Abner scanned the room, as if looking for a reason to leave their group.

She'd make it easy on him. "Jah. Well, I need to—"

Abner flashed a grin at her, but his eyes held an unfamiliar seriousness. "I don't know what Abram's shared with anyone." He waved his hand around the crowded room. "I'll tell you the whole story when I take you home."

She shut her mouth, her words having faded. She stared into the blue depths of Abner's gaze. A girl could get hopelessly lost there. Or drown. A tiny sigh escaped.

"And we'll talk about what brought you here, too."

Right. He'd have to go there. She looked away.

Natalie nodded and patted Abner's arm. "I'm going to get more punch."

Micah reached for her cup. "I'll get it for you. Then we probably should get to work cutting and wrapping taffy."

"I'll send my share home with you so I can have it whenever I want," Abner told Micah with a nudge to his shoulder.

"I'll eat it for you." Micah nudged him back.

Natalie laughed. "I'll go claim our seats. I'm anxious for our date afterward." She turned to Mercy. "Maybe you and Abner would like to join us."

Mercy started to shake her head, but Abner touched her hand, freezing her brain waves.

"Jah, we will. I promised Mercy an eggnog milk shake." He grinned at her. "And I always keep my promises."

She didn't remember that it'd been a promise. More of an offer. It hadn't sounded as certain as his other seemingly offhand remark about marrying her.

If he took the eggnog shake promise this seriously, what would he do about the second promise?

"I think Katie would like to have a chance to get to know her future sister-in-law before we marry." Those words had played in her mind over and over since he'd said them. Coupled with Katie's comment about the Hilty brothers working fast—*"at dizzying speeds."*

Along with something about being married in four months.

Mercy shook her head. Completely unimaginable.

Katie came into the room and surveyed the area before she approached Mercy and the others. Abner's hand was still on hers, and he moved his thumb, sliding it across the back of her hand in a caress, sending shock waves up her arm.

She jerked away.

Katie's eyes met hers, and she mouthed, *"Hang on for the ride."*

Jah, and it'd probably be a bumpy one. Because Mercy didn't want another heartbreak where a man took her heart and shattered it.

Abner was going to Montana. Someplace she had nein intention of going.

But she did love eggnog milk shakes.

And it wouldn't hurt to make a few friends while she was here. Besides, they would be with Micah and Natalie. Not alone.

Abner watched as a variety of emotions played across Mercy's face. He wished that the thoughts going through her head were as easy to read as they had been on previous occasions. Or maybe he didn't, judging by the shuttered look that settled there. One of wariness.

If only he could wipe all that away and end up with nothing but acceptance, welkum, and a desire to dive into the relationship and let it take them where it would.

But nein, he wouldn't be so lucky.

He shouldn't have allowed his thumb to stray across her soft skin. Maybe if he hadn't, he'd still be touching her. He glanced around the room at the other couples who'd paired off, but none of them obviously so. None of the men acted near as forward as he'd been. They'd just formed groupings of equal parts men and women, casually talking. If asked, he wouldn't be able to tell who was with whom.

That wasn't the way der Herr had wired him. He curled his fingers into his palm to keep from reaching for Mercy again.

"I'm with Micah—let's get back to work," he finally said. So that he could be with Mercy. At least until McDonald's. And then maybe they could ride the rest of the way in the secluding darkness.

Sitting in the confines of a small buggy, having a quiet conversation in the dark while cuddling under the quilt, sounded gut.

Maybe too gut.

He'd said he'd promised her an eggnog milk shake, but it seemed silly to order a frozen treat when the mercury on the outdoor thermometer hovered below freezing. But then again, maybe she'd sit closer to him under the heavy quilt, in an effort to keep warm, while they rode the rest of the way to the Yoders'. Her current home.

Too far away from his.

It certainly would be helpful if she lived in the same district. Then he'd bump into her at singings and frolics.

They headed to the sink and took turns washing their hands. Then Abner grabbed a tray of taffy in assorted flavors, while Natalie took the wax paper, and the four of them headed back to the table.

Micah snagged several pairs of scissors. "Abner and I will cut while you two wrap. See if you can keep up." He reached for the butter.

"I'll cut the wax paper," Natalie offered. "Mercy can wrap."

"Right." Abner added a smirk at Mercy, then transferred it to Natalie. "Don't fall behind. I want that eggnog shake."

"I'm thinking of something much warmer," Natalie said. "Maybe a gingerbread latte."

"Or a peppermint mocha." Micah buttered the scissors, then started cutting the taffy ropes into one-inch pieces.

Mercy buttered her hands while Natalie started cutting the wax paper. The other chairs around them started filling.

"I just want to be with my girl," Abner muttered. "What I drink doesn't matter."

Micah kicked him in the shin, but Abner couldn't look away as Mercy's face flamed an alarming shade of red.

He may have just gone too far.

Chapter 5

Mercy looked around one last time, hoping Matthew would appear. Apparently, he had assumed—correctly—that Abner would ask to take her home. In one mittened hand, she clutched her Ziploc bag full of colorful taffy; with the other, she clasped the front of her black coat shut as she hurried toward the buggy.

Abner pulled a beautiful quilt from under the seat and laid it aside, ready to tuck around her as soon as she was settled.

She wasn't ready to sit in a buggy beside a man who wasn't Paul, Daed, or Matthew. None of them was dangerous or scary. Not like Abner. Her heart's reaction to him terrified her.

Mercy set the bag of taffy on the seat, released her coat flaps, and started to climb up, but Abner's hands closed around her waist. She shivered from the unexpected contact. Nobody had helped her into a buggy since she'd been old enough to get in on her own. He lifted her with ease, almost as if she weighed nothing. Maybe she did feel weightless, compared to some of the things he had to lift daily while doing farm work.

His fingers slid away slowly, as if he were reluctant to give up the touch.

She was a tiny bit reluctant for it to end, as well.

She avoided Abner's gaze as he stepped back and adjusted his black hat on his head. Then he turned to Micah, who was climbing into another buggy nearby. "I'll follow you to McDonald's."

Micah nodded, and Abner gathered up the reins and jumped into the buggy.

He was close enough that she could feel the heat of his body next to hers. She shifted to the side so that her hip pressed against the cold metal edge of the seat.

Abner reached for the blanket. With a jerk of his arms, it opened, and he settled it over them. "Comfortable?"

Not really. But she nodded. How could she answer that? She was as comfortable as she could possibly be in a narrow buggy with a dangerous man. How long would it take him to steal her heart? She didn't want to fall in love again. Didn't want the hurt of losing a man she loved. Nein. Never again.

Abner released the brake and backed the horse and buggy out of the space between two other identical buggies.

"I promised to tell you the rest of the story." Abner darted a glance toward her as he trotted the horse between the haus and barn, then turned her toward the road. They paused by the mailbox, and Abner looked in both directions before proceeding into the road after Micah.

The rest of his story—and then hers? Mercy slid her hand a little closer to him under the quilt and picked up her bag of taffy, pulling it back to her lap. She twisted the plastic in her hands. Then paused.

A date. She was on a date. With Abner. A man about as far removed from Paul, personality-wise, as possible.

And the furthest thing from her mind when she'd gotten into Matthew's buggy earlier that evening.

She didn't know how she felt about it. Well, other than the little tingle of expectation tickling her belly. She adjusted the bonnet covering her kapp so she could see him better. "Jah, I'm anxious to hear your story."

"Anxious" may not have been the right word. "Curious" might have been better. Or maybe both.

Abner guided the horse to the edge of the road to let several cars pass them more easily. "My brother Abram, some friends of ours, and I were out in the woods. Mamm had sent us out to collect the first of the wild mushrooms. We wandered into something we had nein business seeing. Someone lay on the ground, dead, beside some men who were arguing. They had guns."

Mercy caught her breath.

"That's not the worst of it. One of the guys there shouted something. I don't remember exactly what he said. In my nightmares, I hear him yell, 'You're all going to die!' That might've been my overactive imagination, though. Whatever he said, it communicated clearly that we needed to leave. We ran, but one of our friends was shot in the back. Dead before he hit the ground."

"Ach, that's terrible!" Mercy's eyes widened. She tried to think back. Hadn't she heard something about this?

"The rest of my friends were gone in short order. Not the same day, though. Abram and I decided we needed to get out of town if we wanted to stay alive. So, I contacted a friend of mine who worked at a ranch in Montana, and the rancher agreed to hire one of us. Me or Abram—not both. That was hard. Abram and I were pretty much inseparable until then. Abram decided to kum to Missouri to visit Micah, which was gut, I guess, because he met Katie. And I went to Montana."

"Wow." Mercy did remember hearing something about multiple murders of Amish youth during the early spring and through late summer. Even the bishop of a neighboring district had been shot. But he'd survived. She'd prayed for the families, knowing firsthand how hard it was to lose a loved one.

"Abram talked to someone here about it. An Amish police officer, he said, but…." He laughed. "That doesn't exactly ring true. Anyway, Abram was lured back to Indiana, and an attempt was made on his life. But because he talked to the law, they caught the man. So I guess it's safe to return now, but…well, I haven't. To be honest, working on a cattle ranch in Montana is pretty exciting. Plus, there are the mountains to hike in, and, believe it or not, there's an Amish community there, too. I'll take you—I mean, you should go sometime. I bet you could get a job as a mother's helper there."

She wasn't sure she wanted to go to Montana—or anywhere— to work as a mother's helper again. This job in Seymour was taxing beyond belief. Not that the Yoders weren't nice. They were. But meeting strangers at the bus station, moving to an unfamiliar haus, settling into a routine she didn't know…not an easy thing. And she hadn't even met the other women in the district yet. That would change soon, as Shanna had mentioned that some friends would be coming over soon to help bake Christmas cookies. And, of course, there was church.

Mercy shuddered, dreading the first church Sunday she'd attend. Everyone would stare at her, wondering why her kapp was different, why her dress was different—unless she got busy and made some outfits to match Shanna's. And found someone to help her make a kapp. Mamm had always bought theirs ready-made at a store in Shipshewana.

"You haven't said anything." Abner nudged her knee with his while the buggy was stopped at a red light. "Weren't you listening?"

Mercy nodded quickly. "Jah, I heard you. Just...processing." She ran his monologue through her mind, trying to find something to comment on. Something to say, other than a flat-out refusal to go to Montana. Or a spilling of her mental ramblings. "Losing your friends must've been horrible."

She should know.

☙❧

"Horrible" wasn't a strong enough word for it. Abner forced the corners of his mouth up in a smile that was so fake, it hurt. He searched for a shrug he hoped was nonchalant. "Life goes on. Might as well make the best of it." He tried to steady the waver in his voice.

The traffic light turned green, he clicked at the horse, then pulled in a shaky breath as they crossed the four-lane highway. He turned down the next street.

Mercy remained silent. He glanced at her and caught the set of her chin as she looked out the opposite side of the buggy, then twisted to look behind them at a car following too closely.

The perfect opening to get her to start talking. "I'm sure you know that all too well."

Her glance was startled, as if she'd forgotten what he was talking about. Hadn't she been listening? Or didn't she recognize that comment for what it was—an opening for her to share her story about her deceased fiancé?

"About life going on?" She swallowed hard, then shook her head. "Look—McDonald's." Was that relief in her voice?

At least he had the return trip to draw information out of her. Though he might need to be more obvious in his questioning. As far as he was concerned, the past needed to be talked about and put to rest so they could move on with the future. Their future. Together.

Though, how could one ever put the past totally to rest? His life had been disrupted, all his closest friends lost, the result of one day in the woods. And considering the grief he still felt over losing them, how had Mercy kept going after losing the man she'd planned to marry? Kum to think of it, how had his friends' girlfriends handled their losses?

He drove around the building to the red hitching post and parked next to Micah's buggy.

Mercy threw off the quilt and stood, leaving the taffy on the seat.

Abner jumped out of the buggy. "Stay there. I'll help you." He tied the reins to the post and hurried around the vehicle.

Mercy accepted his extended hand. "Danki." Once on the ground, she pulled away, not letting him hold her hand a moment longer than necessary.

"Danki for waiting," he said to her. "I know you can get out on your own, but I like being the gentleman." He refrained from reaching for her hand again as they went into the building. She'd made her position clear.

Natalie and Micah waited just inside the doors. Natalie gave an exaggerated shiver. "I think the temperature dropped ten degrees since we left home this afternoon."

Abner glanced toward the gray sky, heavy with moisture-filled clouds. "I hope it holds off awhile." Whatever "it" was. Rain, sleet, snow…. Judging by the current temperature, if it was rain, it'd be the freezing type.

They stood in line with mostly Englischers. Not many Amish here now. Noon was when most Amish men came in, on their lunch break from working construction in town. Or on weekends, when they had to take their wives on long shopping trips in town.

Abner shifted, then glanced at Mercy as they finally stepped up to the counter. He wouldn't assume she wanted the milk shake he'd originally offered. "What would you like?"

She smiled, but it wobbled a little. "The eggnog milk shake sounds gut." She looked around. "Should I go find someplace to sit? Or are we taking them to go?"

"Jah, find someplace to sit. For four."

She turned and headed for the tables, and Natalie followed her. Micah moved to stand next to Abner as he placed his order. "Two eggnog milk shakes, please." He paid, then stepped aside to wait. A moment later, Micah joined him.

"She's kind of reserved," Micah said.

That was an understatement. Abner shrugged but didn't reply.

"She'd keep you settled."

Meaning he was unsettled? Flighty?

Abner frowned. Then he found his grin. "Hey, someone has to keep my feet on the ground."

"Jah. Otherwise, you'll be forever hunting that prize moose."

"Grizzly," Abner corrected him. "I always dreamed of spending my honeymoon on a bear rug in front of a roaring fire."

Micah laughed. "I never know when to take you seriously."

Abner collected the two eggnog shakes the cashier had set on the counter. He shot a smirk in Micah's direction, which was guaranteed to leave his cousin confused.

Then he walked off.

Actually, he had been kidding. Because even he wouldn't be able to sleep, much less focus on anything else, with the scary head of a grizzly bear beside him. Nein, that'd give him nightmares of a different sort.

Like the time he—

Abner shuddered.

He wouldn't think about that. Not now.

Not ever.

❧❧

Mercy jumped when a clear plastic cup full of creamy goodness landed in front of her. Abner slid into the seat beside her. He winked at her, then aimed his thousand-watt grin at Natalie. "Micah will be over in a minute. Fancy koffee takes a wee bit longer than gut old-fashioned milk shakes."

He handed Mercy a straw. As she started to rip it open, something hit her on her temple. She looked into Abner's laughing eyes. Had he really just blown his straw wrapper at her?

She glanced at her own wrapper, swallowed her fear, brought the open end of her straw to her mouth, and blew. The wrapper didn't go anywhere. She pulled it away and frowned, embarrassed by her failed venture in frivolity.

Abner smirked at her. "Takes a special touch." He winked again and rested his arm on the back of the booth, not touching her, but his closeness made her more aware of him.

Micah slid into the booth across from them. "So, Mercy." His gaze met hers. "You're the responsible oldest child, ain't so?"

She blinked at him. Why would he ask that? Did he think she was boring? Not worthy of Abner? "Nein, I'm the middle child."

"That explains a lot. Reserved, quiet. Keeps things to herself." Micah nodded. "A lot like me."

Mercy wrinkled her brow, not quite sure how to take his comment. She glanced at Abner, trying to remember what he'd said when he'd rattled off his list of siblings. Wasn't he also a middle child?

He was anything but quiet and reserved.

Abner chuckled. "Jah, Micah and I, we were the gut Amish buwe." His grin widened, and he raised his voice to a high falsetto. "Why can't you be more like Abner and Micah?" He nudged Mercy with his shoulder. "Abram heard that a lot."

"Probably most of the buwe in our district did." Micah shook his head. "But what they didn't know...." His eyes narrowed with his wide smile. "Fun times. And we never got in a bit of trouble."

"Sometime we'll need to hear about that." Natalie pushed one of the ribbons from her kapp over her shoulder.

"Sometime? How about now?" Mercy took a sip of her milk shake.

Both Micah and Abner shook their heads. "We'll save that story for another time," Abner said. "Don't want to give away all our secrets so soon." His arm shifted closer, his shirtsleeve brushing against the back of her neck.

Delightful tingles shot through her. She should move away. Should...but didn't.

Instead, she took another sip of her shake...and pretended not to notice when Abner's arm settled around her shoulders.

It was gut to be wanted.

As if realizing he shouldn't touch her, Abner pulled away, his arm moving back to its original position. Not touching.

She tried not to miss it.

"You will kum to my haus two Saturdays from now to help make fudge, ain't so?" Natalie leaned forward. "I can get Micah and Abner to kum and crack black walnuts. Or it can be just you and me. We're going to be close friends, I just know it."

"Danki, but it depends. I'll have to ask the Yoders. Shanna said something about having her friends over to bake cookies. I'll be helping with all the kinner if she does." Either that or baking, since Shanna tired quickly this close to the end of her pregnancy.

Natalie smiled. "If she does, then I'll kum there and help, too."

Mercy grinned back. It was nice to have a new friend.

Natalie pulled a piece of paper out of her purse. "Here's my address and the phone number for our phone shanty. Daed doesn't check messages much, though, so it might be better for us to write— or for me to call you." She slid another sheet of paper and a pen toward Mercy.

Abner leaned closer, watching as she wrote her address.

"I don't have a phone number," she said. She didn't know the number for the phone shanty nearby. Shanna had never shared that information, since, as a midwife, she carried a cell phone so she could be reached at any time. Mercy's family had Shanna's cell phone number—for emergency use only.

Not that Mercy expected an emergency, on either end. But Shanna was a nurse-midwife. She'd earned her RN license during her rumschpringe. And she liked to be prepared for the worst. Mercy could respect that.

"Want to make a copy of that for me?" Abner said in her ear. His arm landed around her shoulder again and tightened. "So I can write love letters," he whispered.

Natalie laughed and slid another piece of paper across the table.

Mercy's hand shook as she wrote her name and address, then slid it to Abner. He must've been kidding, though. Why would he want to write love letters to her? His arm stayed around her shoulders, a comfortable weight.

"I saw a flock of geese flying over early this morgen," Micah said. "They were headed south fast."

"Must be something coming in." Abner took a sip of his shake.

"Hallo, buwe, Natalie." An older Amish man stopped by the table, a young Englisch girl beside him.

Abner abruptly moved his arm. This time, completely away, to his side. As if this man was someone to be feared. Mercy straightened her spine.

"Bishop Dave, Meghan," Micah greeted them. "I don't think you've met my cousin Abner Hilty. He came to spend the holidays with Abram and Katie. And me."

"Abner." Bishop Dave studied him. "Abram's twin brother, ain't so?" His gaze moved to Mercy. "And you are? Not from around here, ain't so?" He glanced at her kapp, then at her pink camouflage dress.

Mercy shifted uncomfortably, wishing she hadn't taken off her coat. She really needed to sew some more suitable clothes. And soon. She swallowed. "Mercy Lapp. I'm here as a mother's helper."

"In a different district," Micah added.

"For Matthew and Shanna Yoder," Abner put in, straightening. "She's from Shipshewana, like Abram and me."

The bishop nodded. "That explains much." But his expression remained serious. "You haven't been here long?"

Mercy shook her head. "About a week."

"Nice dress." The teen girl, introduced as Meghan, bounced on her heels. "Grandpa, we gotta go. I'm gonna be late."

"Jah, jah. I know. Even Englisch grosskinner always in a hurry. She's in some play at the high school."

Meghan huffed. "It's not a play, it's a talent show, and—"

"And I'll get you there. It's wrong, exalting yourself. Just a way to appear better than someone with nein talent, ain't so? Der Herr created all men equal. The Bible says, 'For every one that exalteth himself shall be abased; and he that humbleth himself shall be exalted.' It's in the gospel of Luke." His gaze moved to Mercy. "Know the reference?"

Her eyes widened. She wanted to slide down and become invisible, just like when she was in school and the teacher called on her to answer some confusing math problem that made zero sense. "Nein." She shouldn't have admitted that. Maybe it would've been better to kum up with a number. Any number. Wait—she'd need two.

"Luke eighteen, verse fourteen," the bishop said, his expression gentling. "Bishop Sol won't be so understanding about the dress kum church Sunday."

"Jah, I understand." She watched the bishop and his gross-dochter walk away. Then she pulled in a breath and muttered, "If I have five pencils and you have seven apples, how many snowflakes will it take to cover the roof?"

A slow smile spread across Abner's face. He leaned nearer and peered into her milk shake. "Maybe I'd better check to see if they spiked your eggnog."

Chapter 6

Abner flicked the reins, and Savvy's pace increased to a trot. He glanced over at Mercy, buried in a bundle of quilts. Only her head and the tops of her shoulders peeked out. "So, how'd he die?"

She jumped, her eyes widening. "Who are you talking about?"

"Your fiancé." He waited, but she didn't answer, other than to give a sharp intake of breath. "How long ago?" he persisted. "What happened?"

She blew out her breath, making a white puff in the cold air. "Over a year ago. He went fishing on Lake Michigan. There was a freak storm, and only one of the buwe returned."

He listened for a sob, or something, to indicate the level of grief she might feel by talking about it.

Nothing. Not even a sniff.

Encouraging.

Abner reached across the buggy seat and found her mitten under the blanket. She had a tight grip on her taffy bag, so he rested his hand on top of hers. "How close to marrying were you?" He cringed. Hopefully, the question hadn't sounded as tactless to her as it had to him.

"Not very. We talked about getting married right before Thanksgiving this year. But he hadn't gone to the bishop…we hadn't started baptism classes or anything."

Still nein sob. Gut. But her mention of Thanksgiving had made him wince. When they'd met, she'd been dealing with reminders of a missed opportunity more than memories of a particular man.

Her hand flexed under his, and their fingers were nein longer separated by the tiny piece of plastic bag she'd been clutching. A smile started. An open invitation to hold hands. Maybe. He moved his to clasp hers.

She didn't pull away.

"So, tell me about him. When did you start courting? Did you always know him?"

Not that he really wanted to hear about the other guy. He just wanted to know everything about Mercy.

And maybe talking about it would help her get ready to move on.

She shrugged, her arm moving next to his. "Jah, we always knew each other. We went to school together. He used to help me with my math, especially the story problems. They never made much sense to me. When we were older, he took me home from the first frolic I attended. I never went with anyone else." She pulled in a breath. It quivered a little. "Until now."

His smile widened, and he squeezed her hand. If only she would take off the mitten. He wouldn't ask her to. She allowed him this much, and he wouldn't press his luck.

"Did you ever court anyone?" Her hand shifted again, but she still didn't pull away.

He shook his head. "Took a handful of girls home, some a couple of times, but never found anyone who caught my interest." He glanced at her. "Until now."

Her cheeks reddened, and she looked away, the flap of her bonnet hiding her face from view. He didn't much care for that. He wanted to see her expression.

At least she still held his hand. That had to count for something.

Too soon for his liking, they neared Matthew's farm. He swallowed. "When can I see you again?"

"I don't know." She pushed at her bonnet strings. "I'm here to work."

It wouldn't be all work, certainly. She'd already said she would be baking cookies—or making fudge—in two weekends at Natalie's. If she could make tentative arrangements with her, then why not with him?

❧

The week passed in a busy haze. Shanna's baking day arrived too soon. On Saturday morgen, Mercy tried to force her shyness into the background as she cleaned the kitchen in preparation for Shanna's friends to kum over to bake. Matthew downed a cup of koffee, then set his mug in the sink. "Tell Shanna I'll be in the barn if she needs me." He opened the door as a buggy arrived. "Her midwife is here."

Shanna hurried into the kitchen and onto the porch. "Kristi, I wasn't expecting you today. What brings you by?"

Kristi grabbed a cane and climbed out of her buggy as Matthew took the reins with one hand and assisted her with the other. "Danki." She turned to Shanna. "I told you I'd check on you weekly from now on. It's getting near your time. You should know that." She made her way up the stairs, limping slightly, and glanced inside, raising her eyebrows at Mercy. Then she looked back at Shanna.

"My helper, Mercy Lapp from Shipshewana."

"Welkum, Mercy." Kristi smiled. "I'm Kristi Zimmerman. Shanna trained me as a midwife." The smile turned into a smirk as she glanced at Shanna. "Not that you'd know it from this conversation."

Shanna rolled her eyes. "Where's your ehemann today? Shane usually comes with you on weekends."

"Someone called him about a sick cow." Kristi removed her black bonnet, revealing blonde hair beneath her kapp.

"Ach, gut. Then you can stay and help us make cookies."

Kristi hesitated. "Maybe a little while. Not long."

"I'll send some home with you," Shanna said, sweetening the deal. She glanced at Mercy. "Would you clean up from breakfast? I'll send Serena in to help."

Mercy nodded as she reached for the dishpan to fill with water. Not that Serena would be much help. She'd probably bang on the frying pan with wooden spoons—something Matthew discouraged but Shanna laughed at. Mercy's parents would've frowned on it, too. On the other hand, it was a signature move of boppli to bang on things.

Mercy had just finished wiping off the table when the door opened and another blonde woman stepped in, along with a boy and a girl. The woman stood there a second, blinking at Mercy. "Where's Shanna?"

Mercy waved her hand in the direction of the stairs. "With the midwife."

"I'm Becky Miller. These are my kinner, Emma and Jake." The little girl appeared to be not quite school age, and Jake seemed to be about Serena's age. Maybe a little older. "My ehemann, Jacob, is in the barn with Matthew. You must be that helper Shanna hired from Indiana. Nobody understands why she didn't ask one of the local girls."

Were some of the nearby maidals upset to have been passed over? Or had Shanna asked around here first and not found anyone willing or available?

Regardless, Mercy's spirits lifted, extra glad she'd gotten the job at just the right time to provide an escape. She wasn't about to question a blessing. "I'm Mercy Lapp," she finally introduced herself.

Becky took off her coat and hung it on a peg, then unbundled her kinner. "Nice to meet you. Emma, go wash your hands so you can help. Jake, you can play with Serena. Be nice." She reached for the wicker basket of toys, moved it away from the wall, and handed Jake a couple of wooden blocks. He banged them together, and Serena giggled.

Mercy watched the exchange with mixed emotions. She didn't mind the extra work of watching Becky's kinner, and she welcomed the opportunity to make more new friends, if she could open herself up to them. Yet tears burned her eyes. Being in the company of young fraus was a painful reminder that she'd missed her chance.

She was well on her way to becoming an old maud.

Mercy carried the dishcloth over to the sink, wrung it out, and draped it over the edge, then reached for Shanna's recipe box. She pulled out the recipes Shanna had mentioned earlier and started searching in the pantry for the necessary ingredients. She was excited to start baking Christmas cookies, preparing for one of her favorite holidays.

Becky washed her hands, then gathered a mixing bowl, measuring cups, and measuring spoons.

They'd just gotten the first batch of cookies in the oven when Shanna and Kristi came back into the room. And just in time. The silence had begun to get to Mercy, but she didn't know what to say. And Becky had been acting just as ill at ease, studying Mercy out of the corner of her eyes, as if suspecting her of being an alien in disguise.

Kristi set her bag by the door. "Hallo, Becky."

Becky smiled. "Kristi. Have you met Mercy?"

"Jah." Kristi smiled at her. "Shanna's been telling me wunderbaar things about how capable you are. I think I'll hire you when Shanna nein longer needs you."

Shanna laughed. "I have high hopes of keeping her indefinitely."

Mercy forced a smile, even though staying here and not returning home to the pitying looks did hold huge appeal. At least until Abner left for Montana. Then she might face pitying looks here, as well.

A movement caught her eye as she passed by the window. A buggy turned in the drive and continued down the dirt path. Another of Shanna's girlfriends, nein doubt. She didn't know how many had been invited.

But what if it were Abner instead? She almost wished it were. Especially since they'd parted ways without making arrangements to see each other again. He'd said that he would be in contact, but a whole week had gone by without a single word. She was starting to worry he'd lost interest.

If only she hadn't brushed him off with her comments about having to work.

She peered at the buggy. The driver was a woman. Mercy's spirits sagged. Another stranger. More uncomfortable looks and questions to field. If only she could make friends today as easily as she had with Shanna, Natalie, and Katie.

Or what if it was Natalie? In their correspondence this week, she'd said she would try to kum by. Mercy went outside on the porch, wrapping her arms tightly around herself to ward off the chill.

Matthew and another man—Jacob?—came out of the barn to meet the driver. It was Natalie, after all, and Mercy's spirits soared. Matthew took the reins while the other man extended a hand to Natalie as she climbed out of the buggy. "Danki." She started toward the haus. "Hallo, Mercy! Mamm said that if we get done early enough, and you're free, you can ride home with me and help me make fudge to-nacht. Micah and Abner will stop by, and if you kum, Abner said he'll take you home."

Mercy smiled, trying to ignore the way her heart warmed and her stomach fluttered at the mention of Abner. She gave what she hoped was a couldn't-care-less shrug. "We'll see. I don't know what plans Shanna has for me."

Natalie waved her hand dismissively. "She let you go last week to the taffy pull. I think you're restraining your activities more than she is."

That comment hurt, even though there was truth in it. Mercy just didn't want to admit it, not even to Natalie. After all, Mercy would eventually go home to Shipshewana. Abner would leave for Montana. And while friendship was nice, there wasn't any point in making an effort to be part of a group. Nein matter how much she wanted to be accepted, desired, cared for....

She swallowed the pain.

Self-inflicted pain.

She really had to get past this. She swallowed again. "I'm so glad you could kum."

Natalie smiled. "Me, too. And I can't wait until this afternoon. It'll be something to see Micah and Abner helping in the kitchen, ain't so?"

"Jah, it would be." Mercy opened the door, and they stepped inside the warm kitchen, which smelled of fresh-baked cookies.

Natalie pulled her coat off and hung it up, then gave a tiny gasp. "Ach, I almost forgot. Abner said to give you this." She pulled an envelope out of her pocket and handed it to Mercy.

He hadn't forgotten about her. A jolt of anticipation worked through her.

"Oooh, a love letter," Shanna teased. "Maybe you won't be able to hire her after all, Kristi. Some man may steal her away first."

Mercy's face heated. She tucked the letter into her apron pocket and turned her attention back to the cookies.

But she couldn't wait until she had a moment of privacy to read it.

❧

Abner parked his buggy next to Micah's and strode up to the Waglers' front door. His nerves jumped the way they had about two weeks ago when he'd waited for Mercy on the Yoders' porch. Hopefully, she'd gotten his note. Not that he'd said anything important. Just a simple message: "Thinking of you. Hope to see you soon."

Maybe it'd work with her the way it'd worked when Abner's older sister, Anna, was being courted by Thomas, now her ehemann.

Whenever Thomas sent Anna a note, she'd smile all day long—and she had a lot more patience with her brothers.

Hopefully, his note had put a smile on Mercy's face and would give her more patience with his fumbling attempts at courtship.

Had Mercy managed to get away to make fudge at Natalie's? His stomach churned. If she hadn't, he'd make his excuses and go to see her. Maybe she'd be able to take a walk or something.

And maybe he could snag a couple cookies as a bonus. A man could never have too many Christmas cookies.

He opened the door and walked inside.

Micah glanced up. "About time you arrived." His jaw was set, lines of concentration etching his forehead, as he wielded a glass-encased nut chopper. As if the task were hard work.

And maybe it was. Abner had never done anything more than shell nuts for Mamm. Or maybe Micah was just scared of messing up in his desire to impress Natalie.

Abner laughed. "Put you to work, did she?" He looked around. The kitchen was empty, except for the two of them. "Where's Natalie?" *And Mercy? Gott, let her have kum.*

"Natalie went down to the basement for more sugar. And Mercy went with her." Micah winked.

Abner pumped his fist in the air.

Micah laughed. "Way to control your exuberance, Cousin. Careful, or she might think you're happy to see her."

"We wouldn't want that, would we?" Abner rolled his eyes. He didn't have any hesitation in sharing how he felt. A girl needed to know. Right? Open pursuit—that was what his older brother, Aaron, had advised. It'd worked for him and for Abram. Nein reason to believe otherwise for himself.

A step creaked, and Abner's heart went into overdrive. He took off his coat and hat, hung them on a peg, then started washing up.

Mercy came up the stairs lugging a big bag of sugar. Apparently, Abner's mamm wasn't the only one who bought in bulk.

"Let me get that for you." He took the bag from her, then stood there, grinning. Probably looking like a fool, but he didn't care. Especially when her eyes lit up and her lips curved in an answering smile.

Her pink, soft-looking, oh-so-kissable lips....

Micah cleared his throat.

Abner jerked his head up, shifted the bag of sugar, and made an about-face toward the table.

"Glad you could make it, Abner," Natalie teased. She came up beside him with a shoe box. "Guess what I found down there— sprinkles and colored sugar!" She lifted the lid, revealing a collection of glass bottles inside. "Mercy and I decided to make gingerbread cookies, too." She looked at Mercy. "Since Shanna sent a container of cookies home with me, I'll send a tinful of cookies and fudge home with you."

"They won't make it home," Abner muttered. Him, in a buggy with a girl and a tin of sweets...not a prayer they'd make it to their destination. The sweets, that is. The girl would.

Unless he had an opportunity to kiss the girl. Then the goodies could wait.

"You keep your hands off Mercy's treats, Abner," Natalie warned him. "I'll pack a separate tin just for you."

"Me, too." Micah added. "Though mine might actually make it home." He chuckled.

Abner shrugged. "Hey, life is short. Eat dessert first." That had been his mantra since the unexpected, devastating turns his life had taken earlier in the year. He'd determined to attempt to enjoy life to the fullest each day Gott granted him breath.

He opened his mouth to say just that, then snapped it shut. Uttering the words would probably suck the joy out of the atmosphere, because then he'd be forced to explain himself. He'd already given the condensed version to Mercy. And Micah knew only the part of Abner's story that he'd shared with Abram. Any more was unnecessary.

Abner forced down the depression that threatened to well up inside him. He wouldn't allow it to ruin the day. Would not, would not, would not.

He swallowed hard. "Tell me what to do." His voice sounded hoarse, so he cleared his throat. "A chef, I am not." Unfortunately, his voice broke again.

Enough of this foolishness.

But he couldn't think how to change it, except maybe by throwing a handful of sugar at Micah and starting a food fight. And in Natalie's kitchen, that just seemed wrong. He'd end up having to scrub the floor. On his hands and knees.

On the other hand, it might be worth it.

Especially if it meant that his hoarse, broken voice would go unnoticed.

Then again, he'd look more immature than he wanted to in front of Mercy.

He glanced at her. She raised an eyebrow at him.

She'd noticed.

It didn't surprise him. As tuned in to her as he was, it stood to reason she'd be just as in sync with him.

He smiled at her, but he could feel his lips quiver.

"How are you at stirring?" Natalie asked him. "I need someone to stir the chocolate and condensed milk to keep them from scalding."

Abner cleared his throat again. Hopefully, his voice wouldn't crack this time. "What's scalding?"

Mercy gave him another questioning look, as if she couldn't believe he didn't know. Or maybe she was simply impressed that he'd kum into the kitchen for reasons other than eating.

"I thought you'd say that." Natalie grinned. "You know how to read. Here's a recipe for making caramel." She handed him a card. "Follow the directions to measure out the ingredients, and then I'll tell you what to do, jah?"

Abner scanned the recipe, then glanced at his cousin. Micah dumped the chopped nuts into a measuring cup, eyed it with a frown, and put another handful of nuts into the glass chopper. The lines of concentration reappeared on his forehead.

Apparently, baking really was hard work.

But it was clearly worth it for the yummy treats at the end.

And for the opportunity to spend time with his girl. The girl he wanted to be his.

Chapter 7

*M*ercy glanced at the round wall clock in Natalie's kitchen. Back at the Yoders', supper needed to be prepared and the laundry taken down and folded. Serena would need a bath, too. "I need to get back to Shanna's."

"Just a moment. I need to pack up the cookies and fudge I'm sending with you." Natalie headed for the basement. "I'll get a couple tins for Abner and Micah. Would you mind putting the cookies you brought into the cookie jar?" she asked over her shoulder.

Mercy picked up the Christmas treats she'd brought with her and scanned the counters for the cookie jar. A big ceramic teddy bear sat in the corner. That must be it. Shanna's was a plain brown crock with the word "Cookies" scrawled across it.

Mercy lifted the teddy bear's head and carefully lowered the assortment of cookies—sour cream cutout, peanut butter, and chocolate chip with walnuts—into the jar. Then she filled the tin from Natalie with some of the fudge and gingerbread cookies to take with her.

Natalie reappeared from the basement with two more tins.

"I'll wash them for you," Micah offered. He filled the basin with water and squirted in a little dish soap.

Abner smiled. "Then I'll dry." He grabbed a dishcloth.

Mercy's mouth dropped open. She forced it closed before someone could comment about her trying to catch flies. She'd never seen men so willing to do women's work—baking, washing dishes. It was nice.

"Danki." Natalie filled the clean containers with cookies and fudge. "Don't eat them all at once. Share them with your family." She handed one to Abner, then placed the other on the counter, since Micah planned to stay and eat dinner with the Waglers.

Mercy glanced at Abner. Maybe he would stay and eat dinner with her.

Immediate regret filled her. She shouldn't encourage a relationship with him. Not when she...he...well, it was impossible.

If only she could allow him to get closer. If only she could stop worrying about the eventual pain usually caused by falling in love. The pain that would kum when they both went their separate ways....

Too late. It already hurt, and it might eventually shatter her heart. With the intensity of her feelings already, it would go beyond anything she'd felt for Paul.

Mercy swallowed the lump in her throat that threatened to choke her, and went to grab her coat and bonnet.

She and Abner must have only friendship. Nothing more.

Even that would hurt when it ended. As it inevitably would.

"Katie can bake—she doesn't need these," Abner said, nodding at the sweets. "Besides, if I give them to her, they'll be added to the endless list of things I'm not allowed to eat whenever I want. You'd think I was on a diet, the way that woman watches me around food. So afraid I'll ruin my appetite." He rolled his eyes. "Not happening."

"I'll tell Katie when I see her," Natalie warned him with a grin.

Abner wrinkled his nose, handed his tin to Mercy, and grabbed his coat. "I'm *so* scared. Besides, these will be long gone by the time you see Katie."

"I'll make him behave," Mercy said, holding the tin behind her when Abner reached for it. "You won't get this back until you promise not to eat them all."

Abner chuckled. "That sounds like a challenge. We'll just see about that." He added a wink and opened the door. "After you."

"Danki." Mercy turned to Natalie. "This was fun."

Natalie smiled. "Jah, we'll have to do something again. How about—"

"My time isn't my own," Mercy reminded her. "It depends on so much more. I'll have to see." With that, she stepped through the doorway. She hated cutting Natalie off like that, but when Shanna's boppli came, Saturday evenings spent with new friends would cease to exist. She paused on the porch and looked back. She hadn't meant to be rude. "I'm sorry. It's just that the boppli could kum at any time. Before Christmas, according to Kristi—that's Shanna's midwife." Ugh. Now she'd shared too much. Especially in mixed company.

"I understand," Natalie said quietly.

Abner shut the door. "So, we won't be able to make plans, either?"

Mercy shook her head. Then she cringed. Salt in the wounds.

"How about if I toss some pebbles at your window some nacht? We could go for a walk."

"That sounds nice, but…." Mercy pulled in a breath. "You're going back to Montana after Christmas, aren't you?" It hurt to speak, but he needed to be reminded. They had nein future.

"What does it matter?" He shrugged. "We have now."

She slid both tins of cookies under the buggy seat and allowed Abner to lift her up. His hands lingered on her waist a beat longer than necessary.

"Don't shut me out, Mercy." He flipped the quilt over her lap, and she snuggled beneath it.

Something in her body language must've clued him in to what she was thinking. Was it wrong to reject someone who understood her every emotion as well as Abner did?

She turned her head away, her eyes burning.

◦◦◦◦◦

The first girl who'd attracted him in, well, ever, was brushing him off? Abner let out his breath in a huff. "Suit yourself." He wouldn't beg. If she didn't want to be seen with him, then so be it.

Still, he'd thought they could really have something.

He started around the buggy, struggling to keep his chin up. Head high. Posture straight.

Hadn't he seen a welcoming light in her eyes when he'd arrived at Natalie's? And hadn't she let him hold her hand?

Was she stringing him along? It just wasn't right.

He untied the reins from the hitching post and climbed into the buggy.

Next to her.

He pulled in a shuddery breath.

If that was how she wanted it, then he'd have to let her be.

Her hand brushed against his hip as she attempted to scoot away. He sucked in another breath at the unexpected contact, then reached under the quilt to snag her mitten-covered hand in a moment of bravado. He had to try once more to get an honest answer. Where did they stand?

"Mercy…." He glanced at her as he flicked the reins, and the horse moved toward the road.

She chewed her lower lip. Tears glistened on her lashes. She wouldn't meet his eyes.

So, she didn't want it to end any more than he did.

He exhaled. Did her comment about his plans to leave mean she was afraid to grieve a lost love again?

For that matter, how would he feel when he got back to Montana and couldn't see her anymore? What did he expect to accomplish by courting her now? Would she drop everything and kum to Montana to be with him?

Jah, in a perfect world.

In reality? He didn't know.

He probably needed to figure out the answer and find some middle ground so he could continue living for the moment and she could keep trying to protect herself from future pain.

Pain he would cause her by loving and leaving.

Abner swallowed the lump in his throat.

He was nein better than her dead fiancé. The difference was, he wanted to marry her. Well, maybe what's-his-name had wanted to marry her, too.

Okay, modify that: Abner was *alive* and wanted to marry her.

Apparently, he still moved too fast for her comfort level.

But he had a limited time to woo and win her. He supposed he could hold off his return to Montana until after New Year's, but then he would have to give up his trip home to meet his boppli brother.

One way or another, she *had* to kum to Montana to be with him.

Either that, or she'd nurse a broken heart when he left.

For that matter, he would, too.

He gave a frustrated growl and slapped the reins. They made a whoosh that spooked the horse. Savvy increased her pace to get ahead of the sound.

Mercy had won. They would be friends. *Just friends.*

How could he possibly be just friends with her? He sighed, released her hand, and rubbed his jaw, feeling the beginnings of his whiskers peeking through. He hadn't shaved today, so he'd need to shave tomorrow for church Sunday.

Speaking of which…. "Have you had a chance to make any new dresses?" She wore a dark brown one today—not a color he would've chosen for her.

"Nein, but Annie—she's a friend of Shanna's—left all her brown dresses in the closet at her parents' haus, and she had a spare kapp. She lives in Pennsylvania half the year, and, well…." She shrugged and bit her lip. "She doesn't want them back."

Abner could see why. "So, you'll be wearing a lot of brown."

"A lot." She sighed. "Not my favorite color. But I do have one green dress that's suitable." Her face flamed red. "Maybe we shouldn't be talking about my clothes."

"I'm going to miss the pink camouflage." He let that comment hang as he tried to think of something else to talk about.

She shivered and drew the quilt beneath her chin.

If only he could pull her closer and let his body heat help warm her. He looked away until the urge passed.

"In Montana, I live in a bunkhaus with a bunch of other men. There are bunk beds built against the walls. It doesn't smell too gut in there, with all the cowboy boots, and some of the cowboys aren't real clean. They toss their dirty, smelly clothes on the floor and don't do their laundry often." Of course, neither did he.

He grimanced and glanced over at her.

She wrinkled her cute little nose. "Do you wear cowboy boots?"

"To work in, jah." He also wore jeans, a belt, and a Stetson, but that admission would be for another time. He was in his rumschpringe, after all.

"There's a cabin not too far from where I work," he continued. "Well, I guess it's not really a cabin; it's more of a remodeled corn silo. It has a bedroom and a kitchen and a living room, but it's really compact. And I thought…if it's still available…we—I mean, I—" He coughed and stumbled to a stop.

Just friends. Jah. Who was he kidding?

So much for not threatening her involvement issues.

❧

"A remodeled silo? I've never heard of such a thing." Mercy tilted her head at him, ignoring his fumbling words. "Is it habitable?"

He clenched his jaw, then raised and lowered one shoulder. "They're gaining in popularity."

"You said there was an Amish community in Montana?"

Abner nodded. "Jah. Plus lots of bachelors during part of the year."

"Including you." She fell silent. Had he spend time with a lot of Amish girls in Montana? "Do you intend to stay there forever?"

Ugh. She shouldn't have asked.

A small part of her wanted him to answer in a way that would be conducive to her plans. But that would be unlikely, considering that she didn't have anything concrete in place.

He chuckled. "I doubt it. For now, maybe. I've considered moving here to be near Abram, but there's a bigger draw to go back to Indiana where the rest of my family lives."

Jah. Shipshewana was home. It was just.... Well, it might be easier to return with a man by her side. That would eliminate the pitying looks she'd fled. Her heart warmed. She loosened her choke hold on the quilt and scooted a tiny bit closer to him. Close enough to feel the warmth radiating from his body.

He looked at her and smiled. His eyes softened.

"How do you think I'll look with a beard?" He rubbed his jaw again, then laughed. "Don't answer that. Let's talk about you. You said you're a middle child. Tell me about your family."

She shrugged. "There's only three of us. Mamm had some trouble after my younger sister was born and couldn't have any more kinner. Patience is married, and Joy soon will be." Not that anyone was courting Joy. She'd just turned sixteen and had taken a job as a mother's helper. But she was beautiful. And smart. Mercy would be the only one without prospects. Without—whoa. She might have a prospect, after all. Or might have had one.

Her heart gave an unexpected lurch as she studied the man beside her. A man who claimed to always keep his promises—and had declared his intent to marry her on the day they'd met.

It was only her issues that held her back.

But Montana? Really? Abner was a wanderer; she was a homebody. Moving to Missouri had taken her far from her comfort zone. She still didn't feel settled, despite the friendliness of everyone she had met so far.

It didn't help that she kept pushing them away. Natalie, for example. She needed to try to make return overtures of friendship.

Even the bishop she'd met at McDonald's had been kind. Would the bishop in the Yoders' district be as nice? Considering the warning Bishop Dave had issued her, maybe not.

She would find out tomorrow. Church Sunday. She'd missed the first one, two weeks ago, to stay home and tend a sick Serena while Shanna and Matthew attended services. Luckily, she'd had a twenty-four-hour stomach bug that had cleared up quickly.

Mercy surfaced from her mental rambles in time to realize Abner's mouth was moving, and she didn't have the foggiest idea what he was saying.

She frowned. "I'm sorry. I wasn't listening. What did you say?" She hated to acknowledge her failure to pay attention. Maybe that was why she'd struggled so much with math in school.

He chuckled. "I asked how your parents felt about you moving so far away from home."

"Ach, they tried to talk me out of it. Daed especially. He actually cried. Said I'd meet some young man, and he'd never see me—" Her voice broke. She'd promised him she wouldn't. Assured him she'd return. Someday. When her heart had healed.

But maybe Daed had been more upset that she'd thwarted his plans. He'd had it in mind for her to go live with an old-maud great-aenti and disappear from the picture.

Just to get her out of her bed. Get her to stop crying. And force her to live again.

He should be happy she'd chosen her own path and now got out of bed every day. That she actually had some fun. And had begun to discover how to live again.

Which was more than she could have said if she'd gone to live with Aenti Clara.

She shook her head. Life was more complicated than the toughest math problem she'd ever encountered.

Math made her think of her comment at McDonald's, when Bishop Dave had warned her about the other bishop.

"Have you heard anything about the bishop in the district where the Yoders live?"

Abner's glance was startled, probably due to her sudden change of subject. But there was a hint of a smile.

"Uh, nein. Not a word. Other than what Bishop Dave said two weeks ago."

He drove the buggy into the Yoders' yard and stopped in front of the haus.

"That's your window, ain't so?" he asked, pointing. "Right above the porch roof?" He grinned. "I'll be by."

She swallowed her fear. "Want to join us for supper?"

Chapter 8

*A*bner shifted on the buggy seat to face Mercy. He couldn't keep his smile from growing. "Supper? Jah, I'd be glad to stay. If Matthew's Shanna won't mind."

Mercy shook her head. "Shanna will be thrilled to have you join us. But I need to take the laundry down and start supper."

Right. Her job.

But at least he'd be with her.

"Maybe we could go for a walk afterward."

"I'll need to give Serena a bath first. But after that, probably." She gave him a shy smile and glanced away.

He understood her desire to protect herself, but her flip-flopping made him want to hold his heart back. Still, he'd take what he could get.

Abner climbed out of the buggy and went around to Mercy's side. Nobody came out of either the barn or the haus to meet them. "Are they home?" It'd be nice to have more time alone together.

Mercy glanced around. "I guess not. Shanna did say something about taking cookies to her family. But I thought they'd be home by now." She looked up at the sky. It was already beginning to get dark. "I'm sure they'll be back soon." She sounded like she was trying to convince herself.

He reached up to help her out of the buggy, his hands again lingering on her waist for a moment before he released her and turned away. He lifted her tin of cookies from under the seat and handed it to her.

"Danki," she said. "I need to take the laundry down. Not a gut drying day; it's too cold." She gave an exaggerated shiver.

"Nein, but it's windy. They might've already dried." Abner shifted. "I'll take care of Savvy, then kum help however I can." He reached out a finger and let it trail over her cheek. "You're so beautiful." He tried to keep his gaze from straying to her lips.

Tried. But failed.

Mercy blinked, the color deepening in her cold-flushed cheeks. She looked down, then shyly stepped toward the haus. "I'll put this inside."

He couldn't look away. Instead, his feet seemed rooted to the ground as he watched her climb the porch stairs. Her skirts swayed enticingly against her hips and legs, then she paused and glanced over her shoulder. His face warmed as she met his gaze. After a moment, she opened the door and disappeared inside the haus. When the door closed behind her, he pulled in a shuddery breath, then unhitched Savvy and started toward the barn.

Hopefully, Matthew and Shanna would return soon.

Or, hopefully, they wouldn't, and he'd be able to kiss Mercy the way he longed to.

Although that might ruin everything.

Including his not-so-well-laid plans.

Mercy set the tin of cookies on the counter next to the brown crock cookie jar and inhaled a ragged breath. What was it about Abner that made her forget to breathe? She must be suffering from oxygen deficiency. She'd never felt this degree of attraction to Paul. He was familiar—someone who'd always been a part of her life and, she'd assumed, always would be. But Abner...*wow*. The feelings overflowing in her were, in a way, scary. Exciting. Exhilarating. All emotions Paul had never evoked.

Hopefully, it was a sign that her heart had started to heal.

The haus was chilly, as if Matthew had been gone long enough to let the fire in the outdoor wood-burning furnace die down. Maybe Abner would build it back up.

She went outside and headed for the clothesline. She quickly took down the laundry, dropping the garments, unfolded, into the basket. She would fold them inside, where it was a little warmer. She shivered a bit as the biting wind picked up. Several snow flurries drifted past as she unpinned the last shirt.

Natalie had said they didn't get much snow here. Mercy would miss having a white Christmas. At home, she'd always enjoyed taking her young cousins sledding and ice skating.

Abner crossed the yard from the barn. "Let me get that for you."

For a moment, she was tempted to allow him to get close enough to take the basket, but then she decided against it. Better to keep him at a distance so she could continue breathing.

"Nein, I've got it." She picked it up and clutched it tightly to her side. "Would you mind checking the wood furnace?" She pointed toward the boxy thing in the side yard. "The haus is chilly."

"Sure." He turned away, long strides taking him toward the outdoor furnace.

Mercy carried the basket into the haus and set it on a chair beside the kitchen table. She folded the laundry, then made the deliveries to the appropriate rooms.

Abner came in as she started peeling potatoes. "I got the fire going. It'd died down to embers. Should warm up soon. What's for supper? And how can I help?" He leaned against the counter where she worked.

She glanced at him, taking in the shadow of a beard on his chin, his muscular arms casually hanging at his sides, the smile curving his firm, nicely shaped lips. What would it be like to kiss such a man? To be married to him?

From somewhere inside, warmth started spreading through her.

His gaze dropped to her lips. They tingled with want—with need.

He glanced up, his gaze holding hers. An unhurried smile began as he slowly moved toward her. She couldn't keep from leaning into him as his hands settled on the curve of her waist and he pulled her to him. His fingers seemed to sear her skin through the thin material of her dress.

"Ach, Mercy...." Her name escaped his lips on the slightest of whispers. His breath caressed her, causing her heart rate to increase in anticipation.

She didn't dare breathe as her eyes drifted closed.

Outside, a horse whinnied. A board creaked on the porch.

Abner released a sigh of frustration, released her, and stepped away. *Perfect timing.*

Color rose on Mercy's cheeks as she turned her attention back to the pile of potatoes on the counter. The door opened, and Shanna came in, carrying her sleeping boppli.

"Ach, gut, you're home. And dinner is started. Fantastic." Her gaze landed on Mercy, then skittered over to him. "Hallo, Abner. Are you staying for supper?"

He managed a nod and opened his mouth.

"Wunderbaar! You can help Matthew with chores. That way they'll get done faster. It's nice and warm in here. I was afraid the fire would go out."

"I built it up." Abner clenched his jaw as he moved away from Mercy. If only they hadn't picked that moment to arrive home. A delay of even a few seconds would've allowed him to touch her lips with his. A few minutes' delay would've been better. An hour's delay would've been perfect.

Or too much temptation.

Well, nein point wishing for things that weren't. He opened the door and went outside. His boots clomped down the steps, echoing the pounding of his heart.

So close...so very close....

Chapter 9

$\mathcal{M}$ercy listened as Shanna's steps carried her down the hall to the first-floor bedroom. She'd probably lay Serena in the middle of the bed, since her crib was upstairs.

Gut thing they'd returned when they had. Her cheeks still flamed. Hopefully Shanna hadn't noticed her flushed face, or she would probably fill in the gaps and tease Mercy.

She'd almost allowed Abner to kiss her. She'd wanted him to. She brought her finger to her still-tingling lips.

They'd kum so close to making a serious mistake, especially so early in the relationship. Mamm had always told her never to let a bu kiss her until they were promised to each other. And Paul had honored that. Even after he'd asked her to marry him, he'd never done more than peck her on the cheek. He'd said he wanted their first kiss to be on their wedding day.

Which had kind of disappointed Mercy. She'd wanted to experience it immediately. See what it was like.

Her eyes burned, whether from a lost opportunity to kiss Abner or a lost honeymoon with Paul, she didn't know. Maybe a combination of both.

Abner and she were far from promised. They weren't even courting.

Shanna came back in the kitchen, rubbing her lower back. She stopped beside Mercy, watching as the last long strand of potato peel dropped to the newspaper below.

Mercy placed the potato into the bowl. "Did you have a gut visit with your family?"

"Jah, I did. But my back hurts so badly today. It started aching when I arrived at my parents' haus. I could hardly sit for the buggy ride home. I wonder if I did something to injure myself. Or if the boppli is resting on my spine." Shanna balled up the newspaper of potato peels as Mercy moved to the sink to rinse the vegetables. "Or it might be labor. Especially since the weather changed."

Mercy reached for a knife and started cubing the potatoes with warm water running over them from the faucet. "Do you think the boppli *might* be coming?" She almost asked what the weather had to do with it, but that might be a dumb question. She didn't want to be teased any more than necessary.

If the boppli was coming, then it'd be a bad time for Abner to join them for dinner. But since she'd already stepped so far out of her comfort zone to invite him, she hated to rescind the offer.

Maybe Shanna would hold off having the boppli for another day or two.

Shanna tilted her head, her forehead furrowed. "If I am in labor, it's different from when I had Serena. And it might mean the boppli's in the wrong position." She sighed. "Walking is the best thing, then."

Mercy shrugged. Mamm had said that labor had been different with each of her kinner. "Maybe you should call Kristi, just to be sure."

"Nein, I'll wait a bit and see if it stops. Call me when dinner is ready. I want to lie down awhile. I'll curl up—on my side—next to Serena." She grasped her lower back and gasped, as if in pain.

"Okay." Labor did last awhile, right? Hours, maybe?

"If that doesn't help, I'll get up and try some repositioning exercises to see if I can get him to move." Shanna turned away and started toward her bedroom, then stopped. "And, speaking of *him,* is Abner courting you?"

Mercy's cheeks flamed. "We're...friends."

Sort of. Beginning friends, maybe. But it seemed as if they were so much more, too.

"I wondered, because I got the distinct impression I interrupted something when I came in."

"Ach, nein. Nothing."

She must've answered too quickly, because Shanna gave a skeptical frown. "Are you sure?"

"Positive. I told you, I'm not looking for a relationship here."

Shanna shrugged, her hand returning to her back. "You don't have to go looking for a relationship. Sometimes, love comes looking for you. Trust me, I know."

"I'd like to hear that story sometime." Mercy filled a pot with water and carried it over to the stove. Sometimes an indirect answer was best, right? She couldn't think of anything else to say.

Besides, asking questions was a gut way to shift attention away from the answers she wasn't giving, with the side benefit of getting to know the other person better.

Shanna groaned. "I'll be back. Wake me if I end up falling asleep. On second thought, maybe you should let me sleep. I don't feel too hungry."

Should Mercy ask about Abner joining them? Well, Shanna knew the plan. She'd asked about that when she'd first kum in. If it wasn't okay, she would've said so. Mercy watched her waddle from the room. A few moments later, the bedsprings creaked.

Shanna might not want to call Kristi, but something was definitely going on. Mercy grabbed her coat, shoved her arms into the sleeves, and hurried out into the cold.

The barn door was open a crack. Just wide enough for her to slip into the dusty gloom of the interior. She sneezed. "Matthew?"

"Up here."

She raised her head and saw Abner peering over the edge of the loft. He grinned down at her. "What gives us the pleasure of your company?"

"I need Matthew to go for Kristi. I think Shanna's in labor."

Matthew appeared beside Abner. His brows drew together in a frown. "I thought she was acting a bit off, but she said she was fine. Are you sure?"

"Nein, but…." Mercy shrugged. How much was suitable to say in mixed company?

"Get her cell phone and call Kristi. Tell her to kum." Matthew moved out of sight. "Abner, help me finish up so I can go be with her."

Abner winked at Mercy before disappearing from view.

Mercy flung her arms in the air as she stared at the empty space the men had just vacated. They wanted her to take Shanna's cell phone—a device Mercy had never used—and call Kristi? How would she even know which numbers to push?

They might as well have asked her to hang the moon.

After Matthew left the barn, Abner finished the chores. He milked the cows, fed the animals, and refilled the water troughs. On the way to the haus, he stopped to check the outside wood furnace and tossed in a few logs.

He rubbed his hands together briskly as he came up the porch stairs. He should've worn gloves, but he had unwisely left them home that morning. He hadn't figured he would need them to make fudge. Matthew didn't have a spare pair of work gloves; or, if he did, he hadn't offered them to Abner.

He opened the door and coughed as he came into the haus. Black smoke billowed from the kettle on the stove. Abner frowned and crossed the room. He grabbed a couple of pot holders hanging from a hook near the stove, then moved the kettle. The potatoes had boiled dry. He filled a teakettle with water and set it on the burner. Mamm would have also opened a window and lit a few scented candles to get the burnt smell out of the haus, but a cursory glance around the kitchen didn't reveal any candles. Plus, it was so cold, he hated the thought of opening the window.

Neither Mercy nor Matthew was anywhere around, but he could hear low voices coming from the back bedroom. He belatedly took his shoes off by the door, then washed his hands and sat at the table to wait. For what, he wasn't sure.

Maybe for the water to boil, so he could have a mug full of something hot to warm his hands.

He should check to see if there was something else cooking for supper that might start burning soon. He stared at the stove as if it'd give him the answers. Not that he knew how to cook.

Outside, gravel crunched beneath buggy wheels. Abner stood and moved to the window. A man helped a woman climb out of the buggy, handed her a black bag, then led his horse into the barn. That must be the midwife. Abner opened the door to admit her.

"Matthew called me." The blonde woman gave him a curious glance and headed down the hall without another word.

Abner reached for his shoes. Maybe he should go help the man who'd gone to the barn. He didn't know what else to do. This "date" with Mercy had turned out much differently than anything he'd daydreamed. Besides baking at Natalie's and the kiss-that-wasn't, they hadn't had much time together.

On the other hand, it made for a solid foundation for a friendship. And kept him close, just in case future moments developed.

Mercy came into the room carrying Shanna's dochter. She smiled when she saw Abner. "Ach, gut, you're still here. I thought you'd left."

Abner shook his head and pointed to the stove. "Your supper's ruined."

Mercy wrinkled her nose at the odor permeating the room. "Shanna's not hungry anyway. Guess I can make sandwiches for everyone. But Matthew told me to take Serena for a long walk. *Now.*"

A loud groan came from the back of the haus.

Abner nodded. A walk sounded ser gut. He shoved his feet into his shoes but fumbled with the laces in his haste. Mercy turned the flame down on the stove, then reached for a small black coat hanging on a peg by the door. "The jogging stroller's in the barn."

That was where the midwife's ehemann had disappeared to. Would he join them on their walk? Judging by the way things were going, he probably would.

Abner didn't have any idea what a jogging stroller might be, but hopefully he'd find it. He pulled his coat on, mashed his hat on his head, and headed out the door.

To the right of the barn doors sat a pink and black three-wheeled stroller. Abner hoped it was what Mercy wanted. He pushed it across the yard as she emerged from the haus carrying Serena and a mound of boppli blankets.

A wail followed her. Mercy quieted it by closing the door behind her.

Apparently, Shanna didn't go through labor as silently and stoically as his mamm had. He'd never known when a new boppli had joined the family until he'd awakened the next morgen and found his grouchy, old-maud aenti preparing breakfast with a scowl on her face.

Abner shuddered.

"Cold?" Mercy eyed him as she put Serena in the stroller and messed with the funny-looking black straps. Then she tucked the blankets around the little girl.

"It is cold, jah. But I was remembering the helper Daed always called whenever Mamm was laid up after giving birth. Nothing like you, for sure."

"Nothing like me? How so?" Mercy moved behind the stroller and started pushing it down the driveway.

Abner hesitated. "Hold up. I just realized that man never came out of the barn."

Mercy waved her hand dismissively. "That's Shane, Kristi's ehemann. He's probably taking care of his horse, then he'll wait in the kitchen. Or maybe in the barn."

"And you know this because…?" Abner glanced in the direction of the dark interior of the barn, then slid the door shut.

Keeping a distance from the woman in labor sounded wise. Abner would be hightailing it for home if it weren't for Mercy.

The things a man did to impress a girl.

⚬⟋⟍⚬

Mercy started out at a fast clip down the dirt road, Abner keeping pace beside her. It felt so strange to push a stroller with a man walking alongside, almost as if they were a married couple going for a walk with their boppli, as Matthew and Shanna did almost every nacht. They lived for those times together. Matthew called it "courting his frau," even if they did take their dochter along.

An ehemann courting his frau sounded so romantic.

Mercy sighed. When she married, hopefully her ehemann would love her so much, he'd never stop courting her.

She glanced at Abner. Would he love her that much?

Her face heated. Too soon to be thinking of such a thing. Love, when she'd known the man about two weeks and had seen him only a few times….

"They call these jogging strollers for gut reason, ain't so?" He met her gaze with a grin and reached for the handles, putting his hand next to hers—so close, she could feel it through her mittens. "Let's slow it down some now, jah? I think we're out of earshot."

"Shanna can be a bit dramatic." Mercy didn't know why she felt the urge to explain. Not that she'd tell him everything. Kristi had said that the boppli needed to be repositioned, and she'd told Shanna to get into a more gravity-friendly position. Abner didn't need to know that. Bad enough that Matthew knew. But he'd flat out refused to leave the room when Kristi had gently suggested it.

Probably a gut thing, though. He was so steady and down-to-earth, he'd help keep Shanna grounded.

Something cold and wet hit Mercy in the face.

Soft babbling came from the front of the stroller.

Abner held out his hand. "It's sleeting."

Mercy looked at him. "Matthew told me to—"

"I know. You told me. I'm just saying. We're supposed to get sleet and freezing rain tonight before it all changes to snow by midnight. At least, that's what Mose said. We might want to hole up in the barn with Shane—at least until Serena goes to sleep. Then maybe you could put her to bed, and I'll head home."

She hated the thought of his leaving. Who knew when they'd see each other again? She'd have nein free time after the boppli's birth. It was probably gut that the various frolics were over—the ones she'd been invited to, at least.

"Then again, I could plan on spending the nacht in the barn, if you think Matthew wouldn't mind, and go to services with you. Tomorrow is church Sunday. Maybe a singing, too. Jah?" His warm breath misted in the air between them.

Mercy's voice caught in her throat. "I...I can't."

"Mercy—" He sucked in air and coughed. "Uh, I forgot. We'll work something out."

If anyone could, it'd be Abner.

He moved closer, his arm sliding around her waist, his fingers gently tickling her side.

She jerked away, but his fingers tightened.

"I promise."

"Jah, and you always keep your promises." She hadn't meant to sound so sarcastic.

His other hand caught the stroller's handle and brought it to a stop. He ignored Serena's babbling as he moved directly in front of Mercy.

"Jah, I do," he said softly, his gaze holding hers. "And...."

His fingers rose and slowly trailed over her cheek to her lips. They lingered there on the corner for a long, excruciating moment. Her breathing increased, her heart nearly pounding out of her chest.

Ach, she wanted it. Wanted him. Wanted....

His fingers moved again, lightly tracing the outline of her lips.

Her knees buckled. She probably would've fallen if it weren't for his arm holding her up, drawing her nearer. Her toes curled in anticipation as his head lowered.

His breath caressed her. She caught the scent of oranges. "I promise..." he whispered.

Chapter 10

Abner lowered his head another centimeter, pulling her tightly against him. Her softness pressed against his chest. His heart pounded as his hands settled on the curves of her waist. This was it—the moment he'd been waiting for...dreaming of.

Sleet stung the backs of his neck and bare hands.

Mercy shivered and burrowed a little closer. His hands slid around to her lower back.

Serena's babbles turned into sharp, piercing wails.

Mercy jerked away, leaving his arms empty and bereft.

Abner stifled a groan. Kissing her wasn't to be.

She hurried around to the front of the stroller and adjusted the blankets. With a snap, she opened the canopy, then turned the buggy so it faced the opposite direction.

He moved alongside her. "The barn, then?" Too bad it wouldn't be empty.

"Jah. It'd be best." She almost jogged back as Serena's wails morphed into full-fledged, headache-inducing screams.

Abner pulled the barn door open and then slid it shut behind them.

Shuffling came from one of the stalls. A tall man emerged, followed by a big Siberian husky. "Matthew?" The man hesitated, frowned, and studied them.

"You must be Shane." Abner stepped forward. "I'm Abner Hilty, and this is Mercy Lapp."

The man nodded. "This is Chinook. She didn't want to be left behind to-nacht. Though we did leave our sohn with his grossmammi. Built-in boppli-sitters right next door."

The dog whined, sat, and extended a paw. Abner laughed and bent to shake it.

Mercy unhooked Serena from the stroller, lifted her out, and held her close, bouncing her up and down. The screaming stopped, changing into gasping hiccups.

A boppli seemed to be a lot of work. Not to mention a lot of noise.

"Want me to hold her awhile?" Abner offered. "You could go see how things are progressing. And maybe bring us something hot to drink." He gave an exaggerated shiver and looked at Shane. "Koffee? Hot chocolate?"

Maybe it was too presumptuous to offer Shane something to drink when it wasn't even his home. Nor was it his frau he'd volunteered.

"Something hot sounds wunderbaar," Shane said with a nod, though he didn't specify which drink he wanted.

"I'll be right back." Mercy pushed Serena into Abner's arms, pulled her coat closed, and left the barn. At least she didn't seem to mind.

He let out a breath.

Serena snuggled against his chest, letting out a tiny, contented sigh.

He couldn't keep from smiling. Maybe a boppli was worth the work. What would it be like to have Mercy as his frau and raise a boppli together?

His stomach grumbled, reminding him of a more important topic than his imagination. Food.

"We have cookies and fudge," he said, remembering the tin that waited under the buggy seat. He wouldn't have gotten it past Katie and Ruthie, anyway. Better to indulge in a "picnic" of sorts right now, even if it meant having to share. It certainly seemed that their dinner plans had been waylaid.

His stomach rumbled in complaint again.

Shane chuckled. "Our dinner was interrupted, too."

"I'll get the cookies. Those'll at least take the edge off."

Abner handed the little girl to Shane, then adjusted his hat, dipped his head, and hurried outside. The sleet came down faster now, covering the gravel driveway in a thin coat of ice. It would be bad soon. Maybe he should get word to Abram so he wouldn't worry.

On the other hand, it wasn't as if he'd planned to spend the nacht here. He'd call later.

Abner pulled the buggy into the shelter of the shed, then removed the tin of treats from under the seat and turned to go back to the barn. The front door of the haus opened, and Mercy stepped onto the porch. "It shouldn't be much longer," she told him. "Kristi asked me to fix something easy for supper." She eyed the container in his hands. "Don't go spoiling your appetite, now."

His appetite was impossible to spoil. Still, Abner nodded. For a second, he was tempted to go over to the porch and give Mercy another hug, maybe make a third attempt at stealing a kiss. After all, didn't the saying go, "Third time's a charm"?

He curtailed the urge. Sometime—when sleet wasn't hitting them with stinging force, when things weren't so volatile—he'd try again. Sometime when he'd be almost sure to succeed.

Some things were best left unplanned.

❧∾⌖∾❧

Mercy shut the door, hung her coat and black bonnet on a hook, and went to the stove. She studied the potatoes she'd burned when the excitement had started. They weren't all ruined. With a slotted spoon, she scooped out the ones that were still okay, put them in another pan, and set the kettle in the sink to soak. That'd take some scrubbing, for sure.

She browned some stew meat and added it to the potatoes, then peeled an onion and some carrots and threw those in, along with a few leftover vegetables from other meals. She added a little water, put it on to simmer, then ran downstairs to the pantry for some of the tomatoes Shanna had put up earlier that year.

Back in the kitchen, she opened the jar of tomatoes, added them to the stew, and covered the pot with a lid.

The angry cry of a newborn sounded down the hallway. That *was* fast.

Mercy prepared the glass of orange juice that Kristi had asked her to have ready and carried it back to the bedroom. She knocked softly, then pushed the door open and watched as Matthew took the red-faced, squalling boppli from Kristi, who knelt at Shanna's feet.

Shanna stood to give birth? Mercy's eyes widened. Shanna hadn't been standing when Mercy had been in the room earlier. Though, she did remember Kristi trying to talk Shanna out of bed. Apparently, the gravity-friendly position had worked.

"It's a bu." Matthew turned with a wide smile. "Kum on in, if you want," he told Mercy.

Mercy's face heated. She didn't have any brothers. "I brought juice." She cringed. "I mean, congratulations. Did you pick out a name?"

"Levi, after Shanna's daed."

"I wanted to call him Matthew," Shanna said, smiling sleepily at her ehemann. "After the love of my life."

"The next one," Matthew assured her.

Kristi stood up, took the juice from Mercy, and set it on the dresser, next to a clear glass of pale green liquid.

"Mercy, hold on a moment," she told her. "Shanna, put on a clean nightdress. I'm going to put fresh sheets on the bed." Kristi turned to Mercy. "I need some old towels or rags and a bucket of water to scrub the floor. Then get some water running in the washing machine. I'll wash them."

Shanna stepped backward and headed for the bathroom.

"It's my job," Mercy said. "I don't mind." Though she'd never washed birthing rags before. "What is this?" She nodded at the glass of unidentified liquid.

"Red raspberry leaf tea. It's good for women during pregnancy, delivery, and afterward. Actually, all women should drink it regularly. It's beneficial for whole health."

"Kristi is also an herbal healer," Shanna called from the bathroom. "Just in case you need one while you're here."

Mercy eyed the liquid. "I'm not much of a tea drinker."

Matthew chuckled. "Neither is Shanna. Koffee, now…."

Kristi made a growling sound. "Caffeine isn't gut for the boppli. Nein more than one cup a day." She raised her voice. "You hear me, Shanna?"

"Jah, I hear you fine. Doesn't mean I'll listen."

The midwife rolled her eyes. "You need to make sure she drinks a glass of red raspberry tea every day while you're here," she told Mercy. "She should also drink juice when she needs an energy boost."

"She'll do it," Matthew said quietly. "I'll see to it."

"May I tell Abner and Shane that the boppli came?" Mercy asked.

"Get the bucket and rags, then start the washing machine filling so we can get this soaking. After that, jah." Kristi turned her back on Mercy and started stripping the bed.

Mercy returned to the kitchen to peek at the stew and give it a quick stir so it wouldn't burn, then went out to the enclosed porch where the wringer-washer and Shanna's cleaning supplies were located. After gathering some rags, she readied the bucket, then started water running into the washtubs.

Mercy delivered the supplies to Kristi, then took the soiled bedsheets, put them beside the washing machine, and stepped onto the front porch. The sleet had changed to freezing rain, coming down fast. The steps were already covered with ice. She shivered and hugged herself. "Abner! Shane!"

The barn doors slid open a crack. Abner poked his head out. "Jah?"

"The boppli is here. You're welkum inside now. Be sure to bundle up Serena."

"She's sleeping," Shane said, stepping into view with Serena in his arms.

Abner grabbed a mound of blankets and draped it over her. "I'm going to check the wood furnace," he told Mercy.

Her teeth chattered as both men came out of the barn and started picking their way across the frozen yard.

When Shane reached the steps, he held Serena with one arm and the rail with the other as he carefully made his way up. "Where do you want her?"

"I'll take her." Mercy lifted Serena into her arms, then turned and went inside the haus. She moved away from the door and started unbundling the little girl.

Matthew stepped into the room and reached for his dochter. "I'll do it. You finish dinner. Make some biscuits to go with the stew." He turned to Shane. "I hope you and Kristi plan to spend the nacht. It's miserable out there. Where's Abner?"

"He went to check your wood furnace. And…." Shane shuffled his feet. "We actually left our boppli with Kristi's parents, since we didn't know how long we'd be. Though I suppose they could bottle-feed him until we return."

The door opened, and Abner came in, rubbing his hands. "Remind me never to go out without my gloves again. I added a few more logs on the fire, Matthew."

"Danki. Plan on staying the nacht, Abner. You can use Shane's cell phone to leave a message for whomever you need to notify. I have some gloves you can borrow while you're here. Would've offered them sooner, if I'd known." Matthew stepped back. "I'm going to put Serena to bed. She can meet her boppli brother later."

Abner nodded. "A bu, then. Congratulations." His gaze moved to Mercy. A slow, knee-weakening smile began with his lips and ended with his eyes. Then he winked.

Her stomach clenched. She spun around and reached for the mixing bowl.

Then she stared at it, unseeing, while butterflies fluttered around in her stomach.

Masculine steps crossed the wood floor. A moment later, Abner's arm slid around her shoulders in a gentle hug. His hands were icy cold.

She shivered and looked up. Shane's attention was directed toward something in his hands—his cell phone?

Her heart pounded. Shane might look up any second. She shifted. "Abner...."

♥

Abner squeezed her shoulders and released her, right as Kristi came into the kitchen.

"Mamm and boppli are settled in bed. I have some paperwork to fill out, but we can eat first. Smells gut. I'll take a bowl back to Shanna when it's ready, if she's not asleep." She opened her black bag and took out a file folder.

"I still need to make the biscuits." Mercy sounded a bit stressed. She raised her fingers and massaged her forehead, as if trying to relieve a headache.

If only he could think of a way to ease the burden of whatever bothered her. Might be the extra work. Or maybe it was because of him?

"Chamomile tea is good for calming nerves." Kristi set the folder on the table, then started rummaging through Shanna's cabinets until she retrieved a box and pulled out a tea packet.

Abner went to the sink and washed his hands with the hottest water he could get. His fingers tingled as they began to thaw. "Tell me what to do. I can set the table, or I could stir the biscuit dough once you assemble the ingredients."

"An Amish man who's not afraid of the kitchen." Kristi smiled as she poured boiling water into a mug, then dipped the tea bag in. "Here, Mercy." She set it on the counter near her. "Want some hot tea, Shane? Abner?"

"Sounds gut." Shane pulled out a chair at the table and sat.

"Something warm would be gut. Koffee would be better." Abner grinned. "I don't know my way around the kitchen, that's for sure. But my mamm made sure I washed my share of dishes and knew how to set the table. She said my future frau would appreciate it. I can also stir." He eyed the mixing bowl. He'd proved that while stirring fudge batter not so long ago.

"That'll help. Danki." Mercy handed him the wooden spoon as Kristi stirred some instant koffee into a mug of steaming water before setting it beside him. Mercy measured ingredients into the mixing bowl, and then, as Abner stirred, she got out a couple of cookie sheets and checked the stew again.

"Is this gut?" he asked. The dough resembled a lump of goo, but he thought it looked similar to Mamm's biscuit dough before she shaped it into balls and dropped them on the sheet to bake.

Mercy checked it. "Perfect. You can set the table now."

Was that a sarcastic tone in her voice? He liked that she could tease some. He raised an eyebrow. "What, don't you think I know how?"

Her cheeks flushed. She reached for a tablespoon and started dropping balls of dough onto a baking sheet.

Abner glanced at the table. Kristi was seated there, bent over her paperwork, while Shane nursed his tea and watched her work. Abner slid his finger along the back of Mercy's hand and waggled his eyebrows at her when she looked up.

He leaned closer and whispered, "It's going to be so fun seeing you first thing in the morgen."

The pink in her cheeks flamed red.

Abner winked, tapped her nose, then opened the cabinet and reached for the dishes.

Chapter 11

Mercy awoke to footfalls outside her bedroom door. She stretched and yawned, listening as the footsteps paused for a long moment, then continued downstairs. Was it Matthew, checking on Serena?

Or...guests! She rubbed her gritty eyes and cast a frantic look outside. It was full daylight. She'd overslept, a result of having stayed up late to help Kristi finish the laundry, which they'd hung on clotheslines Shane and Abner had strung across the enclosed porch.

She sat up. It had to have been Abner outside her door, since Shane and Kristi had spent the nacht downstairs in the living room. She clutched the blankets to her chest, a tad giddy to know he'd slept so close to her. They'd been so tired last night after finishing laundry, she hadn't thought about where he would be sleeping.

Mercy stumbled out of bed, unhooking the straight pins from her nachtdress as she moved to the window. Snow poured from the sky as if it couldn't fall fast enough. Enough of the white stuff covered the ground already that not even a tuft of grass poked through.

The barn door stood slightly ajar, which probably meant that Matthew had gone out to do chores. As she watched, Abner walked across the expanse of ground between the haus and the barn. He was so strong and helpful. Such a wunderbaar man to have around. His boots left deep prints in the snow as he continued along the path Matthew had started.

Horse and buggy tracks led from the barn toward the road. Had Shane and Kristi left already?

Mercy glanced down at Abner again as he neared the barn. He hesitated, as if feeling her eyes on him, and looked over his shoulder. His gaze rose to where she stood watching.

She jumped back from the window, clutching her gown closed. It wouldn't do for him to see her with her hair down and in a state of undress.

She hastily changed into another ugly brown dress, ran a brush through her hair, twisted it up into a bun, and pinned it in place. Then she secured her kapp and went to the bathroom to finish her preparations for the day.

A few minutes later, Mercy looked in on Serena. She lay on her stomach in a curled-up heap, her bottom sticking up in the air, her thumb in her mouth. Still sleeping. With a smile, Mercy tiptoed out of the room and shut the door.

The scent of something cooking filled the air. Mercy headed down to the kitchen, guilt filling her. After Shanna had bragged to her midwife about Mercy's abilities, she'd gone and overslept, neglecting her morgen duties. Great way to make a lasting first impression. She cringed. And what must Abner think? That she was lazy?

The canisters of old-fashioned rolled oats and raisins sat on the counter near the tin where Shanna kept brown sugar. Mercy peeked inside the oven and saw a pan of baked oatmeal, with two servings removed. So, Kristi and Shane had gone.

Today was church Sunday. Mercy glanced out the window again. The snow continued to accumulate rapidly.

They wouldn't be going to services. Not with this weather, and especially not with a new boppli.

And Abner would be leaving soon.

The corners of her mouth drooped with disappointment. He was fun—nice—to have around. When had her view of him changed so drastically? He'd gone from being scary to beyond wunderbaar in such a short time.

Mercy took care of the canisters Kristi had left out, then set out the banana nut muffins she'd made a couple days earlier. They were still gut and would go well with oatmeal.

She set the table, then started spooning the steamy cereal into bowls.

The door opened, and both men came in. They brushed the snow from their jackets and took off their boots, dropping them in the plastic tray.

Abner straightened and winked at Mercy.

"Are you leaving after breakfast?" Inwardly she chided herself for putting it so bluntly. It probably sounded as if she wanted him to go. Nothing could've been further from the truth.

Abner's grin faded. He glanced outside at the still-falling snow. "Jah, probably so."

Mercy dipped her head and distributed the bowls of oatmeal around the table. She started to carry one back to Shanna's room, but the door opened, and she padded out. "Levi's sleeping. Is Serena awake yet?"

"She was asleep when I peeked in on her." Mercy turned back toward the kitchen.

Matthew gave his frau a kiss on the cheek. "I'll wake her."

"Kristi told me not to overdo it," Shanna said as she took her usual place at the table. "I told her that you and Mercy would make me behave."

"You know it." Matthew smiled as he left the room.

Shanna looked at Mercy. "Besides, I plan on keeping you around till I'm back to full speed."

For a moment, Mercy allowed herself to bask in the verboden pride—until she remembered that she'd overslept that morgen. Then again, it seemed everyone else had, too, except for Kristi and Shane.

She squashed the self-satisfied thoughts. "Just doing my job."

"How long till you're 'back to full speed'?" Abner asked. His concerned gaze met Mercy's before he looked back at Shanna.

She lifted a shoulder. "A few weeks, maybe."

Then...*what?* Mercy blinked at the tears burning her eyes. Her time in Missouri would reach its end entirely too soon. She turned away without looking at Abner. She didn't want to see his reaction. Not when she wasn't sure how she felt about it. Not working for Shanna any longer would mean more freedom for her to be courted, but that wouldn't help much if she went home to Shipshewana while Abner returned to Montana.

She poured some juice for everyone, then slid into her chair next to Shanna. Matthew carried Serena into the room, placed her in the wooden high chair, and pulled it close as he sat at the head of the table.

Mercy bowed her head for the silent prayer, but she couldn't focus. *What will I do next, Gott? I can't go home yet.*

Abner's grin slid back into place as he bowed his head. Mercy would be free right about the time he would leave to go home for a brief visit before returning to Montana. Hope flickered that maybe this would work out. If she went home with him to Shipshewana, and if he could win her heart, then maybe...in a perfect world....

He needed to stop flirting, stop trying to steal kisses, and just focus on the one thing that was possible: a temporary friendship.

The realization hurt his heart. He stole a glance at her across the table. Her hands were folded, her head bowed, for silent prayer. So beautiful....

Spoons scraped against bowls. Abner kept his eyes closed. He'd spent his whole prayer concentrating on his problems, not on the One who deserved thanks.

Der Herr, danki for this food, for the hands that prepared it, and for Your many blessings. And for Mercy. Ach, Gott....

How could he possibly leave her behind?

He couldn't.

Abner opened his eyes and raised his head.

Somehow, der Herr would work it all out.

"Too bad I don't have a sleigh, like I did in Pennsylvania." Matthew cut a muffin in half and spread some butter on it. "Not much use for one here. But it would've been nice to take a sleigh ride."

"Perhaps a walk, instead." Abner glanced at Mercy. "Before I go back to my brother's haus."

Shanna grinned. "Ach, you should. Take Mercy for a nice, long walk. It'll do her gut to get some fresh air today. Besides, I'll want to rest and read, and Matthew will be here to help if I need it. As long as you're back in time to fix lunch, Mercy."

He wouldn't be leaving right after breakfast, then. So long as he got home by noon, it should be fine.

"I'll read the Bible after breakfast." Matthew took a sip of his juice. "We might not be worshipping with the others, but we should observe church Sunday." He turned his attention to Shanna. "I expect your family will stop by after services, since we aren't there."

Shanna grinned. "Gut. I can't wait to see Daed's expression when he finds out the name of his gross-sohn."

Abner helped himself to a spoonful of baked oatmeal. Listening to Matthew talk about devotions made him homesick. Daed was a relatively new preacher in their district, having drawn the lot mere weeks before Abner and Abram had left home. And he would've insisted on the same thing. Bible study and prayer were important.

Daed lived that out, to the point of preaching his sermons to—and praying with—cows, chickens, horses, or trees, if he lacked a human audience.

Abner and Abram had found it hilarious—and maybe a bit frightening—to hear Daed belt out to the forest, "Repent and be baptized," but now he missed it.

He shook his head to force his mind back to the present. And to breakfast. He looked down at his bowl. Empty. Either he'd managed to eat all his oatmeal and hadn't realized it, or he'd never bothered to serve himself.

Wait a minute. Mercy had handed him a full bowl, so he must've eaten it. Scraped it clean. Did food stick to the ribs when one couldn't remember having taken a single bite?

He drained his juice, then looked up as Matthew left the table. He returned moments later with his Bible.

"Just a second." Mercy stood. "Anyone want koffee or tea or anything else?"

"Koffee." Shanna aimed an impish grin at Matthew.

He hitched a brow. "Only one cup."

"Koffee sounds gut," Abner said.

Matthew thumbed through the Bible as Mercy prepared the koffee and passed it around. As she slid into her seat, he settled on a passage. "I'm reading from Proverbs three."

Abner shifted on the hard wooden chair. His gaze met Mercy's as he took a sip of his koffee, then listened to the Scripture reading.

"*Trust in the LORD with all thine heart; and lean not unto thine own understanding. In all thy ways acknowledge him, and he shall direct thy paths.*"

His attention shot back to Matthew. Those words were something he'd needed to hear. Understand. And heed.

Something he hadn't been doing very well.

Gott, help me to surrender my will to Yours. I want to trust You and not try to plan my way. I need You in every aspect of my life. Help me to follow You.

Chapter 12

As soon as Mercy finished the breakfast dishes, she went into the living room. Abner had gone outside to add more wood to the furnace, leaving Matthew free to read *The Budget* in the light of the gas lamp. It was still so overcast outside that one couldn't see to read without artificial light. Shanna rested on the couch with a mug of red raspberry tea within reach, as well as the book she'd been wanting to read. Serena played quietly with her wooden blocks on the floor by her parents' feet. Levi slept in an old-fashioned boppli buggy near his mamm.

Anticipation worked through Mercy as she slid on her coat and gloves. She peered out the window, hoping to catch a glimpse of Abner. After donning a black bonnet over her kapp, she headed outside.

Abner stomped a path through the thick fallen snow to the porch. He wore Matthew's oversized work gloves and carried a metal pail full of warm ashes.

"Hold on a moment." He sprinkled the ashes on the icy steps, then extended a hand to help her down.

His sturdy fingers closed around hers, making her feel secure. Protected. Her heart pounded in anticipation of a walk alone with him through the snowy woods. Or maybe the meadows.

With her free hand, she pulled her coat snugly around her. She gave him a sidelong glance, noticing how the snow clung to his hair. How had he worked his way into her affections so quickly? Katie had been right to warn her that the Hilty brothers moved fast.

With him being so quick to give his heart to her, should she trust him? Or would he meet someone else next month and give his heart to *her*?

Daed would tell her to proceed with caution.

But then, it was the same overly cautious nature that had made Daed court Mamm for five years before he'd decided to risk proposing marriage. And he'd taken the chance only because Mamm had told him to either declare his intentions or sit back and watch while she looked elsewhere.

Hardly the same situation.

And yet, they were happy. Though Mamm constantly pushed Daed out of his comfort zone.

Mercy glanced at Abner. He pushed her out of her comfort zone, too. Maybe that was a gut thing.

Mercy had her daed's restrained nature. So did Paul, for that matter. She hadn't thought much about it until now. Maybe someone bolder, more outgoing, would be a better choice for a life partner. And if that were the case, would it be wise to give in to the urge toward madness every now and then—the sudden urge to catch snowflakes on her tongue or to make a snow angel in the deep drifts—or to continue keeping it captive?

She walked in silence beside Abner, thankful that the snow hadn't started to seep through the tops of her shoes. Thoughtful Abner walked slightly ahead of her, stomping out a path.

Still, it was gut Mamm had insisted she take her heavy black socks with her. Mercy hadn't thought she would need anything so thick. Mamm had been right, as usual.

Abner tugged her a little nearer. Their arms brushed. She shivered.

"Cold?"

She shook her head. A snowflake landed on her nose. She tilted her head back and stuck out her tongue.

Abner chuckled.

Mercy instantly pulled her tongue back. Her face flamed. Could she act any more childish? So much for giving in to momentary madness.

His gloved hand moved over her mitten-covered one. "I used to do that in Montana."

Maybe the act hadn't been as childish as she'd thought. And it had felt gut to let loose for a moment.

"Let's build a snowman in the meadow." Could she help it that the words of an Englisch Christmas song swirled through her mind? She didn't dare think about the rest of the words, though—especially the part about getting married by Parson Brown.

A smile quirked Abner's handsome face. "Jah, let's." He hummed the same tune she'd thought of as they walked past the barn and opened the metal gate to the pasture. "Where do you want it?"

Mercy stopped to consider their options. "Maybe there?" She pointed with her mittened hand to a spot about twenty feet ahead.

Abner's grin warmed her. "I knew there was a reason I liked you. Building snowmen and catching snowflakes with your tongue. You're my kind of girl."

Liked?

Not *loved?*

It was too soon anyway.

Too. Soon.

Mercy tried to keep her heart from crashing.

She dug inside her pocket for a peppermint, unwrapped it, and stuck it in her mouth, needing something to keep her mouth occupied.

❦

Abner bent and made a snowball. This snow was perfect for packing. He straightened, surveying the unspoiled field of white. He could almost envision his little sister and her friends running out there and falling flat on their backs to make snow angels. He'd never been much gut at those. His big shoes would always mar the angel with deep footprints at the bottom. Not like the girls. They seemed to be experts.

He, on the other hand, was an expert on the ice. He used to sneak over to the home of an Englisch friend to watch the winter Olympics on television and later try to mimic the fancy moves the professionals made. And he'd been gut at it, too. He turned to look at the pond on Matthew's property. Unfortunately, the ice wasn't thick enough to support skaters.

Maybe he'd get a chance when he went home to Shipshewana.

And hopefully, Mercy would be there.

Abner bent again and started packing the snow to make the beginnings of the snowman's body. When the ball got big enough, he started rolling it.

He parked the finished snowball where Mercy had indicated, then turned. She had already made a slightly smaller one.

"I'm going to find some twigs for his arms," she told him.

"Okay." He lifted her snowball up on top of his larger one, packed it steady, then started rolling the head.

Mercy returned as he put it in place. She stuck the twigs in the middle ball, one on each side, then stepped back and tilted her head as she considered it.

A second later, Abner's black hat was swiped from his head and placed atop the snowman.

He blinked in surprise. "Mercy!" He reached up, feeling his disheveled hair. It was cut in an Englisch style, but nobody had said anything about it. Probably since he worked on an Englisher's ranch. What did she think of his haircut?

She laughed, then crouched down to pack a handful of snow.

Abner liked this playful side of her.

The snowball hit him square in the face. *Sheesh.* Even though he'd stood there and watched her, he hadn't made an effort to avoid the attack. He was a dummchen. A real dolt.

He mopped the snow off his face and grinned. "This is war."

He expected a squeal or something, like most of the other girls he knew would have made. Instead, she remained silent, her expression serious, as she prepared another snowball, took aim, and fired.

He ducked to dodge it, then scooped up a handful of snow and slowly approached her.

Nein need to pack a snowball.

Not for his intentions.

Mercy's heart thudded, threatening to break out of her chest. She fired a third snowball at Abner—one he dodged as easily as the second as he continued his slow approach.

What did he have in mind?

The fervor in his gaze sent a shiver through her. His mysterious grin never wavered.

She threw another snowball. This one veered over his left shoulder. She started backing away. He was too close. Too—

She tripped over something—maybe her own feet—and fell backward. The next second, Abner knelt beside her.

"You okay?"

Mercy nodded as she opened her mouth to reply. The words formed but were drowned in a face full of snow. She couldn't keep a squeal from escaping as she struggled to roll away, but his hand rested heavily on her shoulder, pinning her in place without effort.

Her eyes watered as Abner washed her face with snow, and then he pulled back, his grin still in place, as he released her shoulder. "Sorry about that. Couldn't resist."

He didn't look very sorry. His blue eyes twinkled with merriment.

She wiped her face with her coat sleeve. "You'll pay for that, Abner Hilty."

His smile widened. "That so?"

"Someday, somehow. You can count on it."

He laughed, then raised his hand and wiped her cheek. "You missed a spot." Then his smile faded, his gaze focusing on her lips.

Mercy's heart rate increased, her pulse pounding in her ears. Could he hear it, too? She moistened her lips nervously, then started to roll away again.

His hand moved from her face to her waist, pulling her back. "Stay." His voice was husky.

His lips brushed hers in a move so tender, she could've cried. A shiver—and not from the cold—traveled the length of her spine.

He raised his head to look into her eyes, and then, with a soft groan, his mouth came back to cover hers.

She tasted koffee.

Against her will, she raised her arms, wrapping them around his neck. His kiss, while still gentle, changed into something different. Something...possessive. Insistent. Commanding.

"Ach, Mercy," he whispered, his breath warm against her tingling lips. His hand tightened on her waist, while the other slid around her neck.

She whimpered. Her arms tightened around him as he deepened his kiss, evoking unfamiliar emotions. Foreign sensations.

If she could just stay in his arms forever and not think about....

What was she doing?

With a strangled cry, she pushed him away and sat up.

Chapter 13

*A*bner fell back on his haunches and stared at her. "Mercy? Was ist letz?" He'd never expected their first kiss to end like that.

She struggled to stand. He let her go, tilting his head back to look at her. The falling snow contrasted with her dark clothes.

"I…I promised."

He furrowed his brow. "Huh?" *Promised?* Did she mean…the other guy? Whatever his name was? "He's *gone.*" Okay, he could've sounded a little less callous. But really.

"Mamm made me vow never to let a man kiss me unless we were promised."

Ah. He let out a sigh of relief. At least he didn't have to compete with a ghost.

She'd been promised before. Likely been kissed before. He refused to think about how his kisses compared. He pushed himself to his feet, brushing off the snow that stuck to him. "That's okay, Mercy. We're promised." He took a step toward her and reached out.

She skittered away. "Hardly."

He grinned. "I declared my intentions the day we met, remember?"

Her face turned a little pinker. "How could I forget? But…that doesn't count."

He shook his head and shrugged. "Sure it does. I meant it."

"You don't even know my favorite color. Or my favorite food. Or where I want to live." She attempted to brush the snow off her coat.

Abner considered her, his gaze skimming over her borrowed brown dress. She was right; he didn't know any of those things. But he could guess. "Your favorite color is pink. Your favorite food is pizza. And you want to live in Montana. With me."

She'd been dressed in pink camouflage the day they'd met at the grocery store, and she'd expressed reluctance to stop wearing that unusual dress. And he vaguely remembered her inhaling pizza at frolics in Indiana.

She blinked. "I should probably get back."

So, he'd guessed correctly? Impressive.

Best yet, she hadn't argued his third assertion.

He grinned and reached for her again, snagging her arm. He tugged her to him and settled his hands on her shoulders. "Mercy, we have a lifetime to learn everything about each other." If only he could declare his love for her. But even he could admit it was too soon. Besides, to be honest, while something in his heart might've recognized her, he wasn't ready to say those words. He wasn't ready to commit to a woman who held him at arm's length. "Let's go for a walk before we head back. We haven't been gone long enough for them to miss us." He lifted his hat from the snowman's head, shook off the snow, and put it on. Then he grasped her hand, and they started toward the road.

Abner didn't voice the thought that weighed heavily on his mind: He'd have to leave soon to go back to his brother's haus. And as much as he loved his brother, he didn't want to go. He'd rather stay with Mercy.

Not to mention, he'd probably have to field embarrassing questions from Abram's father-in-law. It was extremely awkward sometimes, the way Mose assumed the role of father figure to Abner and tried to parent him.

Though it was kind of nice to have a substitute Daed around to hold him accountable. Nice to know somebody cared.

He didn't have anyone like that in Montana. He had friends, jah—lots of them. But most of them were Englisch. And the local Amish seemed to turn a blind eye to the activities the bachelors did.

A whole different set of rules applied.

Maybe if someone in Montana had cared, he wouldn't have—

Abner frowned, shook his head, and blinked, surveying the area around him. The unfamiliar landscape. The snow-covered road with recent buggy tracks quickly becoming obliterated by the falling snow. The woman beside him, her hand grasping his as if it were a lifeline.

Speaking of that woman…*wow*. He could've kissed her all day. He smiled, remembering how she'd felt in his arms. Her minty-fresh taste when they'd kissed. Her soft, sweet responsiveness.

He glanced at her, wishing that he dared pull her into his arms again. But while the haus they'd just passed had looked empty, the residents easily could have missed church, too, and might peer out the window and see them.

He'd better behave.

Her mouth moved, forming…words? Sentences. Paragraphs. He stared at her lips, fascinated by the movement, but heard nothing.

Her lips stopped moving. She looked at him, her eyebrows arching. Had she noticed his stare? Or maybe she expected a reply.

He didn't have a clue what she'd said.

He made what he hoped was an appropriate sound, and then, to be safe, he followed it up with a "Jah."

"Really?" Gratitude radiated from her.

Her smile—*wow.* He'd say anything to see it again. It seemed to light up the world around them.

He blinked again and looked down at the ground.

He'd chosen a bad time to get lost in never-never land.

What had he just agreed to?

Mercy moved a little closer to Abner as they walked to the end of the road. They passed a couple of Amish farms but didn't see any signs of life. The residents had probably gone to church services in someone's haus or barn, judging by the buggy tracks leading from the driveways. All of them headed in the same direction—to the intersection where the churchgoers had taken a left.

She and Abner turned to walk back to the haus in silence. He seemed to be lost in his thoughts, whatever they were, judging by his furrowed brow. And her mind went in five hundred different directions. It warred between her to-do list and *the kiss.* Mostly *the kiss* and her overwhelming reaction to it. Who knew kissing would be so wunderbaar? Maybe that was why her parents had told her to wait until she was promised. So she wouldn't get addicted.

Too late.

Way beyond too late.

She'd go insane if she tried to figure out the ramifications of their relationship now. Were they promised, really? He'd never asked her to marry him. Just stated his plan, as if it were a done deal.

Maybe she shouldn't argue. She would write home and tell Mamm and Daed she'd met this wunderbaar man, and....

Who was she kidding? Not even gone a month, and already promised? Nein. They'd be on the next bus down, and then they'd send her to live with Aenti Clara—which had been the only item on their short list of options when Mercy had taken to bed in grief after Paul's death.

Not that Aenti Clara wasn't nice. But she was beyond old—ancient—and set in her ways, and she smelled like garlic, due to the clove she wore around her neck to keep sickness at bay. Not to mention her haus was so piled full of junk, it was an obstacle course to walk through. Since she didn't have any kinner, she'd lived with another widowed aenti, who had recently passed on to glory.

Mercy couldn't think of that.

She forced her mind to shift to things on her ever-lengthening to-do list.

It was gut Abner had agreed to take her to town to do Shanna's grocery shopping. With Matthew working for his father-in-law at the furniture shop, he usually took Shanna—or Mercy—on Saturdays. Unless he needed to make a special trip for something, as he had the day she'd run into Abner.

She'd skipped the shopping trip on Saturday, since they'd been baking Christmas cookies instead. Not that it was a major issue, since Shanna had put up plenty of garden produce now stored in the basement. There was an abundance of vegetables and fruits of all sorts, as well as canned meats. But the hens weren't laying well in this unusually cold weather, despite Matthew's attempts to keep the coop warm. And Shanna wanted some fresh fruit and vegetables, as well as some items to restock the baking supplies, not to mention a few household goods.

Maybe Abner would take her to McDonald's before they headed back, and she could have another eggnog shake before they were discontinued for the season.

A date. She couldn't wait.

Abner's hand shifted on hers, and he cleared his throat a couple times. "Uh, Mercy? I'm sorry, I know I just agreed to something, but I have nein idea what. I was...thinking."

He hadn't been paying attention? He'd merely agreed to get her to be quiet? She pulled in a sigh. "I asked if you'd take me to the store this week. I need to do some grocery shopping that can't wait until the weekend. And Matthew doesn't want me to go alone, since I have to cross the highway."

"Ah. Jah, I'll be glad to." He smiled. "Just let me know when."

"Danki. I'll find out from Matthew. I was thinking Wednesday, since I know Shanna will have a lot of visitors, but he'll need to go back to work, probably." She frowned. "And…." This was awkward. "I wondered about another date at McDonald's." More time alone together, complete with an eggnog milk shake.

His smile widened. "I'll take you on a date anytime, anyplace you want to go."

Ach, she loved him. Or at least was really close to it.

He'd been lost in his thoughts—about what? Was he as focused on their kiss as she'd been? His lips quirked when her gaze settled on them. Had their kissing been as gut for him as it'd been for her? Or had he found her lacking in some way? She had to know. "What were you thinking about?"

He shook his head. "A jumble of things. I thought about how Katie's daed treats me like a sohn and about Montana. And you. Mostly about you. Ach, Mercy." He stopped walking again. "I wish we were more secluded. Back in the meadow. Somewhere private. I want to kiss you again."

She dipped her head. So, she hadn't been that bad, after all. Relief washed through her. But he'd mentioned Montana. Funny how that word sent an ache through her. She pulled in a breath, hoping to find some courage with it. "Montana. Are you anxious to get back?"

Discomfort crossed his face. He shrugged. "I have a job there. I'll need to go back by mid-January, because calving season starts in February. But…it isn't home."

Really? A smile began. He might be willing to return to Indiana. "So, you miss Shipshewana, then?"

Another shrug. "I miss my family. I miss frozen-over ponds to ice skate on—and the free time to do it. But if I were there, I'd miss Abram. This is the first time we've ever been separated in our lives. But, that said, I probably won't settle here near him. It'll either be the Shipshewana area or Montana. Or somewhere else der Herr has yet to disclose."

"I don't want to go back," Mercy said quietly. "At least, not yet. Everyone there pities me. But I'm not sure where I want to go. I feel displaced here."

"They pity you because of *him*, don't they?" After a moment, Abner's grin reappeared. "But now, there's me. Nobody will feel sorry for you anymore."

"Nein, they'll think I rebounded nicely. Landing one of the Hilty buwe." And she *had* rebounded nicely. Abner Hilty...he was a catch.

She'd probably sounded a bit catty, because Abner turned to face her. He caught both her hands in his and held them loosely as he studied her face for what seemed an eternity, his eyes serious. "You aren't on the rebound, Mercy. I'm the one Gott intends for you. I know it, and I think, somewhere deep inside, you know it, too."

She couldn't hold his gaze. If only she could be as sure of things as Abner. It was like he had a special connection with der Herr. Either that, or he was extremely arrogant, since he dared to presume to know the mind of Gott, saying things like that.

But he also avoided use of the *l* word. Either he didn't feel it, or he felt she wasn't ready to hear it.

She was ready.

Or maybe he was right—she wasn't. She didn't know for sure.

Abner released one of her hands, and they started walking again. He inhaled. "Since you don't think we know each other well enough...my favorite color is blue. The shade of the sky on a cloudless summer day. I like pizza, too, but my favorite food is...I don't know. Too many things to choose from. I like food in general. As long as I'm fed, I'm easy to please." His grin turned impish. "But that's the unimportant stuff. What is important is, how long do you want me to wait before I ask whoever I need to ask for permission to marry you?"

❧

Abner waited a beat for her reaction.

She didn't disappoint. Her eyes widened, and her mouth gaped a moment, before she gasped. "You're incorrigible."

He chuckled. "Nobody's ever told me that before. I'm the gut twin, remember?"

"I'm thinking whoever told you that doesn't know you as well as I do."

Abner laughed. "See? There you go. You do know me. My own mamm told me that, as well as my aenti—Micah's mamm. And my grossmammi. Though usually I overheard that statement when they were scolding Abram for getting caught doing something he shouldn't. You already know me better than my family."

Mercy smiled, then sobered. "But I don't know what brings the shadows to your eyes sometimes. I don't know why you force a smile when you don't feel it."

He blinked, shock working through him, even as he fought to keep his grin in place. Nobody had ever noticed that before. Everyone seemed to think he was perpetually happy-go-lucky.

Her gaze searched his. "Like now," she said quietly.

He pulled in a deep breath and nodded. "You're right, Mercy. You don't know. Nobody does."

And maybe it was time to kum clean.

But if he did, would it scare her away?

Chapter 14

Mercy waited, not daring to breathe. An almost palpable fear tingled its way into her fingertips. Was it merely anticipation? Or was it the fear of knowing what Abner was hiding? She glanced at him, afraid he'd change his mind and the moment would be gone.

A muscle worked in his jaw. "I told you about losing my friends."

"Jah." She nodded, just in case he hadn't heard her quiet acknowledgment.

"After that, I...I vowed to live life to the fullest, because life is short."

Really? That was his philosophy? It explained why he tried so hard to play. And life was short, indeed. Paul's premature passing had taught her that. She reached toward Abner but hesitated as he looked away, the muscle in his face flexing again.

"Did I tell you about my ice-skating skills?"

"What?" She didn't want him to change the subject. His ice-skating ability—or his lack thereof—had nothing to do with...*wait*. Maybe it did. "Nein." She repressed a shiver and looked around. Should they start walking again, back toward the farm? Or should they stand here talking in the middle of the road while the snow fell around them, obliterating their tracks?

He rubbed his gloved hand over his jaw, his gaze shifting to her. The shadows were there, turning his beautiful blue eyes more of a stormy shade. "I have some Englisch friends with TVs. They watch some interesting programs, like the winter Olympics. Ice skating is one of the sports they compete in for medals. And the skaters...." He shook his head. "They have some amazing talent. I could skate—forward, backward, whatever—but, watching them, I learned to jump, twirl, do other things with strange names I don't remember right now, and dance on the ice."

She still didn't see what this had to do with what she wanted to know. She opened her mouth.

Abner shook his head and raised one finger in a silent command to wait. She pressed her lips together.

"I also learned to dance off the ice, admittedly in a different style. The point is, I enjoyed it. Probably too much." He swallowed.

She'd never done any of that during her rumschpringe. It sounded as if Abner had been one of the wild ones, and not such a gut bu after all. Dread settled in her stomach.

"At the ranch on Friday nacht, after the work was done, some of the cowboys used to go into town. They had their paychecks and a thirst for something to drink, and they wanted a gut time. They often invited me to join them, and…." The muscle jumped again. "I eventually gave in. It was a strange world, Mercy. The room was almost blue with smoke. The people, both men and women, were loud, and the music blared. It was like Amish parties in the back field, in one way, but it was very different in another. I danced, and there were plenty of women, but none I was interested in having a permanent relationship with."

Had he done things he shouldn't have with women? Something in her chest pinched. She pressed her lips together, trying to keep the hurt and disapproval at bay. Maybe he'd merely danced with them.

"I'm not proud of the things I did, Mercy. I'm very ashamed."

So, it had been more. Bile rose in her stomach, burning in her throat.

She would have been ashamed, too. Her heart hurt. The beginnings of a headache threatened. Abner—*her Abner*—with other women….

She'd heard enough. She didn't want to know anything more. She swallowed a painful lump in her throat. "Abner—"

"I'm not done." Abner's eyes burned, and he wiped the rough material of Matthew's work glove over his jaw again. "The worst thing was when an Englisch friend named Chad and I decided to go hiking after a nacht of drinking. We never should've gone after dark, especially when we were inebriated—and carrying more alcohol with us. We passed out in a drunken stupor in a cave."

Mercy's eyes widened. She opened her mouth again.

He held up his hand, moving his finger forward to rest against her lips. "Still not done."

She nodded. Her eyes were fixed on him, the brilliant greenish-hazel color bright against her drab clothes. But he saw shadow in her gaze that hadn't been there before. Maybe he should memorize her look before he destroyed the last of her illusions about him.

Still, it was gut to get this painful story out.

"I woke to the smell of bear. Don't ask me how I knew what it was. I'd never smelled one before. I think Gott told me. I opened my eyes to a grizzly standing in the back of the cave, looking right at me, as if I were his dinner. I don't know when he entered, if he came from further back in the cave, or why he didn't attack right away. Gott must have been protecting us. I don't know if Chad died or survived. After I tried to rouse him, I fled. I never heard anything from behind me—nein growling or screaming.

"I went back later to check, and the cave was empty. I didn't see any blood, so I assumed Chad had gotten away, too. I didn't work with him, but I asked around town, hoping to find him. Nobody had seen him since that day, so now I don't know...."

Grief pierced him all over again. "I've never felt so helpless in all my life. Chad's disappearance haunted me, and I never returned to the bars after that. I realized I was on the path to destruction. I fell on my knees and confessed all my shortcomings and sins to der Herr. And this is the best part: I know He heard me. I felt... something, deep inside me. I can't describe it. Peace, forgiveness... that and more. I never had the desire to drink again. I could walk away from it with nein problem. I still wonder what happened to Chad. I wonder if he's alive...and I still have nightmares about the bear."

He also still remembered the verse der Herr had brought to mind that day: *"Be still, and know that I am God."* Standing there, staring at the bear, he'd had an up-close-and-personal encounter with Gott. *"Be still, and know that I am God."*

He would look for Chad when he returned to Montana, find him—if he could—and apologize for leaving him in the cave. Tell him about finding Gott. Those were two big reasons he needed to go back.

Abner swallowed and glanced back at Mercy, his gloved hand rising to cup her chin. "I hate that I abandoned Chad. I hate that I dishonored myself and my body the way I did. I wish...I wish...."

His smile was nowhere to be found. In fact, it'd flatlined. All the bad memories were why he didn't talk about it. Why he hid behind his grin. His heart hurt as he searched the confusion, pain, and other undefined emotions reflected in Mercy's eyes. Her fists were clenched around the fabric of her coat, so tight, it'd probably leave wrinkles. Her forehead was furrowed. But her eyes, still wide, were locked fast on his. As if she needed to see into his soul.

To know if he'd bared it all.

"I have so many regrets I struggle to get past," he said. "But… Gott found me there. And if it wasn't for Gott and His infinite forgiveness, love, and mercy…."

Mercy. That reminded him of the question he'd asked Abram soon after he'd arrived in Seymour: *"Where can I find Mercy Lapp?"* That made him smile. He slid his thumb over her cheek. "I searched for mercy all my life. And after Gott found me, after He saved me, He brought me to you."

❧

Mercy didn't know quite what to think. Her emotions ranged all over the board. Mostly, she was in awe. She also felt something warm and tingly that she didn't recognize. Something she'd never experienced before. Not with Paul. Not with anyone.

Nein wonder Abner sounded like he knew the mind of Gott. Der Herr had gone looking for him and had forged a relationship with him.

She wanted to know der Herr like that. Not the one she feared—not the one who insisted on her following all the bishop's rules. Abner's Gott forgave him for making mistakes. Saved him.

Would Gott ever kum looking for her?

Or maybe He didn't need to, because she'd never left the fold.

Still, she didn't have the relationship with Him that Abner seemed to have.

Abner leaned forward and briefly brushed his lips over hers, heedless of the haus less than twenty yards away. Then he released her but kept his hold on her hand. "I need to get back to Abram's. I should be there by the time they get home from church."

Tears stung her eyes. Their time together was short. Too short. But she didn't look away. There was something different in his expression that she hadn't seen before. Trust—because he'd shared his deepest secret with her? Maybe. And maybe—just maybe—love.

Well, she could dream.

And she was falling in love with him.

This was a man she could willingly obey. Submit to. Follow to the ends of the earth.

Except—maybe not to Montana. Grizzlies? Even their name sounded scary. Not like the common omnivore black bears that roamed the woods here.

Abner looked up at the sky, still pouring snow upon them as they started walking back to Matthew's haus. He opened his mouth and stuck his tongue out to catch a flake, like she'd done earlier.

She fought a smile. "What about lunch? Abram and Katie will eat after their service." Her voice sounded husky, shaky, even to herself.

But then, a casual conversation about lunch was the last thing she wanted to have.

"It's okay. I can make a sandwich, or...." He grinned. "I still have some left in that tin of cookies."

"You could stay and eat with us." Did she sound needy?

"That'd be wunderbaar. But I'll have to leave right after."

Mercy nodded and bit her lip to keep from asking when she would see him again. Would he still agree to drive her to the store and to McDonald's, now that she'd made him share his secrets? She would just try to enjoy the time she had with him now. They followed the road back as slowly as possible. But her temporary home loomed long before she was ready.

When they arrived, Matthew was outside tossing more wood into the furnace. Since the porch stairs were covered with snow again, Abner helped Mercy up, then went to talk to Matthew.

She brushed the snow off her coat and bonnet before stepping inside the warm haus. Then she shrugged off her outerwear, hung it on a hook, and slipped off her shoes. She hadn't brought boots with her. Hadn't thought she'd need them. She hadn't known southern Missouri could get snow like this.

Before she started setting out lunch, she decided to check on Shanna. She stepped into the cozy living room, where Serena babbled to herself—or maybe to her rag doll. Levi slept on Shanna's chest. Shanna lowered her book and looked up with a smile. "Did you have a nice time?"

"Nice" didn't even kum close to describing it. Even so, she nodded. "Do you need anything before I get lunch ready?"

Shanna shook her head. "I'm gut, Mercy. Just so anxious to hear about your walk with Abner. You know what I miss most about the time before I was married? The thrill, the rush, of falling in love. Being married is wunderbaar, and I wouldn't give it up for anything, but there's something about the beginning—getting to know each other...the first kiss...the first time you touch...."

Mercy's face flamed. Ach, this conversation, right after their first kiss....

Shanna's smile grew. "I want to hear all about it."

Right. Mercy didn't know if she could put words to the wonder, the emotions, that raced through her. And talking about it? It just wasn't done.

"I'll go get the food ready." She walked back to the kitchen, her eyes going to the Englisch wall calendar. The picture faded into nothingness, but the Scripture verse stood out. *"For God so loved the world, that he gave his only begotten Son, that whosoever believeth in him should not perish, but have everlasting life."* —John 3:16. She'd have to look it up in context after Abner left. Daed always said that she should never take a verse on its own but should pay attention to the verses that came before and after, too.

Mercy opened the refrigerator and pulled out the platter of thinly sliced roast beef she'd prepared the day before, along with sandwich bread, sliced cheese, pickled eggs, three-bean salad, and pasta salad. Everything would be served cold so they wouldn't break the rule of nein cooking on Sundays.

The door opened with a gust of frigid air, and the men came inside. Abner rubbed his bare hands together. He must've relinquished the borrowed gloves to Matthew. They took off their coats and hats, hanging them on wooden pegs by the door, as Mercy set the table.

Mercy went to help Shanna by putting the newborn in the wooden cradle Matthew had made. She covered him with a flannel boppli blanket, then carried Serena to the table while Shanna pushed herself off the couch and carried her teacup to the kitchen.

Abner and Matthew finished drying their hands and came to the table as Shanna slid into her chair. Mercy poured drinks for everyone, then sat and bowed her head for the silent prayer.

Gott, I want to know You like Abner does. Please show me how.

She peeked at Abner, seated across the table with his head bowed, and, once more, something inside her warmed. Despite his story, she was falling in love.

A new romance. A beautiful thing, like Shanna had said.

What could possibly go wrong?

Chapter 15

Wednesday morgen dawned fresh and clear, without a hint of gray overhead, though snow still covered the ground, and the temperature wasn't expected to climb anywhere near the freezing point. Single digits, Mose predicted. He could forecast the weather down to the degree, and he could tell the time of day with just a glance at the sky.

After finishing breakfast, Abner went to the barn to harness Savvy. He'd told Matthew he would kum to take Mercy to the store first thing, and he didn't want to stay away much longer. It had hurt like the dickens to leave her on Sunday. After their morgen together, talking, playing, and kissing, it took all that was in him to drag himself away.

Mose wandered past as Abner clambered up into the buggy seat. "Headed out, bu?"

"Jah. Promised to take a maidal shopping."

Mose raised his eyebrows. "That be the same maidal who kept you away Saturday nacht into Sunday, ain't so?"

Abner's neck warmed. Since neither Mose nor Abram had mentioned his disappearance when they'd arrived home from church the other day, he'd thought he'd gotten away free and clear. Apparently, that wasn't the case.

"I called." He motioned in the direction of the phone shanty.

"Jah. And you thought we'd wander out in the middle of an ice storm turned blizzard to check messages?"

Well, actually, he had considered that. It wasn't his fault that nobody in this household had a cell phone. Abner shrugged. "At least I called." He grinned.

Mose grinned back. "We figured you'd holed up there when the weather got bad. But maybe I'll take a walk out to the phone shanty today and listen to your message. They did put you up in different rooms, ain't so?"

Abner's face heated. "Jah. Plenty of chaperones, too."

Katie opened the back door and stepped out on the porch. "Are you going somewhere, Abner?"

"Jah. Promised to take Mercy to the store."

"Hold up a minute." She disappeared inside again.

Mose chuckled. "Sounds as if you'll be doing some shopping for her, too. Or taking her along."

Abner tried to keep from groaning. Either one wasn't gut.

"Don't worry," Mose assured him. "Maybe she just has something for you to give to...what's the maidal's name?"

"Mercy."

"That's right." Mose nodded. "Have fun." He headed toward the barn.

The door opened again, and Katie ran out, wearing tennis shoes and a coat. "I have a few things for you to pick up. Unless you want to take me along." She gave him an impish grin.

Abner reached for the list—the lesser of two evils—and scanned it. "Eggs, bananas, oranges, and a big bag of flour. Got it."

"Invite Mercy for dinner sometime."

"I will." Abner folded the paper and slid it inside a pocket. "But it might be a while. Matthew's Shanna just had a boppli bu."

The twinkle in Katie's eyes died. "Ach. I'm sorry, Abner. That's going to cramp your style, ain't so?"

He shrugged. "I'll figure it out." He already had a few plans in place, though they might mean a few late-nacht trips back to Abram's.

"I know you will. Maybe I'll have you take Mamm and me there tomorrow so we can welkum the new little one. I'll fix something for their supper."

Abner nodded. "I'll plan on it." It was nice to have Katie in his corner.

Katie touched his arm. "I'll pray, too. It must be hard to find a girl here when you'll both go in different directions soon."

"Danki for the reminder." Abner forced a smile. "I'll be back as soon as I can."

"Take your time. I know how it is."

Jah, he supposed she did. The difference being, she and Abram were married now and never had to be apart again. If only....

Abner made a clicking sound with his tongue, and Savvy moved down the snow-covered driveway.

He didn't want to think about Abram and Katie. He wanted to think about Mercy. And a way to work it out so they could be together—forever.

❧

Working from memory, Mercy made a list of the items Shanna had rattled off to her the nacht before that she needed from the store. Then she started breakfast: drop biscuits with jam, cream of wheat, scrambled eggs, bacon, and orange juice. Water for koffee was already heating on the stove.

Shanna wandered into the room, fully dressed, moments after Mercy put the last dish on the table. "I'm going to be so spoiled by the time you leave."

Mercy smiled. "You'll be fine." But she hated the idea of leaving. She wasn't ready to go home. Didn't want to go live with Aenti Clara.

"Annie Esh asked about you when she stopped by yesterday. She's visiting her family, and she has a boppli due in March. But you'd have to relocate to Pennsylvania."

That'd be an option. Who knew mother's helpers could be such seasoned travelers? At least it'd be somewhere new to go, instead of home, when the time came. But March? She'd need a new destination kum January.

"Mary-Elizabeth Swartz asked about you, too. She's expecting boppli number six, all buwe so far. But her mamm shot it down. She said that whenever she had her kinner, she got up and fixed supper for her family right after giving birth."

Mercy laughed. "I've known fraus like that." She slid the list across the table toward Shanna. "Abner is going to take me to the store this morgen. Anything else you'd like to add?"

Shanna glanced at the paper. "Nein. Looks like you remembered everything I mentioned. We'll probably have plenty of meals brought in, anyway, despite your being here. Some women can't break the habit. But that's gut. Maybe it'll give your 'friend' a little more courting freedom."

Mercy's face flamed. "I'll get Serena up."

Shanna smiled. "I'll do it. Looks like you have the kitchen pretty well under control. Besides, I've missed getting her up the last few days and weeks…well, since you arrived."

Mercy slid the list into her purse, then turned to check the biscuits.

The door opened with a whoosh of frigid air. She glanced over her shoulder. Matthew knocked the snow from his boots, then slid them off into the plastic bin by the door. "Gut morgen, Mercy."

"Morgen. Shanna is getting Serena. Breakfast will be ready in a moment." She took the biscuits out of the oven.

"Might want to set another place. Just saw Abner coming down the road. Recognized the horse." Matthew headed to the sink to wash up.

A thrill shot through Mercy, and she glanced out the window. Savvy turned into the driveway. "He might've eaten already."

Matthew chuckled. "My guess is he didn't. He was probably in a hurry to get here. And even if he had, he'll at least want a cup of koffee."

Mercy set another place at the table as the door opened with another burst of icy wind. She shivered as she turned toward it.

Abner stood there. "Not quite ready to go?" He knocked the snow off his boots, then removed them and his outerwear.

Mercy blinked at the Englisch pants, belt, and long-sleeved shirt he wore. She'd never seen him in anything but Amish clothes. But she liked the new look. "What's this?"

"Flannel-lined jeans. They're warmer. I use them in Montana. Figured they'd be useful for a day like today." He glanced at Matthew. "Gut morgen."

"Morgen. Flannel-lined. Huh." Matthew eyed the jeans. "Hungry?" He motioned toward the table.

"I had breakfast a bit earlier, but I could eat another bite or two. Always hungry."

Matthew winked at Mercy. "Wash up and have a seat." He pulled over a chair and sat at the head of the table.

"Danki." Abner headed for the sink.

Mercy watched him stride across the room. *Wow.* Who knew he'd look so gut in Englisch clothes? They were much more flattering than the shapeless pants and suspenders all the Amish men wore. Far more formfitting.

She shook her head and turned away, her face heating. She had nein right to think like that. He was in his rumschpringe, so he could dress the way he chose. But when he joined the church, he'd have to conform.

In the meantime…. She glanced over her shoulder again.

She could enjoy the view.

❧❧❧

Abner didn't like grocery shopping. Not in the least bit. But he did like to spend time with Mercy. He squared his shoulders, crumpled Katie's list in his fist, and followed Mercy into the store.

She paused in the entry and looked around. "I'm still getting used to the layout here. Every store is different." She walked away without waiting for him to reply.

He hurried after her, smoothing the list he'd just wadded into a tight ball. "Katie wants a few things, too." He held it out to her.

She didn't take it. "Grab your own cart." She added a teasing smile.

He gave her his best sad-puppy-dog look.

She giggled, took the list, and glanced at it. "Ach, she needs pretty much the same things as Shanna. I think people are craving citrus fruits this time of year. For the vitamin C, probably. Shanna asked for oranges—and grapefruit, too."

"Wouldn't want to get the flu or a common cold—nein kissing," Abner said wryly.

Mercy's face turned a pretty shade of pink.

He moved a little closer, but this place was too public. He released a sigh and followed her to the produce aisle as he tried to think of a way to lure her somewhere private so they could share a personal moment.

Since neither shopping list was very long, they finished the trip with relative efficiency, but it still wasn't fast enough to suit Abner's tastes. He handed the clerk some cash for the food items Katie had requested, then waited while the cashier scanned Mercy's items.

He glanced at the store receipt to check the time. It was a little too early for lunch. "Would you like another eggnog milk shake?" he asked her. Though by the time they got home, it'd be late. And it was too cold to take an ice-cream drink to go. "Or maybe something hot?" he added. Anything to spend more time together.

"Can we share a milk shake? I can't finish an entire one all by myself." She gave him a look that almost bordered on sultry.

Except she was too innocent for that.

Either way, his blood heated. He forced his thoughts away from *that* direction and smiled at the mental image of an old soda shop print featuring a bu and a maidal leaning over a table, two straws in the same drink. "Jah. Absolutely."

At least he could rest in the knowledge that his confession yesterday hadn't cooled her feelings toward him at all.

As soon as she'd paid, he added her purchases to his cart and wheeled everything out to the buggy. He wouldn't mind shopping as much if she were his frau. Maybe he would pretend she was, if he ever had the opportunity to take her again.

Abner glanced at the sky. Dark, stormy. The sunshine from earlier that morgen had vanished. Another round of bad weather threatened. "Would you like lunch, too?"

Mercy wrinkled her cute little nose. "I suppose I could eat something. I love the French fries at McDonald's."

"Maybe a sandwich, too?" His stomach rumbled. Thinking about food always seemed to have that effect on him.

She tilted her head. "Do they still have chicken sandwiches?"

He shrugged. "I think so." It'd been awhile since he'd eaten there. He loaded the groceries into the buggy, assisted Mercy up, and returned the cart while she spread out the blanket.

Even though it wasn't quite noon, the parking lot at McDonald's was crowded. Abner maneuvered around the building to the red hitching post and parked next to another buggy. As he hopped out and secured the reins, a white van pulled into a nearby space. The side doors slid open, and a half dozen Amish men filed out. Working construction, nein doubt. Their Englisch driver followed them into the restaurant.

Abner assisted Mercy down, and then they walked to the building, side by side but not touching. A redheaded Amish girl hovered by the door, looking at the Amish men—all of them bearded—then turned to leave. She did a double take when she saw Abner.

He looked away, but not quickly enough. Interest filled her eyes, and she immediately stopped and retraced her steps. "Hallo. You look familiar. Abram Hilty, ain't so?"

Mercy stopped slightly behind Abner as he looked back at the girl. "He's my brother."

The girl's smile faltered a moment, then widened. "Jah? I didn't know he had one. Abram was my beau until Katie stole him away." A touch of bitterness colored her voice. "But you...." She tucked her hand around his elbow. "I'm Patsy. And I'm simply parched. You can buy me a drink while we get acquainted." She ignored Mercy completely.

Abner frowned and gently removed his arm from her grip. "Nice to meet you, Patsy." He didn't remember Abram ever mentioning her, but then, almost a whole year had passed during which the brothers hadn't been a part of each other's life. He'd missed more than he'd realized, and now he needed to get the scoop on Patsy.

"I would like a peppermint mocha." Patsy reached for his arm again.

Maybe Abner could ask Abram how he'd escaped her clutches. She was a bold one. And Mercy seemed to be withdrawing, allowing a bigger distance between him and her. That was wrong.

Abner wriggled free once more. "You can order whatever you want, Patsy." *And pay for it yourself.* He reached out and snagged Mercy's hand, pulling her forward. "Have you met my girl, Mercy Lapp?"

Chapter 16

*M*ercy could've been invisible. The redhead's brown eyes skimmed her dismissively in a once-over, then shifted back to Abner as she fluttered her lashes.

"If you'll excuse us, Patsy...." Abner tugged on Mercy's hand again. "I promised to buy Mercy lunch before taking her home."

She enjoyed the feel of his skin against hers. The way their fingers intertwined. So personal. And so bold, his holding her hand in public.

"Ach, lunch sounds gut. I'm *starving*," Patsy gushed. "My daed dropped me off here to wait while he ran a few errands, and I just might perish of hunger before he gets back."

Mercy blinked. Most Amish used simple words, not complex ones like "parched" and "perish." How was it that this girl missed the meaning behind Abner's use of the words "my girl" and the way he held Mercy's hand? She wished she could help make her understand he wasn't available, but how? She'd never encountered such an aggressive girl.

Abner's frown deepened, but he didn't say anything when Patsy joined them in line behind the construction workers. He nodded to a few of the men but didn't exchange pleasantries with any of them. Mercy didn't recognize them, but then, she had yet to attend services on a church Sunday.

A cashier opened a new line and motioned to Abner. Without letting go of Mercy's hand, he advanced to the counter and placed their order. Patsy pushed her way between them and jabbed her elbow into Mercy's side. "I want a number three, regular-sized."

Mercy caught Abner's eye, then glanced down at their hands, still clasped. He frowned and shook his head, but she released him and stepped sideways as she watched the price on the register display increase. Abner shifted. "Actually, that's a separate order."

The cashier frowned.

Mercy smiled.

Patsy shoved Mercy to the side with another jolt of her elbow and pressed herself against Abner's side. "But I don't have any money. And it's not nice to invite a girl to lunch and not pay her way." She batted her eyelids again.

He invited her to lunch? Mercy mentally replayed the meeting and conversation. Nobody had said anything about Patsy joining them—except for Patsy herself.

Mercy couldn't watch this. She'd never met an Amish girl like this one. "I'll go find a seat." Maybe in the buggy. It might be beyond cold out there, but it was better than being frozen out by a too-aggressive Amish *maidal* making a play for *her* man.

Hadn't Patsy's *mamm* ever told her that men like to do the pursuing? Mercy's *daed* had made that more than clear to his *dochters.*

She "accidentally" stepped on Patsy's toe as she walked away. Payback for the elbowing.

"Ouch!"

Ach, that felt *gut.* But guilt ate at her as she moved further away. She shouldn't have done that. It was unkind. *Forgive me, Gott. Please.*

She turned back, thinking of apologizing to Patsy.

Abner handed over some cash, and Patsy's expression changed from outrage to smugness.

Mercy shrugged and turned away without apologizing. Maybe Daed had been wrong. She found a table—for two—and sat.

If Patsy pushed her way in between them again, she'd…what? Anything she did would go against the way she'd been raised—except for quiet submission. And her heart objected to that.

Abner picked up the tray of food and carried it to the place Mercy had picked, though he doubted the small table would keep the obnoxious strawberry blonde from pushing her way in. Especially given the way she trailed after him, so closely that she almost stepped on his heels.

He set the tray on the table—it took up almost all the space—and slid into the other seat. He started unloading their food.

Pushy Patsy stood beside him a moment, holding her tray of food. "Aren't you going to get a chair for me, Abner?"

"Here, Patsy. You can have mine." Mercy jumped to her feet.

Abner shook his head and opened his mouth to object, but then he saw Mercy stop at another table for two, across the room. Her eyebrows rose as she glanced at him.

He grinned and reloaded his tray. "Jah, you can sit here, Patsy." He walked over to where Mercy sat, and started unloading the tray again.

Patsy pushed her way to the empty seat across from Mercy and claimed it. Mercy slumped, evidently not prepared to move again. Besides, that tactic had proven futile. Patsy seemed incapable of taking any hints. What would it require to get through to her? A two-by-four to the prayer kapp?

Ugh. Mamm hadn't raised him to be rude to women. However, she'd probably never met anyone like Patsy. He'd be sure to ask Abram about her when he got home. Somehow, he couldn't see his brother welcoming her attention. Not when he'd married a wunderbaar girl like Katie.

Abner would be nice. He would be nice. He would be nice. He glanced at Mercy, hoping to catch her eye, but she didn't look up.

Pulling in a breath for fortification, Abner slid his tray to the side. He took Patsy's tray and unloaded it. Smothering another sigh, he pressed his lips together and glanced at Mercy.

She looked as unhappy about the invasion as he felt.

Abner grabbed another chair and sat between the two girls. At least he'd be alone with Mercy on the way home.

Unless Patsy somehow maneuvered her way into his buggy.

Nein, nein, nein.

He couldn't allow that.

Besides, something told him that if he didn't stand up to Patsy, he'd be saying good-bye to Mercy. If only they could leave now and go somewhere else to eat their lunch.

But it was too cold for a picnic in the park. Too cold to eat the food as they rode home.

Staying here was the only option. Maybe praying Patsy's daed would kum for her soon.

Abner glanced out the window, then looked around the restaurant. Nein other Amish were here, except for the half-dozen men who'd arrived in the white van.

And hadn't Patsy been leaving when they'd kum in?

Which meant that her story about her daed dropping her off had been a lie. She'd probably already eaten, which would explain why she was barely picking at her food right now. He gritted his teeth as the truth dawned. He'd been a fool. And he might have risked losing Mercy by going along with this girl's manipulations.

She was on a manhunt. And he was her intended victim.

Abner cringed.

Gullible, Hilty.

He was a first-class fool for giving in as much as he had.

Mercyhad lost her appetite when Patsy had joined them, but she forced herself to eat her lunch. She nein longer wanted the eggnog shake that sat so temptingly in the center of the table—the treat she and Abner had planned on sharing.

It seemed awkward to share a drink with him while another girl flirted shamelessly, even though he did nothing to encourage her attention.

That did make her feel a little better. Especially when he glanced at her and rolled his eyes.

Abner slid the shake a little closer to Mercy. "Have some. Please." Lines furrowed his forehead, and a muscle jumped in his jaw, as if Patsy's infringing on their time together made him ever so close to losing his temper.

That would be a sin, but it seemed that nothing short of a man's temper erupting would be enough to scare away the unflappable Patsy.

"Seemed" was the operative word.

Patsy put her hand on Abner's arm. "I don't mind if I do. Danki." She reached for the eggnog shake with her other hand.

Mercy pushed her chair away from the table. "I'll be back. I… um…I have to go." And she did, before she ended up losing her own temper and doing something that would require her to kneel and confess before the bishop and the church.

Abner took the eggnog shake from Patsy before the straw touched her lips. He caught Mercy's arm as she pushed past. "The drink belongs to Mercy. I was talking to *her*." His voice could've frozen the springs that bubbled up from the ground in the woods near Shanna's haus. "Mercy, let's go."

"I guess my daed isn't coming." Patsy stood. "Would you mind giving me a ride home? I don't live too far from Katie." She fluttered her lashes yet again.

Abner glanced pointedly out the window. "Why would I give you a ride when your buggy is right out there? You want to leave your horse waiting in the cold?"

Mercy's eyes widened. She looked out the window, then returned her gaze to Patsy. The girl's cheeks were tinted slightly with something that might've been guilt, but she recovered quickly.

"You are so *mean*. We're finished, Abner Hilty." She stood and flounced off, leaving her food on the table.

Mercy's gaze shot back to Abner. His eyes followed the other woman, a muscle still jumping in his jaw. Both of them watched Patsy march out the door and over to the waiting buggy. Then Abner turned to Mercy.

"I *am* mean, ain't so?" He grinned. "Do you want to take the milk shake to go or enjoy it here?"

"To go. Please." She'd had enough drama today.

"You sure?"

"Jah." Mercy watched Patsy maneuver her buggy out of the spot before she headed for the door.

One of the younger Amish men high-fived Abner as he passed. "She's been asking for it for a while. Not very nice to say so, but…her daed needs to curtail her, for sure."

And for certain. Mercy swallowed a lump in her throat. Maybe Daed had been right to say that maidals shouldn't pursue buwe.

"I'll be having a talk with a preacher about what we witnessed," the other man added. He nodded at Mercy before turning back to his meal.

Mercy followed Abner out the door. He'd handled himself well. Made his relationship with her clear. Fought for her without actually fighting. Something welled inside her. Tears pooled in her eyes. She wanted to throw herself in his arms and hug him tight.

She accepted his help into the buggy, then snuggled next to him for the ride home.

And not just for the warmth, though that was a definite plus.

Chapter 17

Abner drove Savvy as slowly as possible back to the Yoders' haus, not wanting the time spent snuggling with Mercy to end one second before it had to.

Yet all too soon, they arrived. The haus seemed quiet. He parked the buggy in front of the barn, but he didn't bother unhitching Savvy, since he wouldn't be able to stay long. Unfortunately. He shouldn't have told Katie that he'd return as soon as he could.

"Kum with me." He would help Mercy unload the groceries later. First, he wanted—needed—a moment of privacy. Just long enough to kiss her. To hold her. Before he tore himself away.

Mercy trailed him into the barn without asking any questions. He led her to a stall at the back, one that wasn't occupied. Shanna and Matthew were just starting out, so their farm was small, with just a few animals, as well as a blueberry patch. Matthew's dream. Or so he'd told Abner.

Several hay bales had been arranged on the dusty floor, and a lantern hung from a hook in the ceiling. An old blanket was spread halfway across one of the bales. "Matthew told me about this room," Abner said. "On visiting Sundays, this is where the older men talk while the younger men wrestle."

It looked like a cozy sitting room. Matthew probably waited there when an animal was in labor and he needed to stay close.

Maybe this was where Shane had waited it out while Kristi had assisted Shanna with labor—or whatever a midwife did. Abner shrugged and glanced at Mercy.

"You wrestle, ain't so?" She eyed his arms.

He resisted the urge to flex his muscles. He was young and strong, and, like most young men, he enjoyed showing off his strength for the maidals.

Abner rubbed his forehead, then raked his fingers through his hair. He shrugged. "I have wrestled some, jah. But that's not why I brought you here." He sat and patted the space next to him. "Join me for just a second. Please."

❧

Mercy sat beside him, a jolt of anticipation running through her as she tried to imagine what Abner might want to say before he left.

Maybe he would finally ask her to be his girl, even though he'd already declared his intentions to marry her. He'd also told Patsy that she was his girl. Apparently, he chose to disregard the Scripture verse about doing everything "*decently and in order.*"

Not that she minded.

He pulled off his gloves and tossed them on another hay bale, then reached for her hand and gave the tip of her mitten a slight tug. It slid off without resistance.

Her stomach clenched as he repeated the process with her other mitten. He tossed his hat on the other bale, then reached for the black string of her bonnet.

"Uh, Abner?" She pulled back a bit. Why was he doing this? The room was warmer than the outdoors, since it was protected from the elements, but it was far from comfortable. And undressing...?

"Don't worry. That's it." He reached for her again. His hand settled briefly on her shoulder, and the heavy fabric of her coat shifted. But he didn't remove it. Instead, he pulled her closer, his hand sliding down her back, his arm enfolding her snugly, holding her tight. His other hand rose to cup her cheek, and his gaze lowered to her mouth.

A violent shiver worked through her. Any shred of resistance fled the scene at the look of intent in his eyes. "Ich liebe dich." The words formed in her mind and were out of her mouth before she could monitor them.

So much for doing things decently and in order.

His eyes shot up to meet hers, and a slow smile formed on his well-shaped lips. "I dreamed of this moment all last nacht." He leaned forward, closing the slight distance between them, and his lips settled firmly on hers—as if he knew they'd be welkum, since they'd kissed Sunday in the meadow. His hand lowered to cup her jaw, gently holding her in place.

He wasn't wrong. Her mouth instinctively softened and molded against his, her lips parting slightly, as she responded to his kiss.

His arm tightened around her, and she could feel the strength of his muscles through the fabric of her coat and dress. She wrapped her arms around his neck, her fingers threading through his hair, as one kiss morphed into two. It became impossible to tell when one kiss ended and another began.

He groaned, his hand leaving her jaw, lowering to her waist, sliding beneath the fabric of her coat. She felt herself moving, shifting, and her arms tightened around Abner as he lowered her to the hay, his upper body coming to rest on hers.

His kisses changed, becoming more insistent. And his hand started a slow northward migration.

"Ich liebe dich," Mercy whispered against his lips.

His only reply was another firm kiss before his mouth left hers and trailed fire to her ear and down her neck.

"Abner," she moaned. A weak protest.

His lips came back to claim hers.

"There you are."

It took Mercy a moment to recognize Matthew's voice as Abner rolled off her in one smooth move and rose to his feet. Even in the dim light of the stable, she could see the red flooding his neck and face. He looked down, avoiding her gaze, and raked his fingers through his hair, then reached for his hat and slapped it down on his head.

Mercy scrambled to sit, her face heating. Abner reached out his hand for hers, caught it, and pulled her to her feet, then lowered his gaze back to the floor. "Sorry."

She wasn't sure to whom he was apologizing, her or Matthew. Maybe both.

Matthew nodded once, frowning, his gaze on Abner, then backed up a step. "Mercy, we need to talk to you inside. Now." He turned and walked away.

She caught her breath. Her heart stuttered to a stop, then started up again with an erratic beat. Her hands shook as she reached for her bonnet and mittens. This was it. She would be fired, sent home in disgrace, and, as soon as Daed had his say, put on the next bus to Aenti Clara's.

Abner's hand clasped hers. "It was my fault. Don't worry."

She was just as guilty as he was. Maybe more so, because she could've said nein. Tears burned her eyes but didn't escape, thankfully. Daed would scold her for even allowing the tears to form; he'd mock her for behaving like a boppli. He'd upbraided her harshly for giving in to her grief over Paul by staying in bed, crying, all day. Mamm had been more sympathetic, but even she had reminded Mercy that Amish were stoic. *Show nein emotion.*

Her breaths came rapidly, and a wave of dizziness washed over her.

Abner's hand left hers and slid around her waist.

She stiffened.

His arm stayed. "You're turning white. Are you okay?"

She forced the wave of dizziness to recede and pulled away from him. "They're going to send me home, I just know it." She inhaled and exhaled in short gasps as she balled the items in her fists.

"Don't worry, Mercy. I'll explain everything. I'm to blame. And if they do send you home, I'll go with you. It's about time for me to declare my intentions to your bishop, anyway." He lifted one shoulder, then let it fall. "I didn't talk to the bishop here because I… well, I didn't know what to do. Or even who your bishop is."

He would declare his intentions? Relief flooded through her. As did a sense of acceptance. But she didn't know who the bishop was, either—only that, whoever he was, he wouldn't understand pink camouflage.

That made her smile. "The bright spot of being sent home in disgrace would be leaving these horrid brown dresses behind."

Abner blinked, his gaze lowering to her outfit. Then he grinned. "Leave it to you to find the sunshine behind the clouds."

He leaned toward her, as if intending to kiss her again. But that was what had started the whole mess to begin with, so she stepped away. "Might as well get it over with." She straightened her spine, raised her chin, and marched out of the stall.

Abner followed Mercy, his heart heavy. He hadn't meant to get her in trouble, especially since it was his less-than-stellar motives that had landed her there. He'd wanted only a brief moment to kiss her, but that kiss had escalated out of control far too quickly after her breathless admission of love and her quick, hungry response.

She loved him.

Twice, she'd said those magic words. And he hadn't responded either time. It'd seemed wrong. He'd allowed the words to lodge in his throat, unsaid, because it would have been as if he'd returned her affections solely to gain favor in his unplanned and unintentional seduction. He despised men who did that. *Just tell the girl what she wants to hear. You'll get lucky every time.*

Well, truthfully, he hadn't been looking to "get lucky." All he'd wanted was a brief moment of privacy before they joined the family. There would be plenty of time for everything else after they'd said their wedding vows and knelt before the bishop and preachers in front of their family and friends.

It had simply gotten out of control.

His fault. All his fault.

However, he'd mentioned his desire to declare his intentions to the bishop. That should count for something.

He put his hand on her shoulder and stopped her just inside the barn doors. "Mercy, I'm sorry." He sighed. "Ich l—"

A shadow came out of the darkness and joined them. *Matthew.* "I took care of your horse, Abner. You're going to want to be here."

Here? Jah, but what Abner wanted most was to tell Mercy he loved her. Uninterrupted. She needed to know, didn't she? And then, when they got home to Shipshewana, he would go with her, to hold her hand and support her during the disgrace of having been let go by her employer, all because of her—their—wanton behavior. And he would ask permission to marry her, and all would be fine. Beyond fine. Perfect.

Well, practically perfect. They were human, after all.

Matthew led the way across the barnyard, and Mercy trailed behind him, head lowered, as if she were about to face a military firing squad. Abner tried to think of words of encouragement to cheer her afterward.

Katie would take Mercy in until they could arrange bus passage. And he would be overjoyed to have Mercy in the same haus as he.

He followed the others into the kitchen.

When they entered, they found Shanna pacing the floor, a horrified expression on her face. Her cell phone was clutched in one hand, the newborn boppli tucked against her other shoulder. His thumb was in his mouth, and he made sucking noises. His blue eyes were wide open, looking around.

Shanna's gaze narrowed on Mercy, and she extended the cell phone toward her.

The first indication that this wasn't about *them*.

The heavy hand of dread landed hard on Abner's chest, threatening his oxygen supply. Whatever it was, it was bad. Worse than he'd imagined.

His throat closed up.

Shanna opened her mouth. The phone shook in her hand. "Mercy—"

"I'm sorry. So sorry. It won't happen again," Mercy said. "Please forgive us. Forgive me." Her breath caught, as if she were on the verge of tears.

Abner studied her. Why such a guilty conscience? He didn't feel quite the same weight of sin. Should he? It would probably happen again, though he would certainly try harder to keep his hands from wandering where they shouldn't go.

Shanna snapped her mouth shut. The hand holding the phone fell to her side, and confusion colored her face.

Abner put his hand on Mercy's shoulder. "Shhhh." That was the only sound he could manage in his oxygen-deprived state. Hopefully, the news wouldn't be as bad as he feared. But judging by the horror on Shanna's face when they'd entered....

Still, he couldn't imagine anything that could be so terrible to warrant that.

Unless something had happened to one of their family members.

Wait. One of *her* family members. His family would have contacted Abram, not Shanna.

"What are you talking about?" Shanna asked, tilting her head. "You have nothing to be sorry for."

Matthew cleared his throat. "I did find them in a...compromising position...in the stable."

"Ach," Shanna said. Then she shrugged. "Mercy, I'm not going to scold you for that. Courting couples, that's...well, you know, normal. Matthew and I—"

He cleared his throat again.

Well, at least Shanna would forgive them. Abner glanced at Mercy to see how she was handling the gift of grace.

A slight smile appeared as she met his gaze. He grinned back.

Shanna's face had colored. "Right. Well, it's normal. Just so long as you don't anticipate your marriage vows. And even if you did, Gott will still forgive—"

"Shanna." Matthew's voice held a tone of warning. "Get to the point."

"Right. The point." She raised the phone again and looked at Mercy. "Your daed called, and...Paul is back in town." There was a touch of skepticism in her voice.

Mercy swayed. The pretty pink that had colored her cheeks faded to nothingness. "What? He's...dead."

Abner firmed his grasp on Mercy's shoulder. When she swayed again, he moved behind her and wrapped both his arms around her, drawing her against his chest for support. His arms brushed against her—

He took a deep breath and slid his arms down a few inches.

"He's alive," Shanna said, with hesitancy in her voice. She searched Mercy's face.

Abner tightened his arms around her. Maybe he was the one who needed the support.

"How can he possibly be alive? It's been a year. Over a year. And...and we had a memorial service for him. I moved on."

Abner nodded. It was a bit inconsiderate of the man to kum back to life now.

"All I know is, he went to your daed's haus and asked to see you, and your daed called and asked you to kum home," Shanna said. "Well, he didn't exactly ask—he *told* me, in nein uncertain terms, to send you home." Her voice firmed. "I told him that I couldn't possibly spare you now, and you'd be home after the first of the year. He refused to accept that and said that you'd be on the next bus... or else."

Or else...what? Abner frowned. Mercy had to stay here. She *had* to. She'd told him she loved him, and....

"I'm staying here," Mercy stated. "He stayed away a year. He let me believe he was dead. And...and I'm not about to drop everything and run back to him now." Her voice sounded firm, but it wavered a little.

"Gut girl," Abner whispered. But his heart felt like it wanted to pound right out of his chest and shatter on the ground. Paul—

her old beau—was *alive?* He still couldn't wrap his mind around the notion.

"Gut." Shanna smiled, but her eyes were sad. "It seems to me we have options now. Abner is courting you, and—"

"Shanna." Matthew cleared his throat. "We won't interfere with matters of the heart."

"But you said they were in a compromising position," she pointed out. "We could claim that Abner dishonored her, and—"

Jah, and then he'd be forced to marry her—a gut thing, but....

"Nein," Abner spoke up. "I want Mercy to choose me because she loves me. Not because she's forced into it because of a lie." He swallowed, released her, and stepped away. "Besides, we only kissed. Hardly a compromising position."

Matthew quirked his eyebrows but remained silent.

"Maybe it was a little more than a kiss. But still...." Abner shrugged and took another step backward.

"Are you going to be in trouble with your daed for disobeying orders, Mercy?" Shanna asked, her voice gentler.

Mercy nodded, a mixture of resolve and dismay in her expression. "But I have a job and other obligations, and I'm old enough to make my own decisions."

Abner raked his fingers through his hair, dislodging his hat. It fell to the ground. He let it lie. "Not to mention, this...*Paul*...has been dead a year. He really should've had the decency to stay dead."

Chapter 18

Mercy stared at the cell phone Shanna pressed into her palm, waves of panic washing over her. Bile burned her throat as her stomach rebelled, threatening to lose its contents. She didn't want to face this issue. "What am I—"

"Call your daed," Matthew said. "Tell him you'll be home as soon as you can get there."

She looked up. "But I'm working for you until the end of December. Then I might be going to Mary-Elizabeth's haus, if she talks her mamm into letting me kum, and—"

Shanna waved a hand in dismissal. "Ach, whatever. First finish your obligations here, then go. Your daed will just have to understand."

Daed would never tolerate such a measure of disrespect. Not that she was second-guessing her decision, but it was reality. She would be punished. Mercy frowned. "I don't even know how to use this thing." Not that it mattered. She didn't know what to say, either.

"Avoiding the inevitable return will give you and Abner more time together," Shanna said. "Anyone can see you're perfect for each other, and—"

Matthew grunted. "You're interfering...."

"Right." Shanna rolled her eyes. "Anyway, the phone is easy to use." She reached for it, took it back, and angled herself so Mercy could watch. "You just push here to pull up recent calls, then you press the 'call' button beside the number for your phone shanty, and voilà." Her thumb moved over the phone as she spoke.

What?

"Don't look so confused. Here, it's ringing." Shanna shoved the phone back into Mercy's hand.

"But what do I say?"

"Hallo?" Daed's gruff voice came through the device.

Mercy started and almost dropped the phone.

"Daed, this is Mercy. Shanna said you'd called—"

"I wasted enough time out here in the phone shanty waiting for your call. You know how busy I am. Where were you?"

"I went to town, and—"

"When are you coming home?"

"I don't know. I have—"

"Stop this foolishness. You'll be on the next bus out of town. First thing in the morgen. Did that woman tell you Paul returned?"

"Jah. But I'm in love with—"

"Of course, you are. And it's been a year since you've seen him."

"Abner." Her gaze moved to meet his.

Sympathy filled his eyes. Or maybe it was pity, along with something else. She couldn't quite decipher his emotions before he concealed them again.

But then, he hadn't said he loved her. She was the one who'd blurted it out. Not once, not twice, but three times in less than an hour.

And he hadn't said…. Her throat threatened to close. But then, he had held her. Steadied her. Said something about wanting to declare his intentions to the bishop.

"What?" Daed's reply was just shy of a roar. "Who?"

Mercy sucked in a mouthful of air that didn't seem to hold even a thimbleful of oxygen. She wasn't sure what to say now. The damage had already been done. Her hands shook. "Abner Hilty. His family lives near you—"

"I know the Hiltys. How can you be in love with him? You barely know the bu. You didn't grow up with him; you didn't go to school with him. Pure nonsense."

"He's here, visiting family. We got reacquain—"

"Foolishness, plain and simple. Stop the nonsense and kum home."

Maybe Matthew's approach would be best. "I'll be home as soon as I can." It just wouldn't be on the next bus.

Nein, the next bus she planned to catch would be to Pennsylvania.

"Gut, gut. Glad to hear some common sense from you. About time. Tell Matthew Yoder I'll reimburse him for the bus ticket."

"Daed, I—"

Warm hands closed over hers, and the cell phone was pulled away from her ear. She looked up at Abner. He gave her a sympathetic smile, but it didn't reach his eyes.

He brought the phone to his ear. "Mr. Lapp, this is Abner Hilty. I love your dochter and intend to marry her."

Something inside Mercy sprang to life, and she straightened, her spirits brightening. She hated that Abner and Daed were going head-to-head, albeit over a long-distance line, but what else could be done?

"Since it's not an emergency, there's nein point in her coming home now," Abner went on. "She can finish her obligations here first. It'll be only a couple more weeks, and then she can visit, if you'd like." Abner's brow furrowed as he listened to whatever Daed was saying to him. Then, "Danki. Bye." He pulled the phone away from his ear and pressed the screen. "First of the year."

Mercy stared at the phone as he handed it to Shanna. Then she looked back at Abner. "He agreed?" Daed had really allowed someone else—other than the bishop or the preachers—to tell him how it would be? Inconceivable.

Abner shrugged. "What choice did he have? You're here, he's there. He said he'd have a talk with Paul…and tell him."

Really? This was gut. She wouldn't have an uncomfortable meeting with Paul, where she'd be forced to tell the man she'd once believed she would marry that while he'd been presumed dead, she'd fallen in love with someone else.

That sounded so strange.

Though, she would like to hear his story. How had he managed to survive a violent storm on Lake Michigan, and where had he been for the past year? It was improbable. Impossible. Unrealistic. Unheard of. And inconvenient.

Weeks ago, she would have welcomed the news. But that was before she'd met Abner. Everything was different now.

Abner's temples pounded, a slow throb that worsened with every beat of his heart. Tension, nein doubt. And nein wonder. Between encountering Pushy Patsy at McDonald's, getting caught "making out" in the stable, and learning that Mercy's deceased beau had kum back to life, he was dealing with almost unprecedented stress.

Not only that, but while he'd nein idea what was said to Mercy, he'd seen her shoulders slump, despair washing across her expressive face. Too bad her daed hadn't listened to her but had kept cutting her off mid-sentence. Just like Shanna sometimes did.

And Mercy was nice enough to let him. And Shanna.

And even Abner.

That was how she'd been raised. Amish girls were taught submission at an early age.

Abner's eyes moved to Shanna. She didn't fit the mold. Though he remembered hearing something about her running away from home and living with the Englisch for a time. Matthew certainly had his hands full with her, but he didn't seem to mind.

His gaze returned to Mercy. He wished he could go to her, hold her, even wake up and find that this all had been nothing more than a terrible dream. But it was real. Too real. Bile rose in his stomach, and he pressed his hand against it. "I...uh...I should probably go."

"Don't we need to plan what we're going to do first?" Shanna laid Levi in the boppli buggy. "If I were Paul, I wouldn't accept this, especially since he went to Mercy's daed's haus right away, looking for her."

Abner had to agree. He'd be the same way. But how could he and Mercy make plans? The ball was in the other man's court. Well, in Mercy's, too. Abner had already interfered far more than he should have by telling her daed to leave her alone.

Not exactly conducive to a gut relationship with the man he hoped would be his future father-in-law.

He sighed.

He didn't regret declaring his love for her, but he would've liked to have told her privately first.

Matthew frowned. "We really should've talked this through before any phone calls were made. Mercy, we can send you home now if you need to go. Shanna can hire a local girl for a few weeks."

"Nein, I want her to stay." Shanna paced the floor. "I prayed about putting that ad in *The Budget*, Matthew."

His gaze softened. "I know. It was the right thing to do. It helped Mercy start to heal, I think."

Abner glanced back at Mercy. She stood quietly, head bowed. Waiting submissively for someone to make a decision for her, nein doubt. He twisted his hat in his hands. The decision was hers to make. Nobody else's. And she'd already said she wanted to stay. Said she loved him. Told her daed so.

"Mercy already said what she wanted," he reminded Shanna, the implication being there was nothing to discuss. Nothing to decide.

Except for the possibility of Paul traveling from Shipshewana to Seymour to retrieve her.

They'd cross that bridge if they came to it.

His eyes met Mercy's as she raised her head. She looked relieved that he'd spoken.

She was such a beautiful girl. And when she let loose a little and allowed herself to laugh and have fun, she was incredible.

His stomach hurt.

If they came to that bridge? It wasn't a matter of *if* but *when.*

Abner plopped his hat on his head as he crossed the room to Mercy. "I'll unload your groceries from the buggy, and then I should go." He shut the door behind him, boots clomping down the porch steps.

She looked down at the wood floor. They'd left snow melting in puddles beneath their shoes, as neither of them had bothered to unbundle, but it wouldn't take much to clean up. She went to the broom closet for the mop. It would give her something to do while her thoughts whirled, her stomach churned, and her emotions ran all over the place—relief that Paul wasn't dead, anger that he'd left her for over a year without any contact, heartbreak over falling in love with Abner, only to face the possibility of being torn away from him.

Shanna was right—if she didn't go to Paul, he would kum to her. *Probably.* On the other hand, he'd kept his existence a secret for so long. Maybe he'd gone to see Daed to officially call it quits so he could marry someone else. When he found out that Mercy had fallen in love with another man, he'd be relieved, and that would be the end of it.

Nein, he wouldn't kum. That scenario had to be right. Because unless der Herr had worked a modern-day miracle of outrageous proportions, there was absolutely nein way someone dead could kum alive again. Paul had hidden on purpose. A coward, afraid to face his girl and break up with her, and then, finally....

Her thoughts flip-flopped worse than a fish out of water, dangling at the end of a hook.

Which was exactly what she felt like. A fish. Out of water.

Confused. Hurt. Angry. Scared.

She could go on indefinitely with the adjectives.

"Mercy?"

She snapped her spine straight at the roughness in the male voice. Had he been calling her for a while?

Abner stood in the doorway, holding two plastic bags of groceries. His lips were turned down slightly, his jaw set. His blue eyes were still dark with pain. Hurt. Confusion. Then they shuttered.

She swallowed. This couldn't be any easier on him than on her. She hurried over to take the bags from him. "Sorry."

"It's okay. Be right back with the flour." His voice was still rough with emotion.

She carried the bags to the table and gazed around the empty kitchen. Sometime during her mental wanderings down multiple rabbit trails, both Shanna and Matthew had vanished.

Mercy unloaded the bags and put away the food, all of it fresh produce and baking goods. Oranges. Bananas. Rice. Sugar. Salt. She unloaded the last item just as Abner reappeared.

He crossed the room, carrying the heavy bag of flour, snow still on his boots. "Where do you want this?"

She pointed to the basement door. "I'll show you." She grabbed a flashlight, flicked it on, and led the way down into the darkness.

Shanna's jars of garden produce were neatly lined up against one corner of the basement, at a right angle—fruit on one side, vegetables on the other. Metal coolers for storing flour and other dried goods were stacked against one wall. The idea was to keep bugs out. It seemed effective. At least, Mercy hadn't noticed any bugs in the foodstuffs.

"Nice." Abner laid the flour bag gently inside the cooler Mercy had opened. "Katie and her mamm could learn something from Shanna."

"It is nice," Mercy agreed as she closed the lid. The flashlight flickered and died, so she slipped the worthless light into her apron pocket. "One of the few basements that don't spook me."

"Gut." Abner reached for her, tugging her gently into his arms. "I won't let him win, Mercy. I can't. Ich liebe dich."

A whimper rose in her throat and escaped. She wrapped her arms around his neck and leaned into him.

"Ach, Mercy." His head lowered, his lips brushing hers.

She kissed him back with reckless abandon, feeling desperate to have some sense of security in her life. Needing to know that, in spite of everything, he still wanted her.

He pulled away, physically as well as emotionally. "Nein."

Her eyes burned. Paul's return had changed everything.

"Do you need help getting upstairs?" He glanced toward the dim light at the top of the stairs.

"Need…to be…alone." Tears burned her eyes. At least the darkness hid them.

"Okay. I'll toss pebbles at your window tomorrow nacht. Wait for me."

Then he was gone.

The light faded as he reached the top of the stairs. All she could see was his shadow. Then the shadow left, and she heard the outside kitchen door close.

She sank down on the concrete floor, covering her face with her hands, and rocked back and forth.

He'd said he loved her. Said he couldn't let Paul win.

But….

She couldn't think clearly. And she couldn't find the strength to get up off the floor. But maybe that was where she needed to be.

In the dark cold of the basement, alone with der Herr.

Ach, Gott. What am I to do?

Chapter 19

*N*umb, Abner drove back to Abram's haus. He parked the buggy in the drive, unhitched Savvy, and let her out to pasture before carrying Katie's groceries inside and leaving them in a jumble on the kitchen table. Then he headed out to the barn to clean out the stalls—mindless work that would allow him to muddle through the rest of the day.

He thought of nothing but Mercy. His mood drifted toward an ever-widening, swirling black hole of fear. At any moment, he might collapse within himself, never to be seen again.

It reminded him of the time he'd leapt foolishly into the murky, cold water of a neighbor's pond. He'd sunk beneath a tangle of roots and weeds before fighting his way back to the surface. His lungs had nearly burst from want of air.

Like now. When his whole world threatened to close in around him. He'd never wanted anyone, felt for anyone, loved anyone, the way he did Mercy. The moment he'd first seen her in the grocery store that day, his heart had recognized her. And he was completely, 100 percent, gone.

And now…. Now, he had to give her space.

Right?

Or maybe now would be a gut time to push.

He frowned, recalling the confusion in her eyes. The angst. Indecision.

Nein. She had to decide. Because if it were up to him, he'd tell her to pack her things and kum with him to Montana. Someplace Paul would never think to look. He'd marry her as soon as he was allowed, and then they'd inform her family and friends of their location.

But that would be wrong.

He slammed down the shovel outside the stall. It banged against the wall before resting there. Then he stomped off, steered the wheelbarrow out, and dumped it, then came back inside to start on the next stall.

Abner's peripheral vision picked up two sets of boots standing in the entrance. He glanced up and met the gaze of Mose, then Abram. His twin brother had deep concern in his eyes, while Mose wore an expression somewhere between amusement and a smirk.

"You left that last stall 'bout clean enough for a picnic on the ground, bu," Mose remarked.

Abner raised his hand and squeezed his neck. "I'll go back and spread out fresh—"

"Not the point. Something's bothering you."

Abner looked away from Abram's too-knowing father-in-law and dumped another shovelful into the wheelbarrow.

"You want to talk?"

"Nein." There was nothing to talk about. Except his feelings. And what were his feelings? Well, he didn't *feel* like losing Mercy. He hadn't *felt* like getting up at o-dark-thirty, either, especially after a late nacht, but he'd done it anyway.

He shut his eyes against the sudden burn.

"Lovers' quarrel?" Abram's question was barely audible.

"Nein." Abner let the shovel fall against the wall, resisted the urge to stomp like a bu having a temper tantrum, and forced his eyes open. Willed the tears to stay put and not cause him any further embarrassment.

"Not a quarrel. She…. He…." His throat clogged. "I…."

"Slow down, take a deep breath, and start at the beginning," Mose advised.

Abner attempted to follow his instructions. He couldn't help that his voice cracked, and he had to clear his throat a couple times. "Mercy's former beau, he was missing for a year. Presumed dead. But apparently he's alive."

He waited in the almost suffocating silence for words of wisdom. For some advice.

For what seemed like an eternity, nothing came.

Then Mose turned away. "Sounds like you have a bit of a faith issue, bu. Wait and pray."

❧❧

Mercy didn't know how long she'd stayed in the dark quietness of the basement, just that a chill had seeped into her bones and she'd cried herself out. Her prayers were a tangled mess. Abner…Paul… she loved them both. Paul first, and then, when she'd thought Paul was gone forever, Abner.

Paul, with his quiet stability. Going fishing that day had been the only crazy thing he'd ever done, as far as she knew. She'd always been able to count on him, to know he'd be there to help her with those confusing math problems when fuzzy purple one-eyed octopuses took over her brain and left her without a coherent thought. At least, that was what Paul always said had happened. She never would've imagined fuzzy purple one-eyed octopuses.

Then again, maybe she would have. She used to have a ragged-looking plush toy octopus that had lost an eye. She'd dragged it everywhere, even to school, when she was little. Maybe that *did* account for her struggles with math.

But it didn't solve anything now.

Nein fuzzy purple one-eyed octopuses were anywhere in the vicinity, so her mental confusion must be attributable to something else.

Unless Paul had been right, and the silly thing had taken up residence in her brain the day it had gone missing.

She slowly pushed herself off the cold concrete and made her way upstairs to the warmth of the quiet kitchen. She passed through the room and traveled upstairs to the privacy of the second-floor bathroom, where she scoured her face with soap and water, wanting to erase every remnant of the tears she'd shed.

After drying off, Mercy took a moment to compose herself, then started toward the stairs. Her open bedroom door snared her attention. She stepped into the room and spied her Bible sitting on the dresser beside her bed.

Right where she'd placed it when she'd first arrived. Where it had stayed ever since, without being disturbed. A thin layer of dust covered it.

Shame ate at her. She wiped off the cover with the hem of her apron, sat down on the edge of the straw mattress, and let the Book fall open.

The passage that caught her eye was Proverbs 3:5–6. *"Trust in the* LORD *with all thine heart; and lean not unto thine own understanding. In all thy ways acknowledge him, and he shall direct thy paths."* Matthew had read it aloud just that past Sunday.

She studied it again, tracing the words with her fingertip. Did she trust der Herr that much? In all her ways?

She was reminded of the verse from Shanna's wall calendar for the month of November, when she'd arrived. She hurried downstairs, Bible in hand, turned back a page to the previous month, and reread Psalm 61:2: *"From the end of the earth will I cry unto thee, when my heart is overwhelmed: lead me to the rock that is higher than I."*

Exactly the spot where she was now.

She returned the calendar page to December, then reached for the notepad and pen Shanna kept on the hutch, and wrote down both references. Then she tucked the paper in chapter three of Proverbs and thumbed back to find the Sixty-first Psalm.

Her hands shook a little as she drew a blue line beneath the words.

Gott knew her. Understood her. And, even now, ministered to her.

She looked up at the calendar again. At John 3:16, written in the shape of a cross.

"For God so loved the world…."

For Gott so loved Mercy….

Tears burned her eyes again.

Gott, my heart really is overwhelmed. Please lead me to the rock that is higher than I.

Abner stared after Mose, watching his steady steps as he headed out of the barn. Then he looked at Abram, who'd moved farther into the stall.

Abram chuckled. "I know, right?"

A modern phrase, but one they'd both heard. It seemed to fit.

But Abner couldn't quite produce a reciprocal chuckle. He shook his head. "I fell in love the moment I saw her, Abram. Seriously. It was as if one of those fancy neon lights went off inside my head, flashing, 'Here she is. She's the one,' and I had to meet her. To know her. I asked her to kiss me."

Abram's eyes widened slightly. "You're the bold one, ain't so?"

Abner looked down at his boots. "Mose is right. I *am* suffering from a bit of a faith issue." A "*bit*"? *Who are you kidding?*

Abram frowned. "Do those flashing neon lights ever lie?"

Abner shrugged. "A bit of an exaggeration, maybe. Not that I ever spent much time around them." He struggled to find a smile.

"I have been praying for you, but now that I know how things stand, I'll pray more specifically. And maybe you should, too." Abram pulled at the short strands of his beard.

"Danki. Jah, that's the truth of it." Abner watched his brother walk away. Then he looked down at the stall floor—which *was* practically clean enough to picnic on.

He crouched down, lowering one knee to the cold ground, then the other.

Mercy's face flashed in his mind's eye. *Here she is. She's the one.*

The harsh sound of her daed demanding she return replayed in his thoughts.

Abner pulled in a deep breath and bowed his head.

Lord, I believe; help my unbelief.

Chapter 20

*M*ercy yawned, stretched, and glanced toward the dark window. She returned her bookmark to her Bible and placed it on the end table.

Abner wasn't coming. She slumped as sadness washed over her. She would've liked to see him, liked to have him kum courting after dark, but something had probably arisen. Either that or he'd changed his mind.

Mercy walked to the window. Nothing moved in the darkness—at least, not that she could see. Matthew and Shanna had long since gone to bed. She should do the same.

She carefully took off her kapp, laid it beside her Bible, and started unpinning her hair. As it fell, she shook it to dislodge any tangles, then reached for her brush.

If only he hadn't said he'd be by. Then she wouldn't have stayed up, reading and waiting.

Yet reading the Bible hadn't been a waste of time. She'd reread all of Proverbs three, as well as several chapters in Psalms. Confirmed her decision to trust. Renewed her faith. Or tried to.

She'd just finished brushing her hair and had started to unpin her dress when she heard a soft tapping at the window. Pebbles? Her breath lodged in her throat. She'd probably imagined it. Or maybe it was a tree branch brushing against the glass. Still, she hurried to the window, straight pin in hand, and peered out.

Abner aimed his flashlight up, under his chin, so that his face was illuminated. Then he pointed toward the front door.

She set the pin on the sill, slid the window open, and leaned out. The cold wind was a shock. She shivered. "I'll be right down," she whispered as loudly as she could.

He nodded.

She shut the window and watched him walk away as she replaced the pin she'd removed. Then she started to twist her hair

136

back up but hesitated. As long as it was covered, it wouldn't be a sin. Especially since she was at home. She pulled it back in a ponytail and covered it with a scarf. Nobody would see her except Abner. She could let go a little around him. She grabbed her lantern and made her way downstairs, avoiding the step that creaked. Hopefully, Shanna and Matthew wouldn't wake up.

She opened the kitchen door as quietly as she could. Abner waited on the porch. She wrapped her arms around herself, trying to keep the cold at bay. "Kum in," she whispered.

He shook his head and looked over his shoulder. "Want to go for a walk?"

"Not really. It's, what, fifteen below zero?" She shivered as the wind howled around the haus.

He chuckled. "Mose said low of ten, but the windchill makes it feel colder." He shrugged. "Bundle up. You'll be fine."

"Maybe after riding in the open buggy, you've gotten used to the cold. Please kum on in." She opened the door wider.

Abner eyed her skeptically. "Are you sure that's okay?"

She nodded.

"I guess it would be nice to warm up. I'm not quite acclimated." He stepped inside, shed his boots, and set them in the plastic tray.

"We can go up to my room, if you like."

His eyes widened, and he paused in the midst of shrugging off his coat to stare at her. "What?"

"We can go—"

"Nein, I heard you, Mercy. Just don't think that's a gut idea. Not considering everything."

"Everything. Jah." Though she wasn't sure what they were supposed to be considering. Paul's return? Or…. Her face heated. Maybe he meant the out-of-control kisses in the stable. Jah. Being alone, near a bed, wasn't a gut idea at all.

"Cookies and milk?" she offered. "Hot cocoa?"

"Hot cocoa, please. I think I'm chilled all the way through. Can't believe I said you'd be fine if you bundled up." He chuckled. "You actually have cookies left? My tin's been empty awhile."

She giggled. "Maybe you shouldn't admit to that, since it's been only a few days."

Days that had seemed like an eternity.

Mercy arranged an assortment of cookies on a plate, then mixed the ingredients for hot cocoa in a saucepan and set it on the stove. She turned the burner on, grabbed a wooden spoon, and stirred the mixture so it wouldn't scald.

Abner finished unbundling and hung up his outerwear. The floor creaked as he came across the room to stand beside her. "You left your hair down." He picked up a section of strands and gave a gentle tug. "So long and pretty. Soft. Wish it were loose and uncovered."

Should she uncover it? She expelled a breath. *Nein.* If he could be firm about not being alone, she could resist the temptation. "Not until we're married." She wanted only Abner to see her hair, nobody else.

"Wise. Gives me more to look forward to." From behind, he wrapped his arms around her waist and hugged her against his chest.

For a few blissful moments, she allowed herself to imagine they were married.

He must've been imagining the same thing. His lips nuzzled the side of her neck, right under her ear.

All coherent thought left her. "Ach, Abner," she whispered, twisting around in his arms.

He reached behind her. Something on the stove clicked, and then his hands moved to her lower back, pulling her tight against him. His mouth moved over the tender flesh of her neck, nibbling, kissing. Her toes curled; her knees weakened. She wove her fingers through his hair.

With a groan, he untangled himself and moved away. "That's why I can't go to your room." His grin was wry. "I'll get us both into trouble."

Was it wrong that she wanted to? That she wanted to keep pretending they were ehemann and frau?

She'd never pretended, or wanted to pretend, with Paul.

Abner sat in a chair, reached for a gingerbread cookie, and took a bite.

Her wobbly legs somehow managed to turn back to the stove. She stirred the hot cocoa. At least Abner had had the presence of mind to turn off the heat. It was ready anyway.

A floorboard creaked, and Mercy glanced over her shoulder as Shanna came into the room. Her pink knit slippers scuffed on the floor. She cinched her robe more tightly closed. "Something smells ser gut. Cocoa? Mmm. The chocolate ice cream wasn't enough?" Her gaze went from Mercy to Abner. A smile appeared and slowly widened. "Hallo, Abner. I suppose I need to go back to bed without any hot cocoa and pretend you're not here."

"Nein, you can have some." Abner stood and pulled out a chair for her.

It probably would be better for Shanna to chaperone them, anyway. Especially since their kisses had the bad habit of getting out of control.

"Please stay." Mercy took a third mug out of the cabinet. *Just don't talk about Paul.* She had enough to worry about. Trying to turn it over to Gott and leave it to Him was difficult to do.

"Danki." Shanna winked at Mercy. "I won't stay long. I was having trouble getting to sleep. An overdose of ice cream, maybe. If there is such a thing. But this will help, I'm thinking."

Mercy ladled the hot drink into the three mugs, then dropped a handful of miniature marshmallows into each one.

It was a gut thing Abner had stopped their kisses when he had.

Paul had been right about wanting to wait until after the marriage vows had been said to start kissing. Because now that she and Abner had started, she didn't want to stop. Ever.

෴

Abner took a cautious sip of the hot liquid. It didn't burn his throat, so he took a longer one. Shanna settled the a chair across from him and smiled as she lifted her mug. "This is why I love Mercy so much. She likes chocolate as much as I do. Did you know that she and I stayed up awhile after Matthew went to bed and ate a whole pint of chocolate ice cream? Two girls, two spoons, one carton."

Abner raised his eyebrows at Mercy. "Really?"

Her face turned a delightful shade of pink. She settled in the chair next to him and reached for a chocolate chip walnut cookie, but then she hesitated and pulled her hand back. "Jah, but—"

"It's a must-have," Shanna said with a nod. "When life hits like that, a girl *must* have chocolate."

Abner blinked, not sure how he was supposed to respond to a confession of gluttony. "A *whole* container of ice cream?"

"Technically, half a container each. And it was only a pint to start with. Is that why you're here, Abner?" Shanna grinned at him.

"Ice cream? Nein, danki. I'm just beginning to thaw from being outside." He looked at his cocoa and frowned.

Mercy made a kind of choking sound.

Shanna laughed. "Nein. To discuss what you're going to do."

"Ach, nein. I'm courting Mercy." He'd said it pointedly, hoping she would hurry up and finish and go back to bed.

"Well, jah, I know that. I meant with Paul being alive."

Apparently, she hadn't gotten the hint. He sighed and glanced at Mercy. "Right. We've got three choices: Give up, give in, or give it all we've got. I choose the last one."

Shanna grinned. "I like your attitude. Fight to the finish."

"Then again, there's also 'give it to Gott,'" Abner added quietly. He'd been reminded of that earlier by Mose.

"Is that how you feel, Mercy?" Shanna asked. "Give it all you've got?" She took another sip of her cocoa.

Mercy gulped, confusion washing over her face. "I...I don't know. I don't want to discuss it."

What? After he'd laid it all out there, she didn't want to discuss it? After those heated kisses by the stove, she still didn't know? Hurt filled him, followed by confusion.

He pulled in a breath. *Give it to Gott.*

"You *have* to discuss it," Shanna insisted. "What don't you know?" She leaned back in her chair, as if preparing to stay awhile.

Mercy shook her head.

Abner didn't really want to talk about it, either. He didn't have answers. And he was afraid of what Mercy might say. But he supposed Shanna was right—they needed a game plan.

Shanna leaned forward. "You have to choose, Mercy. You can't wait for someone else to tell you what to do. This isn't up to your daed, or anyone else. It's your life. What is your heart telling you?"

Mercy's mouth opened and shut several times.

Abner frowned. Did that mean he most likely didn't want to know what her heart was telling her? The swirling black hole of fear threatened again. He forced it back. He chose to trust that it would be okay somehow.

"Just tell us what you're thinking," Shanna urged her.

"I...I...." Mercy shifted. She didn't look at Abner. Another bad sign. "Paul is steady and dependable, and he'd be a gut provider. Abner is...fun. Exciting."

Ouch. "Fun" didn't begin to compete with "steady," "dependable," and "gut provider." But hadn't he shown Mercy he could be steady and dependable, as well? As for providing, he worked hard. She should know that, too. He wasn't entirely happy-go-lucky.

"But Abner's also steady and dependable," Mercy said, as if reading his thoughts. "And smart. He's about as gut as they kum. And I love him." Mercy peeked at him through partially lowered eyelashes.

Ach, that made him feel much better. He smiled. "Danki."

She nodded, blushed, and dipped her head.

He reached for her hand, threading his fingers with hers.

Shanna drained her cup and stood. "I'll leave you two alone. Danki for letting me join you for a little while. Ach, I know—maybe we could talk to Bishop Sol. He might have some wisdom."

Abner raised his eyebrows. "He's the one who doesn't understand pink camouflage, right?"

"What?" Shanna laughed. "Never mind; I don't even want to know where that came from. Nein, he probably wouldn't. He can be a bit gruff and unbending, but if you try hard enough, you can win him over."

"I think that gift is yours alone, Shanna. He has a soft spot for you," Matthew spoke from the doorway. "Kum, my love."

"Coming." Shanna carried her mug to the sink and rinsed it before joining her ehemann. "Gut nacht."

Abner and Mercy sat in silence as the footsteps receded down the hall, and then the bedroom door clicked shut.

"She's convinced Paul is going to kum down here," Mercy told him. "She plans to contact a few of her friends to see if he could stay with them, if he does."

At least Paul wouldn't be staying in the same haus with her.

Mercy shrugged. "I'm not so sure he'll waste his time."

"Why not?" Probably foolish to ask, but he wanted to latch hold of whatever doubt she harbored and hold it near. Especially if it would keep Paul away.

"I told Daed that I loved you. And you told him you wanted to marry me. Besides, Paul left for a year, with nein contact! If he does kum, I'll want to know why he went a year without letting me know he was alive. That's all." She frowned. "I don't want to talk about him anymore."

"Me, neither." He needed the reassurance of her love. Needed to hold her. He probably should go, but instead, he turned sideways in his chair, reached for her, and pulled her close. "I'm sorry for what I'm about to do." He tugged off her scarf and removed the elastic band from her hair as she caught her breath. "Forgive me." His voice was husky as he threaded his fingers through her loose tangles. "So beautiful. I can't wait to see it spread out on a pillow."

"Ach!" She grabbed for her hair. "I didn't mean to tempt you."

"Nein, don't. Leave it. Ich liebe dich, Mercy."

She obediently let her hand fall away from her hair. His stomach clenched at the unfamiliar and oh-so-wunderbaar sensations of his fingers threading through her long, silky tresses.

She leaned into him. Into his touch. "If only life weren't so complicated. What are we going to do?"

Abner lifted a shoulder. "Your daed said some not very helpful quote about December love melting with January snow. I don't remember his exact words."

She sniffed.

"Are you crying?" He pressed his lips together. Maybe he shouldn't have been surprised. It did sound pretty depressing. "I don't know, Mercy. I haven't quite worked it out in my head yet. I haven't joined the church yet, so we have all the classes to go through before we can declare our intent to marry. And if I'm in Montana, and you're...wherever you are...I guess we'll need to write. Call. Maybe try to visit each other occasionally."

"Daed would also say something about long-distance relationships being doomed." Her voice broke.

Not very encouraging. Abner pulled her nearer. "We've got now. Let's just enjoy each other. Maybe I'll figure it out before we part ways." *If Paul doesn't intrude in our lives.* "*He's* not here. I am." That he'd said more for himself than for her.

"I'm not worried about him. He won't kum." Mercy sat back and looked at him.

"I'd kum. What makes you think he won't?"

"Because, as I said, he left me for over a year. Without contact. He lost interest. I'm more worried about you losing interest when we're apart."

"Not." He dropped a kiss on her lips. "Going." Another kiss. "To happen." And a third….

She leaned into him again with a soft sigh. He wound his hand through her hair and cupped her head, drawing her closer. Her arms wrapped around his neck, her softness pressed against his chest, and….

His brain cells packed their bags, caught a bus, and left on vacation. Nothing mattered, except him. And Mercy. And the moment.

⁂

Mercy wasn't sure how long they kissed. When they finally surfaced for air, she realized she was practically in his lap, lying against his chest. Their breathing was harsh, uneven. Her face heated.

It was a gut thing nobody had kum into the kitchen. Not that they'd done anything wrong, but the kisses were getting more… intimate.

"I want to get married." That had kum out of nowhere. She sat there in the circle of his arms, blinking at the audacity of her own words. But then, being married would eliminate all their problems: the threat of Paul, Daed's control, their upcoming separation….

It was probably too soon. Their relationship had started with a bang, and it would probably end in flames. Would it even stand the test of time? What about after the passion faded?

"Jah. Me, too." He blinked. "Wait. What?" He released her and straightened in the chair. "We already talked about that. Unless… unless you're talking about what Abram and Katie did. Or do you have another idea?"

Mercy looked at him. "What did they do, exactly?"

"I don't know, exactly." He chuckled. "But I could find out. All I know is that in September, Abram was in Shipshewana because he was supposed to marry his former girlfriend, and in October, he and Katie were married."

"I thought she said four months." Mercy remembered that comment. And how much it'd scared her at the time. Now…. Now, all she knew was four months would be too long.

"Jah. Four months."

"September to October is…one month. Less than one."

"Since they met." He exhaled. "I need to go, Mercy. Because if I don't…. If I don't, I'll be taking you up on your offer to go to your room." He stood. "And that just wouldn't be a gut idea. But I'll see you again soon. Katie said she and Ruthie are bringing over a meal, and they want me to drive them here."

It was getting harder and harder to say good-bye, even knowing she'd see him again soon. Because the day was too quickly approaching when he'd catch the bus to Montana. And she wouldn't.

It was strange not having even the foggiest idea where she'd be in two weeks.

But in a little over a week, Christmas would be here. She'd focus on her future later. Now, she needed to focus on that holiday. And the reason for celebrating. *The Christ child.*

Plus, she needed to make Abner a gift.

Mercy pushed to her feet and followed him to the door. "I want to bake more cutout cookies, to send to my family in time for Second Christmas…and to yours, too. Want to help?"

He pulled his coat on. "I think you're the sweetest girl ever. I need to call home and tell my parents about you. Especially before you send them cookies." He smiled. "When do you want to make them?"

"I should get them in the mail this weekend."

Abner's gaze skittered over her. "Friday? Will that work? As soon as I finish my chores, I'll kum over. Okay?"

Mercy nodded. A tear escaped from the corner of her eye and ran down her cheek.

Abner groaned, reached out, and caught it with his thumb. "Ach, don't cry. What's wrong?"

She shook her head, then leaned into his touch. "I don't know. Nothing. Everything. I just feel like everything is changing. I don't know what or how. And Daed was so difficult…." A couple more tears followed the first. "He's not going to stand for me not coming home when he ordered me to." Daed's anger was a fearsome thing. She cringed at the thought.

Abner pulled her into his arms. "Give me time to think and pray. And to talk to Abram." He brushed a kiss across her trembling lips. "It'll be okay, Mercy. Trust me. But, most important, trust der Herr."

But she heard the uncertainty in his voice. As if he didn't quite believe what he said.

He flashed a smile as he stepped away. It didn't reach his eyes. "I'll see you soon." He put on his hat and gloves.

She nodded.

He walked out the door. She watched until he disappeared around the side of the haus—probably going to the road, where he would've left his horse and buggy, so as to not disturb the family.

Mercy closed the kitchen door, wrapped her arms around herself to stop the shivering, and walked back over to the calendar. She lifted the page again to read November's verse. *"From the end of the earth will I cry unto thee, when my heart is overwhelmed: lead me to the rock that is higher than I."*

Oops. Her kapp. She reached up and touched her bare head. She didn't want to show disrespect to Gott by not having her hair covered when she prayed. She hurried up to her room, made sure her head covering was in place, then fell on her knees beside the bed. She longed for the elusive peace she'd felt earlier, before Abner had kum. Before Shanna had forced them to talk about "what if" scenarios.

Instead, it seemed as if she was in the middle of a lump of bread dough, and she was being folded and punched down, over and over, as if being kneaded.

Over, and over, and over.

Then she'd be set out to rise. And bake.

Not a pleasant image. And not a pleasant experience, being stretched and kneaded.

Gott, my heart really is overwhelmed, she prayed again. *Please lead me to the rock that is higher than I.*

Chapter 21

*T*he next day, Abner waited until Mose headed for an upper level of the barn before approaching his brother. He didn't want any unsolicited advice or discouragement from the too-seeing older man. He looked for his twin and found Abram sitting on a hay bale, sorting through a big, grimy white plastic bucket full of what appeared to be junk. "What are you doing?"

Abram nodded toward a nearby hay bale. "Have a seat and help some. Tyler brought by these buckets of miscellaneous stuff he found at a rummage sale. He thought we might be able to use it." He tossed a handful of nails into an empty koffee can. "I suppose, when I have nothing else to do, I'll straighten nails." He sighed. "I have to keep reminding myself that he means well when he comes by with trash. Or says nonsensical words that mean nothing to us."

Abner nodded. He remembered Tyler calling him and Abram "Thing One and Thing Two," and he still had nein idea what that meant. He'd never ask, though. He reached for a handful of junk. "Do you have time to talk? I have a question for you."

"What's on your mind?"

He pulled in a deep breath. "You and Katie got married less than a month after you returned from Indiana. How did you get the bishop to agree to that?"

"Hmm. Looking to marry soon?" Abram teased.

Abner shrugged. "Maybe." He wiped his damp palms on his pant legs and focused on the junk to keep his gaze off Abram's knowing smirk.

"I asked the bishop for permission to marry Katie less than a week after we met," Abram explained. "Bishop Dave and Mose met and talked some, not to mention, the bishop pretty much involved himself in our lives, always watching us, talking to us." He tossed another handful of nails into the can. "They gave us permission to marry after I stopped running from my past. But they didn't know what I was running from."

Abner shuddered. He didn't want to remember that terrifying time. "If I go ask him for permission to marry Mercy...?" He dumped a handful of bent nails into the can and frowned. "They all need straightening."

"You can try." Abram's forehead furrowed. "I'm honestly not sure if you'd need to talk to him or to the bishop in the district where she lives, or whether you'll need to speak with her bishop back in Shipshewana. Though I think I'd start with Bishop Dave. He could tell you where to go and from whom to ask permission."

Abner nodded. "Where would I find him?"

"Down the road about a mile." Abram pointed east. "There'll probably be a pickup in the side yard."

"The bishop has a pickup?" Abner blinked.

"Nein, it belongs to his sohn-in-law, the Amish policeman. Or did. The gross-dochter uses it now. She's Englisch."

Abner shook his head.

Abram chuckled. "It's complicated. I haven't quite figured out the whole story yet. Katie is close friends with Janna—she's the policeman's frau."

Abner remained silent as he sorted through three more piles of nails, discarding the rejects in the garbage pail and putting the bent nails in the koffee can. Then he stood. "Well, enjoy, Brother. I'm going to pay a visit to your bishop."

"Hope it goes well for you." Abram glanced up.

"Jah. We need prayer, for sure." Abner headed out of the barn and toward the road. A mile wasn't too far to walk—hardly worth hitching up the horse.

The bishop's farm was quiet. A pickup was parked in the side yard, as Abram had predicted, but a horse and buggy also sat in front of the barn. Abner hesitated at the front door, undecided as to whether he should knock, since they were virtual strangers, or enter unannounced, as he would at home.

He was still trying to make up his mind when the door opened.

"I've been expecting you." Bishop Dave held a steaming mug in his hand.

Abner blinked. "You have?"

"Abner Hilty, ain't so? Abram's twin and Micah Graber's cousin. I'm going to sample some cinnamon rolls my gross-dochter made. Her first attempt, mind you. Kum on in and have yourself a sit-down."

Cinnamon rolls? Abner's stomach rumbled at the memory of the wunderbaar cinnamon and caramel delights Katie had made for breakfast that morgen. She'd allowed him only one.

"Don't mind if I do." Abner followed him into the kitchen and nodded at the girl in blue jeans who stood by the stove. He tried to remember her name.

Another man, the one who must be the policeman, sat at the table, a cup of koffee in front of him. He gave Abner a hard look, as if distrusting his motives.

"That's my sohn-in-law, Troy." The bishop pulled out a chair.

"The Amish policeman." Abner nodded. He had certainly mastered the interrogation stare.

Troy shook his head. "Former policeman. It takes a while for the reputation of being *the law* to die down."

"It may never die down," Bishop Dave pointed out. "You're the first in our district to ever work with the law." He stirred some sugar into his own koffee. "This is Abner Hilty, from Shipshewana. He's Abram's twin. We met him at McDonald's a few weeks ago. Remember, Meghan?"

The teen set a small plate holding a cinnamon roll, in all its sticky glory, in front of Abner as he lowered himself into the chair. She considered him a moment. "Yeah, he was with the girl in the pink camouflage dress." She set a cup of koffee next to his plate.

"Danki." Abner grinned as the other two men laughed. "Already being identified by my companions, ain't so?" He looked at Bishop Dave. "Actually, that's why I came by. I need to talk with you about Mercy." He looked around for a private place to converse.

"The girl in the unusual dress." Bishop Dave dipped his head in acknowledgment. "Like I said, I've been expecting you. Didn't think you'd take as long as you did to get here, though."

Okay, the bishop talked in riddles. Abner frowned, tasted the koffee, then added a spoonful of sugar.

"Abram waited all of three or four days after meeting Katie to ask to marry her," Bishop Dave explained.

Abner squirmed in discomfort for his brother. The bishop back home knew everyone's secrets, too.

"Not that I can say two or three weeks is much better." The bishop chuckled. "I saw how you looked at her."

This was getting uncomfortable. But Abner didn't think it was too soon to ask for permission to marry Mercy. He looked down, gave the koffee a stir, then took another sip. Better. "Uh, could we go somewhere to talk? Maybe after we eat the cinnamon rolls?"

Bishop Dave shrugged again. "Talk now or talk later. Up to you. We all know why you're here."

There was that. Abner glanced around at the curious faces and frowned. "Okay. Who do I talk to in order to get permission to marry her? You? The bishop in the Yoders' district, where she lives? Her home bishop? Someone else?" He took a bite of his cinnamon roll while he waited for the other man to answer. "Mmmm. This is almost as gut as Katie's." Not quite, but definitely almost.

"It is gut." Troy nodded and held out his plate for another.

"Just 'almost'?" Meghan huffed as she took Troy's plate.

Heat crawled up Abner's neck. "Uh...."

She laughed. "I know Katie has the reputation of being the best baker in the district. It's nice to know I'm almost as good."

Abner smiled. Maybe Meghan would allow him more than one cinnamon bun, too. Still, he put down the treat and forced himself to chew slowly. Savor it. Just in case.

"You should talk to her bishop at home," Bishop Dave finally said.

Abner slumped, and Troy gave him a sympathetic glance. "I was afraid of that. I was kind of hoping you'd be okay to talk with, because it's a tangled-up mess. Her former beau, believed to be dead for over a year, is alive and reentered the picture. We're going our separate ways in about two weeks, and...well, I'm terrified I'll lose her. I'm trying to trust, but...." He released a heavy sigh as the earlier bite of cinnamon goodness turned into a hard knot in his stomach.

Troy said nothing, but the look he gave his father-in-law communicated something Abner didn't understand. The older man frowned, shook his head, and turned his attention back to Abner. "Then if your love is meant to be, it will stand the test of time, the test of distance, and the test of—"

"A love triangle." Meghan set another plate on the table. "Sooo romantic."

"Hardly that." Abner sighed.

"That's not the term I was going to use." Bishop Dave frowned at Meghan. "But it works."

Abner polished off his cinnamon roll in silence. Jealousy churned his stomach, thinking of Mercy and Paul. It'd been easier to accept her loving a dead man than finding out he was alive and well.

"Want another?" Meghan reached for his plate.

He shook his head. "Nein, one's enough. But danki. It was ser gut." And one was enough. Especially after he'd lost his appetite.

"Sorry I wasn't more help." Bishop Dave patted his shoulder. "I will be happy to pray for you. I sense the other bu is the root of the problem."

"I'll pray, too," Troy said.

"Appreciate it." Abner had already made the problem clear—at least in his mind—and the bishop was plainly going to be of nein help. "I need to get back. I promised to take Katie and Ruthie visiting."

"Stop by anytime." The bishop drained his koffee. "Just a thought before you go, though. Der Herr gave it to me just now. A human heart is unable to bear a Gott-sized burden. This one isn't yours to bear; it's yours to acknowledge, to battle while dressed in your spiritual armor, but you can't bear it alone. You must give the situation to der Herr and leave it at the cross."

Abner stood, hat in his hand, silent. His mouth hung open, unhinged. He snapped it shut. "I want to do this—give it to Gott. But I'll probably struggle every day."

"Of course. You are human, ain't so? But Gott will prove Himself faithful, even when things go wrong."

"Danki." Abner nodded at the older man, who appeared as wise as Mose for having identified his trust issue. "I need to go."

"I'll see you out," Troy offered, then stood and followed Abner outside to the buggy. He glanced back at the door, then eyed Abner with a look of urgency.

Abner tried to imagine what Troy might say. Maybe he had some advice that would prove more helpful than the bishop's.

"Janna and I eloped," Troy said quietly. "He didn't want you to know because it opens up a whole slew of problems that didn't exist before. But it is an option if you're prepared to deal with the fallout."

"Elope?"

"Something to consider. You can apply for a license and marry today if you want. But there will be repercussions, both here and wherever your home district is." He frowned, his brow furrowing as if he were deep in thought. "It also eliminates the need to trust. That is something we all struggle with at times. Something we need to learn to do." Troy lowered his head, turned, and strode toward the barn.

Elope? Something about it scared him.

But it mostly excited him.

❦

Hearing the scrape of wheels over the frozen snow, Mercy turned to peek out the window. When Abner jumped out of the buggy, her heart leapt, and her pulse increased steadily as she watched him help Katie and Ruthie out. Such a gentleman. He reached in the back of the buggy and grabbed a big plastic bag, which he handed to Katie, followed by a large wicker picnic basket—the promised dinner. He handed that to Ruthie.

Mercy couldn't keep from grinning. She hurried to the door and flung it open. She found herself wrapped in Katie's arms, the soft bag bouncing against her back. She returned the embrace.

"It's so gut to see you," Katie said. "It's hard to become acquainted when we don't see each other much, and if you're going to marry the twin of my ehemann, we need to be friends, ain't so?"

Mercy blinked and pulled away, not sure how to respond. "Kum in, please," she managed. "Let me take your coats."

"He talks about you all the time," Katie continued as she stepped into the haus. "Ach, it's nice and toasty in here. Have to keep it warm for the wee one, ain't so? Where is he?" She set the bag down on the floor.

"Asleep in the other room." Mercy took Katie's coat and hung it up, then turned to accept the wicker basket from Ruthie. "Danki. I'll tell Shanna you're here." She carried the basket to the table.

"Nein need." Shanna came into the room. "I heard you all talking. Danki for coming. I agree, Abner is obviously smitten with

Mercy. And she with him. She definitely needs to get to know you. You don't have need for a mother's helper, do you? Mercy needs a place to go in January."

Katie blushed. "Ach, nein. I don't. Janna is due about then, but she doesn't have need, either. She has her mamm and her niece, and—"

"Gott will provide." Mercy was surer about that than she was about Abner's love enduring an extended separation. Look where that hope had gotten her when she'd waited for another bu to return. All she'd been left with was a broken heart. She took Ruthie's coat and hung it next to Katie's.

"Jah, He always does," Shanna affirmed. "Mercy, would you please unpack the meal they brought and put it in the oven to warm while I take them to meet Levi?" She didn't wait for an answer but motioned to the other women. "Right this way."

Katie scooped up the bag and handed it to Mercy. "I'll hope we have a chance to talk later. Maybe you can kum over and join us for a meal soon."

Mercy nodded and opened her mouth to speak.

"That sounds wunderbaar," Shanna answered for her. "I'll make sure she can. How about tomorrow nacht? Abner is coming over to help her bake cookies again. At least, that's what she said this morgen."

"Jah, Abner mentioned that." Katie followed Shanna from the room. "Sounds perfect."

The kitchen door opened again. This time, Abner entered. His gaze caught Mercy's, and he grinned as he bent to take off his boots.

Mercy abandoned the bag and basket—still loaded—and hurried over to greet him.

He pulled her into his arms, engulfing her inside his coat.

She breathed deeply of his scent: freshly washed man. A hint of peppermint clung to his breath.

"I spoke to Abram." Abner kept his voice barely above a whisper. "He sent me to talk to his bishop." He leaned forward, brushed his lips over hers in an achingly sweet, too-brief kiss, then stepped back and shrugged out of his coat.

"Jah?" Butterflies fluttered in her stomach. He'd talked to the bishop? Really? So now their future was decided?

He hung his coat on a hook, put his hat on top of it, and then went to the table and started unloading the food Katie had brought. Mercy took the casserole from him and slid it in the oven to warm, alongside a pan of peach cobbler.

Still she waited for his news. Her breath stalled in her throat. Why wasn't he saying anything? Had they been refused? Ach, she hoped not.

"I need to talk to your home bishop in Shipshewana." Abner's voice was still hushed. He closed the empty hamper, looked up, and caught her eye with a look of disappointment. "I expected that. But...his sohn-in-law, Troy, had an interesting suggestion." He came around the table and caught her hand. "He said he and his frau, Janna, eloped."

Mercy frowned. "What?" *Oops!* That had been louder than she'd intended. She looked toward the doorway to the living room. Was it her imagination, or had the conversation quieted in there?

Apparently, Abner had noticed it, too. He moved nearer still and bent to whisper in her ear. "He did warn against it...said it'd open up a whole slew of problems. But I guess you and I could be married by to-nacht."

The thought warmed her to her toes. "Really?"

"Jah. But I...well, I think we need to pray about it before we take that leap. I want to learn to trust Gott completely, wholly, in all areas of my life, and not just jump blindly into whatever solution I see as best."

Wise.

Mercy nodded. "I'll pray, too." She glanced at the fancy calendar hanging on the wall. She wanted—needed—to learn to lean on der Herr completely, too. It seemed He was telling her to. After all, He'd gotten her to read the verses she needed via a calendar when she'd neglected to pick up her Bible. *Gott, help me to learn to trust You completely, to lean fully on You and not unto my own understanding....*

"Abner, you want to see the boppli?" Ruthie came to the kitchen door, her gaze going to Mercy and Abner's clasped hands. She looked up with what might've been a smirk. "So, this is the young maidal you're bringing to supper Friday nacht."

Abner grinned, released one of Mercy's hands, and stepped away. "What's this about supper?"

"Katie invited Mercy for dinner. And since you'll be here helping bake cookies, you can bring her home with you. Shanna gave permission."

Abner's smile widened as he looked back at Mercy. "Then Friday is ours. I can't wait." He kept hold of her hand and tugged her nearer. "We'll go see the boppli together."

Not that she hadn't seen Levi every day since his birth. Still, it warmed her heart that Abner was willing to humor Ruthie and visit the boppli. If he was this gut to the mother-in-law of his twin brother, he would surely treat Mercy's mamm with honor and respect.

Mamm always said you could tell how a man will treat his frau by how he treats his mamm.

His frau. Abner's frau.

He wanted it to be Mercy. And she was more than ready to agree.

She smiled, allowing Abner to intertwine his fingers with hers, as they went to see Levi together.

❧

"Here. Hold your arms like this." Ruthie's cold hands settled on Abner's arm. She positioned one of his hands in the crook of the opposite arm and then folded the other arm across so it almost touched his other elbow. "Stiffen up a little. Don't flop."

Abner tried to hold his arms the right way as he waited for Katie to lay Levi in his arms.

"Be sure to support his head, now," Ruthie directed him. "You'll probably be a daed in a year or two, so you need to learn."

A daed.... Abner's heart swelled as his gaze sought out Mercy. A grin lifted one side of his mouth. Maybe he would be a daed that soon...if Gott willed it. With Mercy as his frau. His stomach clenched as his gaze moved over her soft curves, covered by one of those brown dresses she hated. Ach, he loved her.

She busied herself straightening the blankets in the boppli bed, but the color rose in her cheeks, as if she sensed his gaze.

The boppli made a soft sigh. Abner looked down at Levi and pulled him closer. "He's so sweet."

"You'll be a gut daed." Shanna grinned at him. "You look comfortable with a boppli in your arms. Matthew was so nervous.

He was afraid he'd break Serena right after she was born. He's the youngest of twelve, so he didn't have much practice holding little ones."

"I have younger siblings." Abner glanced up. "One was just born in September. I haven't met him yet."

"Are you going home for Christmas?" Shanna tilted her head.

Levi made sucking noises in his sleep.

Abner shook his head. "Nein. Staying here until after Second Christmas. Then I might go home for a bit. Before I return to Montana."

Shanna's gaze shifted to Mercy. "Too bad you couldn't find a job out there. I guess there are always letters and phone calls."

Mercy shrugged.

Abner's smile died. He lifted one shoulder and lowered it. "We haven't decided what we'll do." He hated rehashing it, but—

"They'll probably elope." Katie's mouth curved upward in an impish grin.

"What?" Abner frowned. He hadn't mentioned that idea to either Katie or Abram. "Where did that kum from?"

Katie blushed. "Just…my two best friends both did."

Mercy's color brightened to an unusual shade of red. She straightened, an unexpected spark of anger in her eyes. "I am standing right here, you know."

Had she just snapped? Because of the gossip and speculation as to what they might decide to do? He liked her show of spunk. And appreciated her desire for privacy.

Abner's grin returned, full force. He handed the boppli back to Shanna and winked. "Our future plans are ours to decide. Mind if I take Mercy for a walk while you ladies visit?" He didn't wait for a reply but reached for her hand, tugging her toward the kitchen, their coats, and a possible snowball fight in the meadow where they'd shared their first kiss.

Chapter 22

Mercy tugged her mittens on just before Abner grabbed her hand and pulled her out the door. He paused long enough to shut it behind them before he led her toward the meadow where they'd built a snowman four days ago.

She needed the escape from the gossip. From the speculation of what she and Abner would choose to do.

What she also needed was a distraction, a sane moment, and a reason to linger outside—something besides hot, passionate kisses.

"Shanna wanted me to collect some greenery to decorate the haus." She looked toward the cluster of pine trees at the edge of the woods. "She also wants me to bring up her red candles from the basement." Maybe Mercy would make tiny wreaths with the pine branches to wrap around the bases of the candles. That would look pretty.

Abner slowed his pace to a leisurely stroll. "Collecting greenery sounds fun. Maybe we'll find some mistletoe."

She grinned at him. "Like you aren't kissed often enough."

"A man can never get too many kisses." His eyes twinkled. "I called home this morgen. Mamm answered—guess she happened to be out near the barn when I called." He hesitated. "I told her about you. I think she'd about given up hope of my settling down. She started crying. Said she can't wait to hug you."

That was nice. Reassuring. Heartwarming. "But what if they don't like me?"

Abner laughed. "They'll love you, Mercy, because ich liebe dich. Just be your sweet self."

"The one who throws snowballs in your face?"

He gave her an impish grin. "Careful, or I might roll you in the snow again."

"Ach, more threats." Mercy pulled away.

156

"Not a threat. A promise." He winked and reached for her hand. She let him catch it again. "Let's get the greenery you wanted. I don't have a gun to shoot down mistletoe, so we'll have to skip it."

"I'm glad we got snow here this year. I'd miss having a white Christmas."

"Me, too." Abner grinned. "One of the things I loved most about Montana was all the snow. And the brisk, cold air. You know, when you step outside, and all the breath is sucked out of you with a loud gasp? After that initial shock, it's so invigorating. Have you ever gone cross-country skiing?"

She blinked at him.

He chuckled. "Of course not. What was I thinking? When I was younger, my oldest brother used to hook up a pair of old skis to the back of the buggy and pull us along the side of the road. That was the way Abram and I started skiing. In Montana, I learned to use a snowmobile. Part of my job, driving one around the ranch."

The Englischness of his Montana life cut through Mercy.

"Are...are you planning to stay Englisch?" She glanced at his jeans.

He hesitated. Maybe too long. She'd begun to think he was just going to ignore her question when he pulled in a deep breath.

"I don't know, Mercy. I realize this is going to sound strange, and that it goes against our teachings, but being Amish isn't the only way to heaven. Jesus wasn't Amish. He clearly says in the Bible, '*I am the way, the truth, and the life: no man cometh unto the Father, but by me.*' It doesn't say, 'Joining the Amish church is the only way to kum to the Father.'"

It didn't, Mercy knew, but she'd always been taught that if she didn't join the church, then she would be eternally lost. Was Abner right?

"*Trust in the* LORD...." Abner was right. It didn't say to trust in the Amish church.

He veered their path toward another portion of the woods, and she matched his pace, scanning the direction he'd chosen. More pine trees. Maybe with pinecones. A basketful of those would be pretty. She should've brought along something to collect them in.

His hand tightened around hers. "I like many things about the Englisch. Such as snowmobiles. Jeans. But I also enjoy the Amish way of life—the sense of community, the emphasis on family, the way we all work together. The peace and tranquility of the countryside where we reside. Working in the dirt growing gardens, plowing fields, tending animals. And if I—we—were to marry, I'd probably join the church, because I'd want our kinner raised that way."

"And if we didn't marry?" Ach, why'd she said that? Maybe she wanted to know his real convictions.

His brow furrowed. "There'd be nein hurry to join, I guess." He shrugged. "I could continue straddling the fence between Amish and Englisch until I decided which side I wanted to land on."

She swallowed. She was his deciding factor? What about his stated desire to wait, pray, and trust der Herr? Had he meant it?

"What about you?" he asked. "What would you do if you were free to do what you wanted? You came here so your daed wouldn't send you to live with your great-aenti. If you had your choice of a job, what would you do? Do you like being a mother's helper?"

She shrugged. "It doesn't matter whether I like it. I don't have a choice." She shook her head. "It's not as if girls have a lot of options. But I do like it...mostly. I like caring for boppli more than I do aged aents who find fault with everything." Her face heated. "I shouldn't have said that. The aenti Daed wanted to send me to is just...a bit difficult."

"So, if you were to be a maidal for the rest of your life, and had to support yourself, you'd be a caregiver of some sort?" He raised an eyebrow.

She glanced at him, startled. That put a different spin on his question. "Nein. If I had to support myself, I'd start a greenhaus and raise seedlings, like some of the Amish garden centers in Shipshewana that are so popular with tourists. I enjoy working in Mamm's garden at home, and Daed even allowed me a makeshift greenhaus so I could get a head start on my tomatoes." Wouldn't it be wunderbaar if she did have a chance to do what she truly enjoyed?

"This morgen, Mamm told me the farm next to theirs is for sale," Abner told her. "Or will be soon. It hasn't been listed yet, but the farmer mentioned it to Daed, just in case one of us kinner might want it. It has a greenhaus, just a small one, already in place."

Her breath caught. His tone sounded so casual, so...nonchalant. She wasn't exactly sure of his intended message. But it seemed as if maybe he might consider buying that farm for himself...for them.

She didn't want to misunderstand him. Bad enough that she'd blurted out that she wanted to marry him during the heat of their kisses last nacht. She wouldn't make that mistake again. He'd have to propose.

The frozen snow crunched underfoot as they neared the woods. The accumulation was thinner there, as the thick trees had protected the ground. It also seemed less stable, as the dead vegetation under the snow shifted with their every step. She tightened her grip on Abner's arm.

"Would you want to live next door to my parents?" He stopped walking, studying a tree with several gut branches. He released her hand, pulled out a pocketknife, and flicked it open. He'd apparently collected greenery for his mamm before, if his confident approach was anything to judge by.

"What about Montana?" She hoped he didn't hear the trepidation in her voice. She wasn't feeling nearly as carefree and relaxed about this as he sounded. Her entire future would ride on his decisions.

Maybe. He hadn't exactly asked her to marry him. But they were definitely talking about it. Eloping…future plans….

He shifted to get a better grasp on the branch he wanted. His shoulder lifted and fell as he cut it. "I could use the money I earn in Montana to make payments on the farm. Daed and my brothers could handle both properties until I get there. We wouldn't be able to marry right away—as Amish, anyway—since neither of us has joined the church yet. I have commitments, Mercy. Besides, I always keep my promises." He looked at her and grinned. "Remember?"

Jah, she remembered. "How long are you committed?" Her voice shook a little.

"Through late spring, though I have the option of staying on longer." Turning his attention back to the branch, he carefully dislodged it from the tree and handed it to her. "You know, if I buy that farm, you could go live there, or live with Mamm and Daed, and start working in the greenhaus. Get the garden in and set up hauskeeping. The harvest would help bring in money, and Mamm would let you sell vegetables from the roadside stand."

In the summer, after his commitment was over and he'd joined her? Or to support herself while she waited indefinitely for him as he continually prolonged his stay in Montana?

He turned his attention to another branch.

She liked his idea—the one about buying the farm next to his parents and living there. A lot. It'd save her from having to go home, too, yet she'd be close enough to her family for frequent visits.

She pulled in a breath. It didn't shake as much. "Jah. Jah, I like that idea."

He looked up and grinned, his expression a mixture of teasing and seriousness. "Of course, if we elope, you could kum with me to Montana. We could live in that remodeled silo I mentioned." He extended another branch to her with a wink.

She took it. "Ach, there's an offer I can't refuse." Did he sense her sarcasm?

Abner flicked the knife shut, slid it into his pocket, then cupped her face with his hands. His fingers slid across her cheek, down to the corners of her lips. "I'll call home and tell them to make an offer on the farm. Here's a kiss to seal the deal." He leaned toward her.

Her heart leapt in anticipation of both the kiss and their future.

"Abner! Mercy! Where are you?" Shanna's voice broke the silence.

He sighed and pulled away without kissing her. "Guess it's time to go." All hint of teasing disappeared. "Don't discount Montana, Mercy. Pray about it. Pray about me. And seek the will of der Herr."

Abner pulled up to the Yoders' drive on Friday morgen just as Matthew was driving out. He lifted his hand in a wave, and Matthew inclined his head in acknowledgment before continuing on, probably to his job at the furniture shop.

Abner parked the buggy by the barn, set the brakes, and unhitched Savvy. He put the mare in one of the empty stalls, making sure she had plenty of water and hay before he headed for the haus.

He found Mercy in the kitchen with Shanna and Serena. Mercy had assembled the cookie ingredients and supplies on the big farm table, and Shanna was sorting through cookie cutters, picking ones that were similar in size. As Abner paused in the doorway, Serena knocked over a basket of blocks with a loud crash.

"Morgen, Abner." Shanna glanced up at him. She sounded groggy.

"Haven't had your morgen cup of ambition yet, ain't so?" He grinned at her as he removed his boots and put them in the tray.

Shanna's lips lifted in a matching smile. "Nein, not yet. And Levi has his days and nachts mixed up."

"I'll say." Mercy's eyes twinkled. "Morgen, Abner."

"Morgen, schön." He gazed at her, resisting the urge to kiss her. If only he could've kissed her yesterday in the woods.

"Ooh, he called you *beautiful*. I like that." Shanna abandoned the cookie cutters and went over to the stove. "I think the koffee's hot, Abner. Want some?"

"Sure, danki." He removed his coat and hat and hung them up. He stuffed his gloves into a coat pocket, then headed over to the sink to wash up. As he dried his hands on a towel, he turned. "What do you want me to do?"

"Stir." Mercy had a teasing glint in her eye. She held out a wooden spoon.

"Ach, definitely stir." Shanna's smile widened. "We made the same kind of cookies a couple of weeks ago. They take a lot of strength."

Mercy measured a mound of flour into a sifter and added some other powdery stuff to it.

"What kind of cookies are we making?"

"Sour cream." She pointed to the recipe on the table.

He picked it up and studied it.

"So, kind of like sugar cookies?" He put the well-used card back on the table.

"Not exactly. Old family recipe." Shanna sat in a chair across the table and sipped her koffee. "Ach, I forgot to pour you some."

Abner shook his head. "I can help myself. Do you want any, Mercy?" He went over to the cupboard, pulled out two mugs, and poured some of the dark brew into one.

She shook her head as he held it out to her. "I'm gut."

"Jah, you are." He winked and sat next to where she worked. "I called home after I left here yesterday. Daed's going to make an offer on the farm."

"The farm?" Shanna put down her koffee mug and rubbed her eyes. "Tell me more. Where? Why?"

Abner cringed. He'd forgotten how involved Shanna could get in Mercy's life. But then, he was thankful she'd nudged Mercy toward the taffy pull and had agreed to release her for dinner to-nacht at Katie's. Maybe putting up with her meddling was the price to pay. "The farm next to my parents is for sale." He stirred some cream into his koffee and added a spoonful of sugar. "Mercy and I… well, I…well…." He shrugged.

"Talking marriage, ain't so? Because of Paul? Are you going to elope, like Katie suggested?"

Mercy pulled in a loud, shuddery breath. "I don't want to talk about—"

"Because we've started to make plans, that's all." Abner shook his head as he looked at Mercy. Another spark of anger glittered in her eyes. He didn't want to discuss Paul, or their future plans, and Shanna wasn't gut at taking the hint. But he shouldn't have cut Mercy off. And he shouldn't have mentioned the farm around Shanna. "Nein. We most likely won't elope." He wasn't big on the idea of piling on additional problems. Not to mention, he hadn't felt the approval of der Herr when he'd prayed about it.

Serena pounded two blocks together while spewing a bunch of boppli gibberish that made nein sense to Abner. But it see-med to convey her opinion of the conversation, the way she looked pointedly at him while she blabbered. Then she stood, wobbled a little, and toddled to him, holding out the two blocks. He was glad to look at her rather than at Mercy or Shanna. He didn't want to see their reactions to his statement about not wanting to elope.

He accepted the blocks from Serena. "Danki."

Serena made another nonsensical comment and reclaimed the blocks.

"And there you have it." Abner leaned back with a smile. "Nein clue what her view is, but as long as it doesn't involve my keeping her blocks, we're gut."

Both women giggled. A wave of relief washed over Abner.

Mercy finished sifting the dry ingredients together, then grabbed a whisk and beat together the others. "Your turn, Abner." She pointed to the wooden spoon. "Time to earn your keep. I'm going to start adding the flour to this mixing bowl, and you can stir."

"Okay." He drained his koffee and rose to his feet. Then he picked up the wooden spoon and ran it around the wet ingredients as Mercy slowly added the flour mixture. By the time she had poured it all in, the dough was thick. He chuckled. "I'm thinking it would've been easier to mix this with my hands. Now what?"

Shanna stood and grabbed an old tablecloth. She laid it out on the table and sprinkled it with flour. "Now it gets rolled out." Her cell phone buzzed. She wiped her hands on her apron and glanced at the screen but didn't answer. The phone buzzed again, and she silenced it. "I think it's your daed, Mercy. It looks like the same number he called from last time. You can call him back later. Or not. Up to you."

❧

Without answering the phone—and without waiting for the cookie dough to chill—Mercy sprinkled more flour on the dough and rolled it out to a quarter-inch thickness before pressing in a few cookie cutters. She made a row of stars, cut one right after another, side by side. Her stomach churned. Daed's intrusion into her day didn't mean anything gut, that was for sure. Especially considering his anger the last time they'd talked. She hoped she wouldn't end up getting sick from the nerves eating at her.

She was already jumpy enough from the lack of sleep last nacht, imagining her greenhaus on the farm she would share with Abner, and praying that Gott would make their path straight, and…. Daed's call grated on a sore subject like salt on a wound.

Abner didn't voice any opinion one way or the other, but he did give her a look of concern before arranging the cutout cookies on the baking sheet. When the first sheet was full, he carried it over to Shanna, who slid it into the preheated oven.

A wail came from the other room. Shanna went to wash her hands. "I need to change and feed Levi. Will you keep an eye on the cookies, Abner? When they're done, take them out and transfer them to a cooling rack."

"Jah, I can do that."

"Gut. Set the timer for about ten minutes." She dried her hands and headed for the door.

Shanna's phone chimed again. She'd taken it off silent mode but left it lying on the table.

Mercy's stomach cramped. She didn't want to talk to Daed. Not now. Maybe in a day or two, after she'd had a chance to calm down. To process the disturbing news that had turned her world upside down. Inside out.

Abner picked up the phone, glanced at it, and carried it from the room. Mercy wasn't sure where he put it. Just so long as she didn't have to hear it. Just so long as she didn't have to deal with whatever Daed had called about. Something that he believed warranted another phone call, the second in mere days.

She cut out another row of stars, just as neat and orderly as the first.

At least she had some control over something.

Cookies.

Not her life.

Abner came back into the kitchen. "Shanna said to put her phone in her bedroom and shut the door. So I did."

Gut. Shanna didn't want to deal with the intrusion any more than Mercy did.

He touched her cheek. "It'll be okay, Mercy. Trust me."

She wished she could. She wanted to grab his hands and hold on tight.

"The shortest distance between the problem and its solution is the distance between your knees and the floor." He cupped her cheek, his thumb sliding back and forth in a comforting motion. "That's what Mamm always told me." His Adam's apple bobbed as he swallowed. "Want to pray together?"

She looked at him, startled. "What?"

"I know it's not normal to pray out loud, but I feel we should."

Mercy studied him, his serious expression. "I'd like that."

He dropped down to his knees. After a moment's hesitation, she knelt in front of him. He caught both her hands in his. "Heavenly Father, You say in Your Word that where two or three are gathered in Your name, You are there in the midst of them. Gott, we thank You for loving us. For dying for us. For saving us. And we kum to You now, asking for peace and direction for our future. For Mercy, as she talks with her daed later, that it will go well; and for the uncertain situation we're facing with Paul. We ask for favor. For wisdom. For guidance."

The timer buzzed. Mercy jumped.

His hands tightened on hers. "In Jesus' name we pray, amen."

"Amen," Mercy repeated.

"Amen," Serena said clearly.

Abner grinned at the toddler and tweaked her nose. Then he rose to his feet and reached to help Mercy up.

He was so sweet. So considerate.

Abner grabbed another baking sheet of cookies and carried it over to the oven, where he put on oven mitts and pulled out the first batch. Meanwhile, Mercy arranged cutout stars on another sheet.

Abner carried the baking sheet to the table and set it on a pot holder. "Do I take them off the sheet right away?"

"Let them cool a little first, so they don't break."

"Can I eat one while it's still warm?"

Mercy grinned at his pleading tone. "I want to put icing on them first."

He moved closer and nuzzled her neck. "Please?"

She shivered, glancing at the toddler playing quietly with blocks on the other side of the room, then toward the door Shanna had disappeared through a short time before.

"Please?" His teeth nipped at her ear.

"Ach, you." She barely kept from turning into his arms. They had an audience.

"Danki." He moved away and slid the edge of the spatula under a cookie.

"I didn't say jah." Mercy put her fists on her hips.

Dimples flashed in his cheeks. His gaze lowered to her lips, and he started to lean closer. "Aw, kum on."

Blocks tumbled to the floor in a loud crash.

He jerked away and looked at Serena. Color rose up his neck. "Maybe she'd like one, too."

"You're incorrigible."

"And you love me anyway."

He was right. She did. And she wouldn't want him to change one bit.

She let her gaze slide over him as he went back to check the next batch of cookies baking in the oven. He was wearing jeans again, his tan long-sleeved T-shirt tucked in. Nein suspenders. He didn't appear very Amish, but he did fill out the jeans and shirt nicely.

She forced her attention away from him and went back to cutting out more cookies, circles this time, then lined them up on a baking sheet.

Vehicle tires crunched over the gravel in front of the haus. Mercy wiped her hands on a towel and hurried over to the window. "I wonder who that might be."

Serena tugged on her skirt. "Up! Up."

Mercy bent, lifted her, then looked outside. The back doors of the van slid open.

Paul stepped out.

Chapter 23

*A*bner looked up when Mercy gave a sharp gasp. A niggle of worry began to gnaw at him as he moved to stand behind her, wrapping his arms around her and Serena. Hugging them against his chest, he peered over Mercy's shoulder and glanced out the window. A tension headache took the place of the worry. His stomach dropped to his knees. Maybe lower. But his knees almost buckled from the shock.

Paul Fisher?

Mercy had never told him Paul's last name. And he'd never dreamed that her former beau would be a distant cousin of his. Even though they'd lived in different districts, Paul and some of his friends had joined Abner and Abram for many a party in the back field before the twins had left home and found Gott. Paul had been known to drink more than he and Abram combined.

Abner stared at Paul, studying him, somehow hoping his recognition had been wrong. The auburn-haired man was shorter and stockier than he.

Definitely Paul.

Wherever Abner's stomach currently lodged, it roiled. How had he missed the news that Paul had gone fishing and drowned? Well, there had been a great deal of drama in his own life. And his family didn't always keep up with their distant relatives. But he couldn't believe that Mercy's Paul was his cousin. His family.

It was unsettling to discover he competed with kin for Mercy's heart. It'd been easier when he'd believed Paul to be a complete stranger.

Mercy whimpered, but Abner's eyes stayed focused on the man paying the van driver. She'd said that Paul never had kissed her, that he'd wanted to wait until marriage before doing so. But Abner knew for a fact that Paul had kissed other girls. He'd even kissed Marianna, Abram's former girl, back in Indiana. Abner had stumbled upon them in a hayloft. He'd gone back down the ladder in a hurry....

He shut his eyes against the memory.

Gut thing Paul had respected Mercy enough to wait. For Abner's sake. And for Mercy's. Gut that she wouldn't be haunted by those types of regrets.

Mercy stiffened in his arms. He opened his eyes as Paul turned toward the haus. Serena began to squirm against his tightening grip. With another sound he couldn't quite identify—something between a keen and a wail—Mercy pulled away, spun around, shoved Serena into his arms, and ran.

Upstairs. Not to the front porch.

A door slammed overhead.

Which spoke volumes of her feelings about Paul's arrival.

But he didn't know what to do. Should he go after Mercy and try to comfort her? Or should he call out to Shanna to let her know trouble was approaching?

His own cousin.... *Gott, I'm not laughing.*

Paul picked up a bag and then started for the front porch. Abner swallowed his unease, carried Serena to the door, and opened it just as Paul raised his hand to knock.

Abner couldn't find a welcoming smile. At least, not a sincere one. He did manage to force a friendly look he hoped would appear genuine. "Imagine seeing you here."

Paul did a double take. "Abner?"

The timer on the stove buzzed again.

Abner set Serena on the floor, crossed the room, grabbed the pot holders, and opened the oven door.

"What are you doing here?" Paul asked as he entered the haus. "Baking? Did I land in some alternate universe where my Indiana cousin ends up doing woman's work in Missouri? I thought you were in Shipshewana. Or maybe I'm dreaming, and you really aren't here." He shut the door and dropped the bag with a light thud.

If only it were a dream. A nightmare. Something Abner would eventually wake up from and find that it hadn't been real. "It's been a while since you left, Cousin."

"I thought Mercy Lapp lived here. This is the address her daed gave me."

"Jah...she's busy right now." Abner glanced at the doorway she'd run through. If only he could follow and comfort her. *Ach, Gott....*

"I wasn't aware you knew her." Paul unbundled from his outerwear and hung up his coat and hat.

"It's a small world." Abner slid the next baking sheet into the oven, even though his appetite for sweets had completely disappeared. At least it gave him something to do. "So, where've you been hiding for the past year?"

"I've...well, I'll have to explain myself to Mercy, so I might as well save my breath and tell you both at the same time. What are *you* doing in Missouri?"

Abner shrugged. "I came here to visit Abram for the holidays. He married a girl named Katie in October."

"Really? Abram's here, too?" Paul pulled up a chair and sat. "I know Micah is. I arranged to stay with him to-nacht. Hope to convince Mercy to return home with me tomorrow. Her daed said she'd agree once she saw me."

Jah, but Mercy had told her daed she would stay here until after Christmas. Hadn't he passed along that nugget of information to Paul? She'd also told him she'd fallen in love with someone else—and specified a name. Apparently, that part hadn't been mentioned, either.

That aside, their mutual cousin Micah had known about Paul's impending arrival and hadn't warned Abner? Really? "Does Micah know why you came?"

"Jah." Paul hesitated, his brow furrowed. "I mentioned I needed to see my girl."

So maybe Micah didn't know that Paul's girl was also Abner's girl.

A movement in the doorway caught his attention. Shanna held Levi against her shoulder, rubbing his back. She stopped and looked from Abner to Paul. After studying the newcomer for a long, silent moment, she said, "Hallo." Her eyes widened with unasked questions, then narrowed as she apparently drew her own conclusions. She glanced back at Abner. "Where's Mercy?"

Abner pointed up.

"Does she know?" Creases of worry cinched her brow.

Abner gave a slight nod.

Shanna handed Levi to him. "Burp him, please. I'm going to go talk to her."

"Okay…but I'm watching the cookies, too," he reminded her, awkwardly raising Levi to his shoulder.

"Just put him in the bouncer after he burps," Shanna told him, then left the room.

Paul chuckled. "You're turning into a regular maud. Burping a boppli and doing the baking. What's next? Laundry? Dishes?"

"You never know." Abner glanced at the boppli in his arms, hoping he wouldn't spit up. That was the last thing he wanted. It would further brand him as a laughingstock in his cousin's eyes.

Not that he and Paul were close. They never had been. They didn't have a lot in common, other than being on different branches of the same family tree. They'd probably be farther apart than ever once Paul learned that Abner was courting Mercy. Even Abner's daed would probably insist that he acknowledge Paul's prior claim. Abner's stomach did another dip as a loud belch erupted from Levi. Thankfully, nothing else came out.

Abner looked around for something that might fit the label of "bouncer." In the living room, he spotted a little reclined seat with straps that looked convincing enough. He lowered Levi into it, then carried the whole thing back to the kitchen and set it on the floor. He didn't fasten the straps. Didn't have a clue how to do it. They looked more complicated than a horse's harness. Besides, how much could a newborn boppli move?

Serena toddled over and set down a couple blocks beside her brother.

"So, you never did say what you were doing *here*." Paul leaned forward and snatched a cookie from the cooling rack. "And where Mercy is staying?"

Stunned at Paul's audacity to help himself to the cookies, Abner turned and washed his hands, then dried them before returning to the table and picking up a cookie cutter. A round one.

Round…for the family circle.

He put it back.

Gott, help….

He forced his eyes up, then caught and held his cousin's brown gaze.

"I'm courting Mercy."

◠◠◠

A light tap sounded on Mercy's door before it opened. Shanna stepped in, pushing her kapp strings over her shoulders. Mercy cringed. She didn't want to talk about it. Didn't want to deal with it. If only she could wake up and find that this all had been nothing more than a bad dream.

"Are you okay?" The mattress dipped as Shanna sat next to her.

Mercy looked away. Shame ate at her for running away from her problems and leaving Abner to entertain Paul—her current beau versus her former fiancé. Or was Paul her current fiancé, since they'd actually never broken up? Instead, he'd died.

But hadn't died.

So confusing.

Either way, he'd disappeared. For a whole year. Without contact. That kind of annulled their relationship, ain't so?

"Jah, I think so."

Shanna's comment jarred Mercy. Had she just voiced her entire thought process? She must've. Either that or Shanna had taken mind-reading courses when she'd joined the Englisch world for a time.

"Matthew would say to pray." Shanna's hand closed over Mercy's.

"How?"

"Gott knows."

Mercy huffed. "I'm the one who doesn't know what to do, how to act, what to think."

"Isn't that the best time to pray—when you're clueless? Some of the best prayers I've prayed were when I didn't know how. It seemed that something inside—Gott's Spirit, maybe—took over and prayed for me."

That seemed valid. Mercy had prayed prayers like that. Most recently, on the floor of Shanna's dark basement.

Shanna bowed her head. After a moment, Mercy followed suit. But she still didn't know what to say, and surely der Herr was tired of her constant whining since hearing of Paul's return to life. Besides, she and Abner had prayed together just a short time before Paul arrived, and He hadn't listened. Or had He?

What had Abner prayed for? Peace and direction. Favor. Wisdom. Guidance. *Ach, Gott.* The words turned into a refrain, playing over and over.

Shanna sat beside her, head bowed, as if she were praying silently.

After a while, Shanna's hand tightened around hers. "You ready?"

Hardly. She sucked in a breath. "Jah."

She forced herself to stand, took a moment to gather as much courage as she could, and shuffled out the door.

"Relax, Mercy," Shanna said from behind her. "Things are rarely as bad as we fear."

True. But it was even rarer that dead fiancés came back to life.

When she reached the bottom of the stairs, she stretched her stiff back and rotated her neck muscles as she walked down the hall to the kitchen, hoping to kum across as calm, cool, and collected.

Both men looked up. Two sets of eyes—one gaze blue and filled with shadows, one brown and assessing—rested on her.

Paul grinned. "Hallo, Mercy."

"Paul."

Did her voice sound strangled?

Abner straightened as Paul approached her and stopped mere steps in front of her. Not quite near enough to touch if she extended her arm. Not in her personal space. A relief, because she didn't know how she wanted to react or respond. Truthfully, she didn't want to go through this at all. Especially not with Abner looking on.

"I've kum to take you home."

Of course, that was why he'd kum. And her heart rebelled at his—and Daed's—high-handed assumption that she would go willingly. That she had nein say in the matter. Out of the corner of her eye, she saw Shanna quietly enter the room and stand near her at the doorway. Mercy's tongue stuck to the roof of her mouth as a million questions swirled through her mind before it settled on the obvious issue.

"I thought you were dead."

And she'd grieved her heart out, then finally developed the courage to move on.

Besides, what made him think he had the right to just walk in here and take her home without answering a few vital questions first?

Paul shrugged with a small smile. "That's what you get for thinking." He moved closer.

She resisted the urge to step back when he invaded her personal space. She clenched her fists, her short nails pinching her palms. And his comment? It hurt, even though he'd probably said it in jest.

He tapped the top of her kapp. "That fuzzy purple one-eyed octopus ate up all your brain cells a long time ago."

❧

Abner's jaw dropped. He forced his mouth closed and glanced sharply at Mercy in time to see her wince, slump her shoulders, and nod. "You're right."

"Nein, he's not!"

Everyone turned and looked at him, eyes wide.

He clenched his hands at his sides, prepared to defend himself. And Mercy.

Paul's tiny smile stayed in place. "Nein need to shout, Cousin. I know her a lot better than you do."

"Cousin?" both Mercy and Shanna asked. Mercy's hand rose to her throat, and she looked at Abner, her expression indicating a sense of betrayal. As if he'd known all along and hadn't told her.

"I didn't know," he hastened to assure her. "You never mentioned his last name. I didn't make the connection." His excuses continued pouring out, sounding lame to his own ears. She'd think the same thing he had: How could he not have known that his own cousin had gone missing for a year?

Paul's smile widened as he looked at Mercy. "You'll return home with me tomorrow, ain't so? Your daed said you would."

She sighed. "I can't. I'm working for Shanna until the end of December." She squared her shoulders, but her words lacked conviction. Abner focused on her, willing his courage to transfer to her, yet half afraid he might have lost her already.

Paul glanced at Shanna. "She seems to be getting along well enough. You can't miss First Christmas with your family. Or Second Christmas with your friends."

Serena picked up an armful of blocks and carried them to Paul, babbling. He ignored her outstretched hands holding the wooden squares.

After a moment, she toddled over to Abner and held them up to him. He took them, stacked them together, and offered them back to her.

She grinned as she took them, spouting more gibberish.

At least her presence helped ease the tension in the room.

The timer buzzed. Abner turned to the stove.

"Would you like some koffee, Paul?" Shanna asked, stepping farther into the room. "You could have a cookie, too, and tell us where you've been hiding this past year."

"I haven't been hiding. But some koffee and a cookie sounds gut. Danki."

"So, where were you?" Mercy's voice sounded small. Unsure.

It hurt to hear. Abner had thought they'd made progress, getting her to speak her mind. A little, at least.

Paul's mouth curved into a half smile as he dropped into the chair he'd occupied earlier. "I went fishing on Lake Michigan. Noah Stoltzfus and I joined a friend of ours and a few other buwe on his boat. He knew a storm was blowing in, but he didn't think the squall would get bad so fast, so he opted to stay on the lake. The boat capsized, and I hit my head on something. When I came to, I didn't know who I was."

"For a year?" Abner scowled. "What about your ID?" *Caught in a lie.* He glanced at Mercy. Her face was pale, and she chewed her lower lip as she pressed the leftover cookie dough into a ball, then started rerolling it flat. A mindless job, Abner supposed.

"Gut question, Abner." Shanna hooked the straps on the bouncer so that Levi wouldn't slide out, then poured some koffee in a mug and set it in front of Paul. "What about your ID?"

"I didn't have it on me. And Noah and I got separated." Paul shrugged. "I saw him in Shipshewana, so I guess he made it home."

"So, where were you?" Shanna took a pitcher of cream out of the refrigerator.

"In Wisconsin. In the hospital for a time, and then a local church got me connected with a men's shelter, where I stayed until I started remembering certain details. I'm still not sure I recall everything about my life before the accident, but I know who I am, where I'm from, and that I'm going to marry Mercy in the fall." He grinned at her. "I also remember that fuzzy purple one-eyed octopus."

Shanna set the sugar bowl on the table with extra force. A few granules jumped out. "You were going to marry Mercy a few weeks ago, in November. You went missing over a year ago."

Paul shrugged. "What changed? Abner won't continue this silly courtship, especially since I'm family."

"It's hardly silly." Abner glanced at Mercy. Twin spots of red appeared on her cheeks, and her lips were flattened together. "Tell him, Mercy."

She opened her mouth. Then shut it.

"Do you even know about the fuzzy purple one-eyed octopus, Cousin?" Paul smirked. "She can't marry someone who doesn't know her history."

"Nein, but she should marry someone who knows her heart, and who cares enough to listen."

Mercy lowered the wooden rolling pin with a thud. "A year. It's been a year."

She didn't say it as loudly or as firmly as Abner would've liked. She made more noise with the rolling pin hitting the table. Her voice was barely above a whisper, undergirded with uncertainty.

"I don't need to know about any octopus." Abner pressed both hands on the table and leaned forward. "I've made promises to Mercy, and I'm going to keep them."

But a niggle of doubt arose. He could almost envision his daed, grossdaedi, and onkels lined up with stern expressions, ordering him to give Paul back his toys, as they had when they were kinner.

Mercy wasn't a toy.

But would the elders in the family—the patriarchs— understand that? Or would they just see Abner taking something that didn't belong to him?

Chapter 24

Mercy grabbed the round cookie cutter and pressed it into the last piece of dough, the way she had the stars. One right after another. A neat, orderly row. If only her thoughts were so neat and orderly. She chewed her lower lip and peered at her former—current?—fiancé from under her eyelashes.

She'd always thought Paul was cute. He had unruly red curls and had once had a mischievous streak to match, but he'd outgrown it when he'd entered adolescence. He'd been her neighbor bu who would roam barefoot down to the creek, fishing pole in hand, straw hat askew, and would kum back with a mess of fish that he'd share with her family. He was kind that way. He'd even walked to school with her and her sisters until he'd turned fourteen.

But Abner.... She glanced at him out of the corner of her eye. Light brown hair cut in an Englisch style with streaks of blond mixed in, sun-streaked, thanks to the time he spent outdoors. Brilliant blue eyes, a shade lighter than blueberries, a shade darker than the sky. He was so very handsome—more so than Paul.

She shouldn't judge a book by its cover—or a man by his appearance. If only Gott would show her a clear path, as the Gut Book said He would. But there wasn't one, as far as she could tell. On the one hand was Abner—whom she loved and wanted to be with, who treated her with affection and respect. He treated kinner with kindness, wasn't ashamed to do woman's work, and pushed her to recognize her heart's dreams, such as maintaining a greenhaus. But their relationship had started with a bang; might it end just as abruptly?

On the other hand was Paul, with whom she had grown up. The relationship had begun slowly, built steadily. Was that an indication that it would probably stand the test of time? Or was it simply comfortable and safe?

Either way, the fact remained that she didn't feel the same emotional connection, or the physical appeal, with Paul that she did with Abner.

She couldn't keep from glancing at Paul's lips. Thin, narrow, and—right now—in a cruel twist. She couldn't imagine being kissed by him. Nausea rose in her throat at the thought.

Daed would tell her that she shouldn't trust her heart. That emotions had nein play in life. That she needed to use common sense.

Common sense that Paul—and some others—had claimed she lacked.

Daed knew and approved of Paul. Abner? Probably not so much. Which would be why Paul apparently caught the next bus out of Indiana to kum here to take her home.

Paul balanced his chair on the two back legs, holding the cup of koffee in one hand, his gaze fixed on Abner. "She got that silly purple octopus when the circus came to town."

Abner shifted his weight and leaned one hip and shoulder against the wall. "I don't need to hear about the octopus. She can tell me if she wants." He grinned, but there was something hard behind his expression.

Mercy didn't remember going to the circus. She'd thought she'd gotten the stuffed octopus as a boppli gift—she remembered carrying it around as a preschooler, and it seemed as if Mamm mentioned her using it while teething. But then again, Paul always said she had a faulty memory.

"Dragged it with her everywhere she went. Even to school. Until it disappeared. We think it was sucked into her brain, where it took up residence." Paul either hadn't heard Abner or had chosen to ignore him. If only he would've stopped.

She glanced at Abner. A muscle jumped in his jaw, but he seemed at ease as he leaned casually against the wall beside her, ankles crossed. Or maybe not. His stance reminded her of the seemingly bored appearance of a panther pretending not to watch its prey. Yet every muscle was ready to spring.

Her teeth were clenched so tightly that her jaw ached. She could only imagine Abner's opinion of her, hearing the story behind her lack of thinking skills when it came to math or problems involving "common sense." He was probably shocked speechless, learning all these things.

She'd been heartbroken when the stuffed octopus had vanished. She suspected Daed had taken it and destroyed it, since, just before its disappearance, he'd started talking about how she needed to grow up. Paul had seemed understanding, telling her that since the octopus had taken up residence in her brain, it would always be with her.

In hindsight, she never should've allowed herself to be consoled by Paul's explanation. Gott was with her always. Not a toy. Paul's reasoning had elevated the stuffed animal into something it wasn't. An idol, of sorts.

And she'd allowed herself to believe it.

Besides, now, it didn't seem so kind.

Maybe Abner should know about the octopus. Mercy pulled in a deep breath and a remnant of courage. "I'm not gut at math. At least, not story problems."

Abner lifted a shoulder. "A lot of people aren't. I can help you."

"I can add, subtract, and multiply." Mercy chewed on her lip again. "I can't divide...."

Abner lowered his gaze, his eyes darkening. "I can think of more pleasant things to do with—" He caught his breath and looked away, red creeping up his neck. "Division is the opposite of multiplying. I can teach you."

Shanna chuckled. "I think you're probably better at math than you think you are."

Paul snorted. "I tried. Our teacher tried. She couldn't get it."

"Then she didn't have a very gut teacher, ain't so?" Abner speared Paul with a glare. "You know what? That's enough talk about Mercy's math skills."

As if to punctuate Abner's comment, Serena's tower of blocks fell to the floor with a loud crash.

Mercy glanced at Abner, surprised at his response. Appreciative of his firm support—something she'd never really experienced before leaving home. That muscle in his jaw still jumped. Was he angry over how Paul was treating her?

Abner straightened and moved away from the wall. "You must be tired after your trip, Paul. How about I take you to Micah's haus so you can rest?"

Paul shook his head. "I'm not that tired. I slept on the bus."

"Then tell us about that homeless shelter you said you stayed in. I'm curious." Shanna raised her eyebrows. "I used to volunteer at one in Springfield when I went to nursing school. We had to do some community service as part of our education, and…." She laughed. "Well, it's not important. Anyway, tell us about it."

Paul shrugged. "It wasn't really all that interesting. An old building in the downtown area. I think it was an abandoned church. It had barred windows and a fire escape with stairs that looked as if they'd collapse if anyone stepped on them. We could check in at five in the evening and had to leave by nine in the morning. They had this big room on the top floor filled with bunks and cots. I usually got a cot when it was rainy, because the bunks filled up fast then. They served breakfast—usually oatmeal—and supper, either beans or rice, and they expected us to help clean the dining room, and…." He chuckled. "Guess I did woman's work, then. Scrubbing floors, wiping tables and chairs, and stacking them. We couldn't help in the kitchen because the state wouldn't let us in there—not even to get snacks."

"How'd you sign in and out if you didn't know your name?" Shanna asked. She carried a baking sheet over to the table and set it on a trivet.

"The hospital chaplain took me after I was discharged. He said they didn't check to see if you really were who you claimed; they just needed a name. He suggested I go by something I could remember, such as John Doe or David Smith."

Mercy glanced at Paul, still leaning back in the chair with a gleam in his eye, as if excited to share about his grand adventure as a homeless man who didn't know his identity. Then she turned her attention to filling an empty baking sheet with the last of the cutout cookies.

"What name did you go by?" Shanna slid a spatula beneath a baked cookie and lifted it from the sheet.

"The chaplain felt that David Smith sounded more like a real name than John Doe."

"Hmmm." Shanna placed the cookie on the cooling rack.

He didn't seem curious about Shanna's question, but Mercy was. "Does it matter what name he went by?"

One side of Shanna's mouth curved up. "Just wondered."

Mercy looked back at Paul. "So, you really lost your mind? It wasn't just that you were in your rumschpringe and didn't want to contact me?"

❧

Abner didn't like the confusion in Mercy's voice. His stomach churned, but he didn't know what to do, other than pray. And praying seemed redundant. Every time he tried, he heard, deep in his spirit, *Trust Me. It's going to be okay.*

That left so much unsaid. Jah, he trusted der Herr. But He could answer in so many ways. Not necessarily the way Abner wanted.

Paul smiled at Mercy. "I had what they called amnesia. I didn't lose my mind, I just forgot stuff. Like who I was, where I came from…the important stuff, you know."

She smiled back with a sympathetic softness that shot daggers into Abner's heart.

"Didn't they have questions about your language?" Abner resumed his position against the wall. Forcing himself to remain calm and controlled, hoping to appear carefree. As if he wasn't suffering from a major faith issue.

Paul's brow furrowed as he lowered the front legs of the chair to the floor. "What do you mean?"

"Englisch is your second language." Abner folded his arms across his chest.

Shanna shook her head as she turned away, giving him a pointed look. As in, *"Hush now."* She carried the baking sheet Mercy had just filled over to the oven.

He grinned. Shanna had the same suspicions? It was gut to know that not everyone bought Paul's story. Maybe the truth would kum out on its own. He tried to relax.

Truth will tell.

Paul shrugged. "One can never tell what a man's mind will recall. It's a strange and wunderbaar thing."

Jah, but if a man lost his mind, wouldn't the language he remembered have been the one he'd spoken since birth?

"I'll be right back," Shanna said. "I need help with something. Abner, kum with me, please." She turned and left the kitchen. After a moment, Abner followed, albeit reluctantly. He didn't want to leave Mercy alone with Paul.

"Mama." Serena toddled after them.

Shanna didn't slow down. She led the way to the back bedroom, where Abner had taken the cell phone earlier, and shut the door after Serena had caught up with them.

She turned to Abner. "You didn't hear me say this, and I'll deny it if you tell anyone, but Daed has a computer with Internet in his barn. I'll have him check out a few things. Don't contradict or question Paul. I want to make sure our Mercy isn't misled."

Our Mercy. Abner liked that. He couldn't keep a slow smile from forming. "You don't trust him. That's not our way."

Shanna grinned with a wink. "You don't, either."

Nein. He didn't.

❦

Mercy gathered the dirty dishes from the table and carried them to the sink as Paul talked about all the things a mind was capable of, according to an article he'd read in some medical magazine he'd picked up at the homeless shelter. She didn't listen too closely. His medical talk bored her, so she tended to tune it out, giving him the same level of attention she'd paid her teachers in school. Not very much.

She'd much rather be doing something than listening to someone talk about it.

So, Paul had lost his memory? He hadn't known who he was? If so, then he hadn't remembered her, ain't so? She'd jumped to so many wrong conclusions.

She needed to forgive him. Give him another chance. Daed would be happy.

But Abner.... Something inside her seemed to break, and a lump formed in her throat. Unexpected tears burned her eyes. She kneaded the few leftover pieces of cookie dough into a ball. Mamm always rolled it out and baked it in whatever shape it had formed. Nein sense wasting a cookie. She'd eat it herself.

Abner came back in the room and picked up the pot holders Shanna had left on the table and went to stand sentry by the stove. Mercy didn't know where Shanna had disappeared to, but a low murmur came from the back bedroom.

She looked away from the door, to Paul, leaning back in his chair again, telling Abner about whatever he'd read in the magazine as Abner checked the cookies baking in the oven.

There was a man who wasn't afraid of woman's work. A man who'd be beside her every step of the way. A man who'd be a gut ehemann and daed. He'd asked his own daed to make an offer on a farm and had even offered to let her live there, waiting for him, while he finished out his time in Montana, if she didn't want to go there with him.

Not that she wanted to be away from him.

But Montana?

Her emotions were all over the place.

Paul? Or Abner?

How could she choose?

More important, how had her younger sister, Joy, ever listened to Paul? She'd found his endless babble intriguing. Fascinating.

The man was well-read; she'd give him that. Paul always had gravitated toward medical journals, even when they were kinner. If he weren't Amish, he'd probably be studying to be a doctor.

Joy used to sit in the kitchen with them when Paul came over, pretending to do her schoolwork. In reality, she just wanted to be near Paul.

The memories of Joy's childish claims washed through Mercy.

"When I grow up, I want to marry Paul Fisher...."

Chapter 25

*A*bner's pleasure in spending the day with Mercy had disappeared the moment Paul had stepped out of the van.

Especially with his apparent determination to hang around. Not that Abner minded others, usually.

It was insecurity, plain and simple.

He wanted to leave and take Paul with him. He wouldn't be with Mercy, but then, neither would Paul. She needed time alone. And he needed to get away before he blew up. His lips ached from forcing a smile against his feelings. The same as he'd done after the murders of his friends. After the separation from his twin brother, and the beginnings of forging a new life for himself. *Hey, I'm fine!* had been his demeanor.

Right. Those were rough days.

At least being here gave him the opportunity to gauge Mercy's relationship with Paul. What he saw so far, he didn't like. Especially Paul's treatment of Mercy, as if she were a young child, and he was determined to keep her that way.

Purple octopus or not, Mercy wasn't stupid. Abner had spent enough time with her to know. Besides, being smart didn't make anyone better than others. If Paul was an example of smarts, Abner would take stupidity anytime.

But that was unkind.

He'd been with Mercy while she shopped. Watched as she added prices in her head so that she knew, almost to the penny, how much the purchase would total at the checkout counter. That had impressed him, though he'd never told her so. If he got the opportunity again, he'd say so. Math might not have been her strongest subject in school, but in his opinion, that wasn't the real problem. Insecurity was. Due to Paul's belittling treatment, nein doubt.

He didn't like it. Not one little bit.

184 Laura V. Hilton

Mercy collected a smaller mixing bowl, along with several measuring spoons and cups, and returned to the table.

"What are you making now?" Paul leaned forward.

"Icing. For the cookies." Her voice was flat. "I planned to send some to my parents."

And mine. Abner swallowed but kept that thought inside. Where it belonged. Especially when Shanna had told him to keep his mouth shut.

"You don't need to send them. We'll deliver them in person when we return together."

Mercy pursed her lips.

"They'll get there faster," Paul added.

"If I mail them, jah. I'm staying here till the end of December." Her voice was weak, but the words had been said.

Abner grinned. She *could* stand up to Paul.

Paul straightened. "Well, actually, I have the bus tickets. Already bought. For the day after tomorrow."

Mercy shifted her weight from one foot to the other. Frowned and lowered her head to stare at the mixing bowl. "Then—"

"Nein. She's not going." Shanna came back into the room.

Abner narrowed his eyes. Had Mercy been about to agree? Or maybe she might've voiced another objection. If that was the case, he wished she would have said it, loud and clear.

"If you want to spend more time with her, you're welkum to visit, if she'll see you. But she's not leaving yet." Shanna planted her fists on her hips. "Got that?"

"Her daed said—"

"I don't particularly care what her daed said." Shanna frowned. "I hired her, and she isn't released until I say so." She turned to Abner. "Why don't you take Paul with you and go? As much as I like you buwe visiting, you're distracting my helper."

Abner's stomach fell. Shanna was sending him away, too? But maybe it was just her way of getting rid of Paul.

"I'm allowed to kum courting, ain't so?" Paul pushed to his feet.

Nein. You're not. Abner didn't have the right to say those words. But Mercy could.

She remained silent.

Shanna's gaze met his, almost as if she'd read his mind. She winked before she looked back at Paul. "Ach, I can't stop a bu from coming courting. The usual rules apply. And absolutely nein bundling."

Paul's face flamed red. "Nein. Of course not." He glanced at Mercy. "I'll see you to-nacht, then. We need to talk."

To-nacht? That meant Abner wouldn't see her. And he was supposed to take her home with him to have dinner with Abram and Katie. His heart sank. But then, maybe this *talk* would be a gut thing. Paul would go home, and life would return to normal. Minus the threat of Paul coming back to court Abner's girl.

His girl. Not Paul's.

But he had to step back and let her decide.

And he had to trust.

A verse from Hebrews flashed through his memory: *"Now faith is the substance of things hoped for, the evidence of things not seen."*

He had to trust der Herr to take care of his faith issues.

Abner nodded at Shanna, and she winked at him again. He didn't know what her winks meant. Hopefully, it wasn't his presence she resented.

He moved away from the wall. "See you later, Mercy."

She met his gaze, and he noted the sheen of tears in her eyes.

Regardless of their audience, he let his thumb graze over the curve of her cheek, feeling the softness beneath his calluses. He leaned forward and brushed his lips against her cheek, near her ear. "Since you're not coming to dinner, I'll kum back later, jah?" he whispered.

She nodded with a tiny smile but then shook her head. "I don't want either one of you coming to-nacht. I want—need—a day to think and pray about this."

"Tomorrow then, buwe." Shanna lifted Paul's coat from the wall hook and handed it to him.

"See you tomorrow, Mercy," Paul said.

Abner pulled in a breath. Nodded. Mouthed *"Ich liebe dich"* and grinned as he stepped away. He'd be there. Tomorrow.

Even if Paul came.

She had to decide, but he wasn't going to step out of the picture.

❧

The haus fell silent after Abner and Paul left. Both Serena and Levi were asleep, and Shanna had decided to take advantage of the

186 Laura V. Hilton

quiet by grabbing a quick catnap. Or so she'd said. Instead, Mercy heard muted conversation coming from her bedroom.

Left alone in the kitchen, Mercy finished decorating the cookies. She filled two tins, one for her parents and one for Abner's, and then put the rest in Shanna's cookie jar. She missed the company, the conversation, the help.

She didn't want to send any cookies to Paul's parents. They might look down on her for wasting postage to send cookies when his mamm was capable of making them herself. Mercy had sometimes taken treats to them when she and Paul were courting, and they'd always found something to criticize. Too much icing or not enough. Kum to think of it, her parents would find fault, too. But not sending Mamm and Daed anything for Christmas seemed unkind. Especially since they usually exchanged simple, useful gifts. Would Abner's parents be the same way? Would they find some deficiency in her? Maybe that was just the way of families—at least the ones she'd known. They didn't give praise because it caused pride, a sin. Criticism kept them humble.

Abner and Shanna both were liberal in offering praise. Matthew was, too, though to a lesser degree.

Mercy liked being appreciated. Feeling needed. Not being made to feel like a failure. Abner must have gotten his outlook from somewhere. Had his parents raised him that way?

Maybe not all families were like hers and Paul's.

Mercy moved to the window and stared out. Snow flurries drifted past. Another snowstorm in the offing? Mercy didn't know for sure. Matthew would be home soon; he might know the forecast. The sky was overcast, and the birds that hadn't left for the winter were busily filling their bellies at the outdoor feeder, presumably before hunkering down for the storm. One brave squirrel stuffed its checks full of seeds, but it kept its distance from the birds.

Mercy sighed, watching the flakes float past. If only she knew what to do. It'd be helpful if der Herr would send her a letter telling her what to do.

Wait—He had. The Bible.

And the Bible clearly stated, "*Children, obey your parents in all things: for this is well pleasing unto the Lord.*" Colossians 3:20 was one of the first verses she'd been made to memorize as a child.

Daed wanted her to return home, but that was out of the question until after Christmas. He also wanted her to marry Paul.

Mercy shut her eyes against the burn.

Was this to be her lot in life?

After dropping Paul at Micah's haus, Abner went into town so he could charge his almost-dead cell-phone battery at McDonald's. There he sat, waiting for it to charge, while he munched on French fries and sipped koffee.

And thought.

And tried to ignore the TV that had the weather playing almost nonstop.

He unplugged his fully charged cell phone and fingered it. He needed to call home again.

He took one last sip of his koffee, draining the cup, and tossed it into the trash on his way out the door. Then he climbed into his buggy and started the short drive to the main square. Katie had asked him to pick up a few items at the store. In front of him was a farmer hauling a cattle trailer. Their neighbor back home had a few head of cattle....

Maybe Daed hadn't talked to his neighbor about the farm yet. Abner didn't want to withdraw the offer so soon, but maybe he'd been a bit premature in making it, since Paul had kum back into the picture.

As he parked the buggy, he tried to imagine what Daed might be doing. If it was snowing in Missouri, Shipshewana would be buried, as well. He might be in the barn, but he was likelier to be in the haus.

Abner climbed out of the buggy and walked toward the town square. It'd be a little more private than the store parking lot. He'd take his chances that Daed would be in the barn. Or at least near enough to hear the phone ring. He speed-dialed the number for the barn phone.

It rang once...twice...six times. Abner pulled the phone away from his ear.

"Hallo?" The muted voice floated in the air between Abner's hand and his head.

He pressed the phone to his ear again. "Aaron? It's Abner."

188 Laura V. Hilton

"Hey! Great to hear from you! Are you coming home for Christmas? Mamm's been baking up a storm. She sent a package to Abram today but said she'd send you a separate one if you wouldn't be home, since you've been complaining about rationed sweets. What's up with that?"

Abner chuckled. "Abram's frau and her mamm take delight in torturing a man with baking goodies and then limiting the amount he's allowed to eat. Something about it not being gut for us and ruining our appetite. Pure foolishness."

Aaron laughed. "My frau's the same way. Difficult for a man. I'm getting skilled at grabbing a few cookies when she's not looking. Other than an occasional 'Ach, you,' she hasn't objected too much."

Abner chuckled. "Is Daed around? I need to talk to him."

"Jah. I heard you made an offer on the farm next door. Found a girl to get serious about, ain't so?"

Abner wandered past a store window, ignoring a bunch of young Englisch buwe racing by. He stopped to peer at the display and stared at a grouping of teddy bears holding ornaments and small toys.

"Maybe." He studied a white bear decorated with blue snowflakes. Nowhere near as scary as the grizzly he'd faced in Montana. He shuddered and turned his back to it, shifting to the right and leaning against the building. "May I speak with Daed?"

"Hang on a minute." There were shuffling sounds from the other end of the phone.

"Abner? That you?" Daed said. "The farm's yours. He agreed to your offer and even volunteered to finance it. Says he knows you're gut for it."

"Danki, but I might've been a bit premature. Mercy's beau is Paul Fisher. She thought he was dead, and—"

"Ah. Right. The fishing 'accident.'" Daed cleared his throat. "So, what's he saying?"

"Something about losing his memory and forgetting who he was."

"And your girl...how's she doing with his return to life?"

"Not so well. He came down to Missouri, wants to take her back home, and believes I'll release her from the promises we made—"

Something banged on Daed's end of the phone. "You're not so inclined, ain't so?"

Abner shook his head. "Not even remotely."

"It's her choice. You know that, jah?"

"Jah." The stubborn lump in his throat returned. "Danki for not insisting I give her up."

Daed chuckled. "I think sometimes it's wrong for us men to get involved in childish squabbles. We gave in to Paul too many times and made him expect that whatever he wants will be handed to him. It's time he learns it isn't that way."

Gut to know Daed wouldn't be lining up against him. He wasn't alone in this fight.

Abner shifted against the building as the Englisch buwe who'd run past earlier came back just as quickly. Laughing about something. He grinned at one of them. "Jah. Maybe."

"I'll pray, sohn."

"Danki, Daed. Pray for my faith."

"I will. As the Englisch say, 'Hope for the best, prepare for the worst.'"

Abner furrowed his brow as he considered the phrase. "Wouldn't it be wise to prepare for the best, too?"

There was silence on the other end for a beat. Maybe two.

"Daed?"

"Jah, just thinking. And a verse in Hebrews comes to mind. *'Faith is the substance of things hoped for, the evidence of things not seen.'* And...maybe I simply need to say to you: Keep the faith, bu. Keep the faith. As a sign of that faith, purchase the farm. Gott will honor your faithful action. *'Faith without works is dead.'"*

Abner smiled as he ended the call. He waited for the English buwe as they stampeded past again. Were they running a relay race up and down the sidewalk? When the coast was clear, he stepped away from the wall. The teddy bear in the window caught his attention again, seeming to wave its tiny, furry paw at him.

Even though the store's wares didn't exactly beckon him, he went inside. It'd be nice to step out of the bone-chilling cold for a moment.

And there, across the aisle, leaning against the wall on top of a shelf, was a plaque that read, *"Be still, and know that I am God."* —Psalm 46:10.

The same verse der Herr had brought to mind when he'd had the run-in with the bear. The time when he'd had an up-close-and-personal encounter with Gott.

Abner's legs buckled with a sudden urge to kneel before Gott and just be still. He reached for something...he wasn't even sure what he grabbed to keep from stumbling.

Be still....

Chapter 26

Milk splattered on Mercy's leg and the floor. The lid of the plastic sippy cup flew off, and the liquid spread in a puddle on the table. "Be careful!" Mercy glared at Serena.

The girl's mouth curved downward, and tears filled her eyes.

Mercy winced. It was her own fault—she hadn't attached the lid correctly—and she was terrible for taking out her anger on the innocent little girl.

She was simply frustrated about Paul, and her feelings were spilling over onto others. She needed to keep better control of her emotions.

"I'm sorry." Ignoring the puddle of milk, Mercy scooped up the crying girl and hugged her.

Shanna eyed her, opening and closing her mouth a couple times, before she finally shrugged, grabbed a lantern, and went downstairs. A few minutes later, she heard things banging around in the basement.

Mercy sighed. She certainly hadn't meant to alienate her closest friend and ally.

She cuddled Serena close as she carried her upstairs, then changed her diaper and placed her in her crib for a nap. Next she went to the basement to seek out Shanna, planning her apology. *I'm sorry for snapping at Serena, but….*

Shanna lifted a can from a box and set it forcefully on a shelf with a frown.

"What?" It had kum out a bit crosser than Mercy had intended. She grimaced.

"I didn't say anything." Shanna glanced at her, eyes wide.

"Nein, but you wanted to."

She lifted her shoulder. "I was going to give you my opinion on which bu to choose. But Matthew has strictly forbidden me to say. You need to decide."

"There's nein decision," Mercy said flatly.

"Right. There's not." Shanna's voice was far brighter than it had a right to be. She picked up a huge can of cranberry sauce. Industrial-size. "Where did this kum from?"

Mercy frowned at the can, remembering. "Some people I didn't know came by the other day when you'd gone to see your mamm. They brought boxes of food. Said it was a gift to help out after the birth of the boppli. The ehemann took everything downstairs, and I forgot to mention it. They didn't tell me their name, but they said you would know who they were."

Shanna pursed her lips and looked pensive for a moment. "Ach, okay. I know who it's from. They brought food after Serena was born, too. They own a local salvage grocery and probably were clearing out stuff they couldn't sell. Which explains all these big cans of food I wouldn't normally buy." She eyed the cranberry sauce. "Well, I guess I'll plan on serving this at Christmas dinner at my parents'. With all of us there, it should be mostly eaten, jah?"

"You do have a big family." How could they carry on such a mundane conversation when Mercy's world was caving in?

Shanna went back to work emptying the boxes of food, humming as she put the canned goods on the shelves. "Ach, look." She held up a box. "Some of those snack cakes that have a shelf life of forever. Preservative city."

Mercy forced a smile, then nodded toward the stairs. "I'll go check the laundry and see if it's dry. I like having the enclosed porch to hang it in."

"You going to tell him to-nacht, then?"

She managed a nod. She couldn't speak past the lump in her throat.

Shanna resumed her humming.

Mercy frowned. She'd thought Shanna was pro-Abner, but she seemed awfully cheery over Mercy's obligation to choose Paul. She hadn't thought Shanna was the type to rejoice when a friend suffered.

A few minutes after Mercy went out to the enclosed porch and started folding the dry laundry, a horse and buggy pulled into the driveway, and Matthew climbed out. He nodded at her, then unhooked the horse and led it into the barn.

After sorting and delivering the clean laundry, she checked the refrigerator for something to make for supper. She took out ham to warm, which she would serve with canned asparagus and sweet potatoes from Shanna's pantry. Maybe she'd make biscuits to go with dinner...and a berry cobbler for dessert. Shanna had some canned blueberries downstairs. Homemade Christmas cookies would be gut, too, and would require less work. Or maybe she'd prefer the preservative-saturated snack cakes instead.

Dinner planned, Mercy went to the basement to get the ingredients she needed. Shanna was still sorting through the items the store owner had brought by. She looked up and grinned. "There are boxes of disposable diapers of assorted sizes in here, too, but they are factory seconds. The attachment tape is torn off one side of every diaper. Gut thing I have diaper pins to attach them. I feel I was just handed the moon. Disposable diapers! I'll need to write a heartfelt letter to thank them."

Mercy heard the kitchen door open and shut. A few seconds later, Matthew appeared at the top of the basement stairs. "Mercy? Paul just drove in."

Shanna frowned. "Really? Now? Before supper?" She eyed Mercy. "What time do you do your courting in Shipshewana? Around here, it's after dark."

Mercy shook her head. "Paul doesn't like that. He prefers to join the family for dinner and then stay awhile afterward, usually to play a game of checkers. He'll leave around seven. I should've thought to tell you. Sorry."

"Odd." Shanna put another can on a shelf. "Jah, you should've told me, but I guess we don't need to worry about you and Paul being alone. Matthew muttered something the other nacht about young couples and raging hormones. But you're in our care, and we'll be awake to chaperone." She quieted her voice to add, "But when Abner comes, if it's at the usual time, you'll be on your own. We'll just peek in occasionally."

Tears burned Mercy's eyes as she started upstairs to prepare supper. Maybe Matthew would entertain Paul while she worked. Better yet, perhaps he would invite him out to the barn to help with chores.

She didn't expect him to stay long. Not when he'd never stayed for more than dinner and a game or two of checkers, as if they were still schoolhaus chums. Not when—

She caught her breath with a sob.

Paul waited in the kitchen, sitting at the table. "You doing okay, Mercy? You look kind of...pale. Sick."

Jah, from having to pretend. From having this painful reality thrust at her. From having to.... She closed her eyes. "I'm okay. Just...a sleepless nacht or two. Want a cup of koffee?"

"Sounds gut. And maybe a few of the cookies you made earlier."

She nodded and set them out, then started peeling the sweet potatoes she'd brought up from the basement.

"I'd like those mashed," Paul said.

ᑭᑫ

Abner decided to wait to go to the Yoders', hoping Paul would have left before he got there. He didn't want to compete in person with his cousin. Plus, if the opportunity should arise for him to steal a kiss or two, he wouldn't be above taking advantage.

Though he probably should be above it. Daed would frown on him for trying to cloud Mercy's judgment with passion.

Abner shivered and gathered the heavy buggy quilt more tightly around him. The temperature must've dropped twenty degrees with the setting of the sun. He glanced at the teddy bear on the seat beside him. "You gut? Haven't eaten the chocolates yet, ain't so?" He was almost at the Yoders', so he could soon go inside and warm up—and stop amusing himself by conversing with stuffed animals. He hoped Mercy would have some hot cocoa ready, even if it was leftover from her visit with Paul. A hot drink and some cookies would be fantastic.

Speaking of Paul, he wondered if Shanna had gotten a chance to research him on that computer she'd mentioned. What had she intended to convey with all those winks yesterday?

He couldn't keep a smile from his face as he neared Mercy's temporary home. A soft glow from a lantern lit her bedroom window, and he didn't see a visiting buggy parked between the haus and the barn. Hopefully, that meant Paul had left. Or hadn't kum at all.

Well, it might mean he'd hired a driver to bring him. And if so, he might still be there.

Abner eyed the window again. *Nein.* Shanna had said "absolutely nein bundling." And Mercy had told him that Paul wanted to wait to kiss until they were married.

That pleased him. Greatly.

He parked the buggy, led Savvy into the barn, and stabled her, then grabbed a handful of gravel and headed for the area beneath Mercy's window.

It seemed like forever before her beautiful face appeared. He held the flashlight to illuminate his face, and she opened the window and leaned out.

He pointed toward the kitchen door. After a brief moment, she nodded and ducked back inside. The window slid shut.

Abner crunched his way across the frozen yard, quietly opened the kitchen door, set down the plastic bag of gifts for Mercy, and took off his boots. He was arranging them in the plastic tray when lantern light filled the room with a soft glow. He gave her a grin, then hung his coat on a hook and topped it with his hat.

When he turned to her again, she didn't smile back. Instead, it looked like she'd been crying.

Had Paul hurt her?

His smile flatlined, his lips tightened, and his fists balled. He forced them to relax as he crossed the room in three long steps. He reached for her upper arms and tugged her gently into his embrace. She leaned into him with a sigh, followed by a sniff and then a sob.

"Mercy, what's wrong?" His voice croaked. It broke his heart to see her cry. If only he could spend his life making sure she never cried again.

"Nothing. Everything."

He blinked. *Okay, then.* "Did he hurt you?"

Burrowing closer, she shook her head, then wrapped her arms securely around his waist, as if she would never let go. He didn't want her to. He tightened his grip on her, hugging her against him.

"Talk to me, Mercy. Why are you crying?"

She sniffed again. "B-because...because the B-Bible says I have to marry Paul."

"Huh?" Abner sounded confused, hurt, and...well, mostly confused. He pulled back and studied her face.

Mercy wiped her eyes, catching the tears that had pooled there. She dipped her chin, but he caught it with a fingertip and lifted her head.

His gaze was serious. Sad.

Fresh tears replaced the ones she'd just brushed away, blurring her vision.

And already she missed the comfort of his arms. Her decision would hurt him as badly as it had her. And he would never hold her in his arms again. Ever.

The tears flowed.

"Mercy," he groaned. "Talk to me. Where did you get that idea?"

"I don't know."

"There must be some verse or passage that's led you—misled you, in fact—to believe the Bible says you have to marry Paul."

She tried to compose herself. "It says, 'Children, obey your parents.' It says, 'Honour thy father and thy mother.' It says...." Her voice broke.

He pulled her close again. "Nein, Mercy. It doesn't say that you must marry a man you don't love—"

"I renewed...my promises...to Paul."

He stilled. She didn't feel him breathe for a long, endless minute. Then he sucked in a shuddering breath, released her, and stepped back, like she'd known he would. She tried to memorize his face to keep her company during the long, lonely years ahead. But his expression was set, as though in granite. His eyes were dark, pooling ponds of blue. He exhaled, staring at her, his gaze intent, as if he...as if...she didn't know what.

"Mercy, nein," he said quietly, almost desperately. His gaze roamed over her face again, as if to memorize her features.

She managed to nod. Her vision blurred as she looked down at his stocking-covered feet. They moved.

Away.

He slipped into his boots and grabbed his gear.

She didn't want him to go. She wanted to reach out for him, pull him back into her arms, and hold on tight. Forever.

She'd never have that right.

She would probably never see him again, unless he moved back to Shipshewana and they ran into each other in town.

A tear escaped and ran down her cheek. Followed by another.

"I wish you every happiness."

She barely heard his whisper through the tears that had backed up behind her eyes and flooded her ears.

The door shut behind him as he walked out of her life.

Chapter 27

*A*bner made the return trip to his brother's haus in a daze, numb to the cold air and his broken spirit. The chill had fully penetrated his heart until it seemed like brittle ice that would crack open at any minute. Somehow he took care of Savvy and the buggy, then stumbled up the porch stairs and into the kitchen.

He was in the middle of removing his boots when the floor creaked behind him. He turned, startled. Late as it was, he hadn't expected anyone to be up.

Mose came into the room and headed straight for the cupboard, turning his back to Abner as he reached for two mugs. "Want some warm milk? Might help you sleep."

"Nein, danki." Abner wanted to move toward the doorway leading to the other room. To the stairs. And to freedom—escaping Mose and any questions he might have. Abner removed his hat and scarf.

"It'll help you feel better, too. That, and a little talk."

Abner hesitated. What, did Mose have eyes in the back of his head? "I doubt there's anything that can help." He swiped his bare hands over his face, surprised that his tears hadn't frozen solid.

"Thought you were home awful quick."

He swallowed, painfully. His throat was raw from his efforts to hold back the tears. "Jah."

"Care to tell me about it?" Mose poured milk into a pan and set it on the stove.

Abner shrugged his coat off and hung it up. "Not really." There was nothing to say.

"She rejected you," Mose said bluntly. Tactlessly.

Accurately.

Abner sucked in a breath that went down to his lungs with almost a growl. He was surprised he managed to stand, to breathe, to live. Seemed a broken heart should be a fatal condition.

"Chose the other bu over you, ain't so?"

The words shot through him with arrow-sharp precision.

Abner's feet were wet, chilled from the snow. He'd walked out of Mercy's kitchen without taking the time to fully bundle up. He'd been terrified of completely losing control. Of wailing out his misery, begging her to reconsider.

As if crying like a boppli and then lecturing her would have helped. Nein, that would have merely cemented her decision. It would be impossible to change her mind.

Instead, he'd "manned up," squared his shoulders, forced a smile, and walked out. And recalled with bitterness the bishop's words about trusting....

Ach, Mercy.

What he should've done was follow Troy's example and elope. He should've made the decision for her and snatched her away from her duties before Paul could arrive. Should have galloped the horse to the courthouse and—

"Have a seat." Mose pulled out a chair and motioned to it. Not really giving him a choice.

Another situation where he'd have to man up. Otherwise, Mose would follow him to his room with the mug full of milk, nein doubt.

Abner wiped his cheeks again and dropped into the chair. "How is it you happen to be awake?"

Mose lifted a shoulder. "Sometimes, it's hard to sleep after the...well, I was thinking of my sohn. Noah. Today would've been his birthday. He'd be about your age now. Maybe going through the same things. Brokenhearted over losing his girl."

Abner looked down, his lips tightening. Not much he could say to that, except "I'm sorry."

"Der Herr knows best. We may not like it much, but He knows." He swirled the milk in the pan. "Want this warm, not hot. Think it's about there."

Abner didn't want it at all. Not the milk, not the company, not the platitudes.

If only he could go back to those moments with Mercy in his arms, squeezing him tight, her tears soaking his shirt. Maybe he could've said or done something. He could've aired Paul's dirty laundry...told her how he'd been unfaithful to her when they were courting. Warned her that it would probably happen again. He could've punched Paul. His fist clenched. Why did she have to hide behind Scriptures about obedience to parents when she could've just said she'd chosen Paul over him?

Now what he wanted was to go upstairs, pack his bags, call a driver, and head back to Montana. Hard work would help to ease his pain. But he'd promised Daed he'd kum home awhile, see the family, meet his new boppli brother, and—unfortunately—see the haus he'd so stupidly purchased for him and Mercy.

It was all he could do to keep from slamming his chair back and bolting out of the room. Instead, he swallowed. Hard.

"Faith is the substance…."

Nein. He didn't want to listen, not even to Gott.

"Be still, and know…."

His chest heaved as he struggled to catch his breath, to keep breathing, to keep a stoic demeanor.

Mose's hand landed on his shoulder. "Go ahead, sohn. Don't be ashamed to grieve."

Abner shook his head. But the tears, defiantly ignoring his will, ran a race down his cheeks. "I'm okay." *Right.* Like anyone would believe that choking lie. Especially when the evidence strongly suggested otherwise. Just like nobody had believed he was okay after his friends had been murdered.

"You will be okay. The sun will rise tomorrow. And you'll get up, put one foot in front of the other, and make it through. It may take days, weeks, months, but someday, the world will right itself, and you'll discover you survived. And that it actually made you stronger."

Mose sounded like the voice of experience.

"*Peace, be still….Peace I leave with you….*"

Peace….

Something inside his heart calmed as an overwhelming sense of peace flooded him.

Mose was right. Somehow, he would survive this. Just like he'd survived earlier hardships and traumas.

Tears still leaked out the corners of Abner's eyes, but he inhaled deeply, caught hold of Gott's merciful hand, and took the first step in dragging himself out of the black pit of despair.

✎〜◎

A hand landed on Mercy's shoulder, gently shaking her. She stiffened and stopped rocking herself, but she couldn't bring herself to look up.

"What happened?" Shanna lowered herself to the kitchen floor beside her. "You were going to tell him—ach, nein." The last two words weren't louder than a whisper. She wrapped her arms around Mercy's shoulders, hugging her near.

Mercy leaned into her. She'd thought her heart had broken when she'd gotten news of Paul's death. This was much worse. Her heart was beyond broken. It was shattered.

By her own doing.

She was vaguely aware of Shanna saying something. A handkerchief materialized in her hands, the softness a comfort against her painfully raw, tear-worn face.

Above her, Matthew said something, and Shanna answered back. The words floated over her, but they could've been spoken in a foreign language, for all she knew. They were just sounds.

The numbness was a comfort. Better than the horrific pain of losing the man she loved.

The next thing she knew, she was being scooped off the floor and carried upstairs. Shanna covered her with a quilt, tucked something warm inside the bedding, and extinguished the lantern.

When she awoke with the rooster's crow, her head pounded, and her throat hurt. *Lovely.* On top of everything else, she had to get sick. Or had she brought this upon herself by crying so hard?

She shuffled out of bed, shed her rumpled clothes from last nacht, and took off her kapp to redo her hair. Then she frowned. What did she have to get up for today?

Nothing. It wasn't a church Sunday.

She turned back to the bed and started to climb beneath the covers again, fully intending to stay there until—

The bedroom door suddenly opened several inches, and Shanna peeked in. When her gaze met Mercy's, she pushed the door open wider and entered. "Gut. You're up."

Right. Her reason for getting up was the woman who handed her a weekly paycheck.

Mercy's face burned as she grabbed a robe and shrugged into it. "Jah, I'm up." Did her voice sound as hoarse to Shanna as it did to her? She reached for a comb, then let down her hair and started brushing.

"What happened last nacht?"

"What about not interfering in matters of the heart?" Mercy cringed. When had she become so spiteful?

Shanna frowned. "Sorry. I'm just confused. I thought you were going to talk to him last nacht. And then...he left early, and you were crying, and I got the distinct impression you had refused him."

"Jah." Mercy dropped down onto the bed and bowed her head. The memory of the sadness on Abner's face when she'd rejected him broke her heart anew.

The mattress dipped as Shanna sat beside her and reached for the comb. "Turn a little."

Mercy shifted obediently, her back toward Shanna.

"Don't tell me you accepted Paul." She ran the comb the length of Mercy's hair.

"Jah." She whispered, but it still hurt her throat. She hugged herself. If only she could do it over. Undo it. Undo it all.

Shanna sighed. "Ach, Mercy. What would make you do a thing like that?"

"The Bible says I must obey my parents." Her voice hitched, and the tears boiled over again—as if she weren't already dehydrated enough.

"Jah. And you do. But there comes a time in your life when you are an adult and need to start making decisions on your own. Whom you marry and what you do with your life are two choices that are up to you."

"They'll be upset." Mercy sniffed. Could she really make this decision? Several of her friends had, but they didn't have Mamm and Daed as parents. She'd never stood up to them, with the exception of when she'd kum here instead of going to live with Aenti Clara. Hope began to surface.

"Maybe so. But they're not the ones who'll have to live with Paul. You are." Shanna started braiding Mercy's hair. "We'll leave your hair down in a long braid today. You can cover it with a bandana."

"Is that allowed?"

Shanna laughed. "Nein. But I'm all for relaxing the rules. And we aren't going anywhere—unless I can talk some sense into you and get you to go speak with Abner."

"I need to think."

"You should've thought before you refused him." Shanna stood. "Kum on. I left Matthew in charge of Serena and Levi. He's going to need breakfast, and then I'll tell you a story."

"A story?" Mercy stared at her. She didn't care to hear a story. Not when her life was in shambles.

"Jah, a story. About living dangerously, taking control, and letting Gott work it out."

❧

Abner packed his few belongings into a duffel bag, left it on the bed to pick up later, and went downstairs. Katie and Ruthie were preparing a cold breakfast. He walked past them, shoved his feet into his boots, and headed to the barn. He could help Mose and Abram with their chores one final time.

In the cow barn, he picked up the milk pail and the three-legged stool, then sat beside a cow, resting his head against the bovine's side.

Abram came in several moments later. "Ach, gut. You've started." He filled the water trough with fresh water. "Mose said you might be leaving early. What can I do to talk you into staying through Christmas? It's just a little more than a week away."

"She chose Paul." The three-word admission ripped through him.

Abram fell silent a moment. "You didn't kum here to see her, anyway. You came to see me and meet Katie. She was just a... diversion."

"I fell in love with that *diversion*."

"Jah. I'm sorry. I can't believe she chose Paul over you. Especially since you're far more handsome." Abram grinned.

Abner glanced up at his twin and nearly smiled as Abram pretended to preen. "You're incorrigible."

"So, you'll stay?"

Abner hesitated, watching the milk squirt into the pail. The cow's tail flicked as a cat came mewing between its legs. "Maybe." *If you can promise I won't have to see Paul.*

"You don't need to go out. And if Paul comes by with Micah, you can hide upstairs."

"I'm not going to hide." Not even if he had to sit on his hands to restrain himself from causing bodily harm to Paul if he so much as smirked. Or, worse, if he belittled Mercy.

"So, if Katie invites her over again…?"

Abner adjusted his hands and resumed milking the cow. "I'm not worried."

Katie wouldn't invite Mercy over. Not after they'd broken up. And if she did, and if Mercy actually came, then…well, to parrot an Englisch friend, *Eat your heart out, baby.*

Except that wouldn't work, because he really did love her. And he wanted her happy, even if she didn't choose him.

He thought about the chapter in 1 Corinthians that said that love "*beareth all things, believeth all things, hopeth all things, endureth all things.*"

Abram walked out of the barn.

Abner bowed his head and stared at the floor.

But the words didn't kum.

Just…peace.

Chapter 28

Mercy somehow managed to drag herself downstairs. Shanna assisted her with preparations for their morgen meal, a simple spread of leftover orange sweet rolls and some warmed oatmeal, until Levi woke up, screaming for his breakfast. "I have to feed the boppli."

Matthew came in from doing chores, took off his boots, and unbundled before he crossed the room. Without giving Mercy the customary "Gut morgen," he stopped at the sink to wash his hands and sent her a look she could decipher only as wary. As if he expected her to suddenly burst into uncontrollable tears at any moment. Which reminded her of the soft handkerchief that had been stuffed into her fist last nacht. Her face heated.

But he was right—she might cry. Moisture burned her eyes and caused her throat to constrict. Her lips were locked together. She couldn't have forced out a word if she tried. Even without a mirror, she could tell her eyes were puffy and swollen. Besides, it wasn't a gut morgen. But at least she was up. Functioning. Earning her keep.

Shanna's cell phone rang. She'd left it on the kitchen table. Matthew unhurriedly dried his hands, crossed the room, and picked it up. He glanced at the screen, then answered it. "Yoder. Matthew speaking."

Mercy arranged the sweet rolls on a platter, then carried it to the table in the ensuing silence.

As she walked back to the stove to retrieve the oatmeal, Matthew grunted. "Just a moment. I'll give the phone to Shanna." He left the room.

Muted conversation filtered out from the bedroom as Mercy poured orange juice into two big tumblers, for Matthew and Shanna, and a small sippy cup for Serena, though she'd probably wear most of it. Nein glass for Mercy. She wasn't thirsty. Or hungry.

206 Laura V. Hilton

She glanced at the wall calendar. The words *"God so loved"* stood out, as if mocking her.

Gott so loved. Right. Clearly, He'd excluded her.

Another Scripture she'd memorized came to mind. *"Trust in the* Lord *with all thine heart; and lean not unto thine own understanding. In all thy ways acknowledge him, and he shall direct thy paths."*

She pushed that thought away, too. What did der Herr care of her?

If You really love me, Gott, free me from my stupid mistakes.

She'd made her choice. She'd have to live with it. At least her family would be happy. Except for Joy—and herself.

As for her, maybe happiness was overrated. She'd loved Paul once. She could love him again. Though, comparing her feelings for Paul versus Abner, it seemed that with Paul, she was more in love with the idea than the man. After all, she'd been encouraged throughout her relationship with him. Suggestions had been planted that she truly loved him. She'd been led to believe it for so long, she'd accepted it as fact.

It wasn't. And yet, she'd renewed her promise to marry the man. What had she been thinking? Shanna was right—she should've thought more, prayed more, before making her decision. Should have sought out advice regarding the difference between obeying and honoring her parents and letting them make all her decisions for her.

From the back bedroom, Shanna squealed. Levi retaliated with a sharp wail. After a moment, he quieted.

A few minutes later, Matthew came back into the kitchen without the cell phone. He washed his hands again, poured himself a cup of koffee, and sat at the head of the table. "Gut morgen, Mercy."

Now he'd said it. She tried to find the words in return, but she couldn't. A nod was all she could manage.

"I'll go ahead and eat," he said. "I'm not sure how long Shanna will be, and…"—he glanced at the wall clock—"I need to get back to my chores. You can eat now or wait for Shanna. You choose." He bowed his head in silent prayer without waiting for an answer or acknowledgment.

Just as well. Because she was awful at making decisions.

Mercy went upstairs to wake Serena and change her diaper.

When she returned to the kitchen, Matthew had left, but Shanna was there

"I just had the most interesting phone call," Shanna said with a smile. "Let's pray, and then we'll talk while we eat."

"I'm not hungry." Mercy put Serena in her high chair and pushed it close to the table.

Shanna shrugged. "Okay. Fine. You can eat later." She sat at the table and bowed her head.

Mercy brought over Serena's breakfast, sat down next to the high chair, and bowed her head.

But she had nein words.

After the blatant command she'd issued to der Herr, what could she say? "Sorry"? She wasn't.

Not one bit.

❦

Abner pushed the button to disconnect the call, then slid his phone inside his pocket. Mamm had been ecstatic to hear that he planned to be home for Second Christmas. She'd said she wouldn't send the cookies she'd made, or his gifts. Too bad, really. He wished she would send them via priority mail, especially since he'd eaten every single crumb in his tin from Mercy. Both Katie and Ruthie practically stood guard over the cookie jar in the kitchen.

Keeping sweets from a rejected man should be against the Ordnung. If he ever became bishop and had any say in the rules, that was one thing that he would change. For sure.

Though he might be hard-pressed to find scriptural support for his decision.

Speaking of Scripture, someone needed to find a verse that proved Mercy had to marry Paul. With a growl, Abner headed inside, eyeing the elusive cookie jar and its two guardians before washing up and dropping into his chair. He should get a cookie as reward for self-control.

His phone rang, the tone a classical song that he recognized as the tune of a praise and worship song from the times he'd participated in a non-Amish church service. "Joyful, Joyful, We Adore Thee." If anyone heard his fancy ringtone, he'd probably get a lecture, even though he wasn't yet a church member. If he wasn't getting married, he might as well put off joining. He still believed, but he didn't want the shackles unless he had need of them. For now, he could remain as he was. Free to kum and go. Free to worship as he pleased.

Free to eat cookies.

He stood and glared at Ruthie, not that she noticed. Her gaze focused on his hand slipping into the pocket of his jeans to retrieve his phone as it continued playing.

"I'd thank you to turn that off in my haus," she scolded him. "Fancy music like that…."

He ignored her, glanced at the phone, and headed outside as he answered. "Abner."

"Matthew Yoder here. Shanna asked me to call you. Turns out Paul didn't lie. He did check into a homeless shelter in Milwaukee, Wisconsin, under the name David Smith. He was there almost every nacht for a month, then he left."

So, Paul had told the truth. He had lost his memory. Not exactly comforting. Abner closed the door behind him.

"He spoke Englisch," Matthew said quietly.

Abner stilled. That meant Paul hadn't been completely truthful. That there *was* more to the story. And if Paul had left the shelter after a month, why had it taken him a year to show up in Shipshewana? Paul had told the truth but had omitted vital parts.

"The woman at the shelter told Shanna he left after a month and never returned. She didn't know where he went. But she gave us the name of a person he'd listed as an emergency contact: Joy Lapp. Mercy's younger sister."

Chapter 29

Mercy sat in silence as Shanna talked about the phone call she'd received earlier. Mercy didn't know what to say. What to think.

All she knew was that her sister Joy had known that Paul was alive. Had kept it from Mercy and let her mourn. Let her believe Paul had died. Why would she do such a thing? And what about Paul's parents? Everyone in the community had believed Paul was dead.

Why hadn't he contacted her? He'd been her beau—her *fiancé*—ain't so? Why had he told her sister instead? And, more important, why hadn't her sister relayed the message to Mercy?

Maybe that explained why Joy had left home a month after Paul had supposedly died, and taken a job—supposedly—as caregiver to an older woman in Wisconsin. Had Paul visited her there?

As closely interlaced as all Amish communities were, why hadn't anyone found out and notified Mercy?

"Since you aren't comfortable using the phone, I called the number provided for Joy and left a message for her to call me," Shanna said. "The shelter woman ended up with this Wisconsin number after first calling the Indiana number and receiving a more local one from Joy's parents—I mean, your parents."

Mercy's mind struggled to process this. Then she turned and looked at Shanna. "What does this mean?" she croaked.

As if she didn't know. What she saw was long-term unfaithfulness. And betrayal. She'd been stupid to believe him, and she'd made an even stupider mistake by agreeing to marry him. Was Gott saving her from her mistakes by showing her the truth now? She glanced at the wall calendar. "*God so loved….*" Maybe He did include her, after all.

"I have my suspicions." Shanna lifted her koffee cup and took a sip. "You can hear my speculations, if you want, or you can wait until Joy returns my call and get the truth from her. She may not call, if she thinks she's been discovered. The point is, Paul hasn't been honest. At least one person in your family knew he was alive, and this…affair…situation…deception has been kept from you."

The phone buzzed. Shanna glanced at it and smiled. She picked it up and pushed a button. "Shanna Yoder speaking…. Ach, jah, Joy. Gut of you to return my call. Just a second, please." She glanced at Mercy. "Do you want the honors, or shall I?"

Mercy reached for the phone.

Shanna handed it to her. "It's on. Talk."

Mercy pulled in a breath. "Joy, this is Mercy. What's going on with you and Paul?"

"Gut to hear from you, too, Mercy. How are you?" Sarcasm laced Joy's voice. *Typical.* Ever since they were teens, Joy had been spiteful toward her. Make that, ever since Paul had started coming around.

She'd been so blind.

Maybe she *had* been a little blunt. But she wanted answers, and casual phone conversations were discouraged. She tried to find the words to backtrack without backing down. She opened her mouth and shut it—twice.

"You don't sound so gut. Got the flu?" Joy asked. There was a hint of concern in her tone, as if maybe she cared a little.

Mercy coughed. "I feel ill, but not with the flu."

"To answer your question, Paul has been courting me on the sly for years. Ever wonder why he ended your outings so early? I'm his real sweetheart. But I wasn't old enough, and his parents said he had to marry you if he wanted the farm. So he disappeared and contacted me, and I joined him. But now he wants to settle down. He wants the farm. It's tied with strings to you, but he swears he'll always love me. You're just a means to an end." She sounded a little sad, as if she'd disappointed herself…or was disappointed in Paul.

Mercy stared, openmouthed, at Shanna. There was the answer to the blatant gauntlet she'd thrown down before der Herr. *Danki, Gott, for loving me. For helping me see the truth.*

"Has Paul abandoned you, too?" she asked her sister. The questions continued in rapid-fire succession. "Were you living together after you joined him? Did you lie about being a caregiver? Will you continue your affair?" Joy was still in Wisconsin…. "Do Mamm and Daed know?" She realized she shouldn't make so many assumptions, but she couldn't help herself.

Joy pulled in a sob that echoed through the phone. "We were living as the Englisch. He left me. He said...he said he'd be back. Often. But I can't bear the idea of him and you. You needed to know, Mercy."

Jah, but who would have told her? And when?

"I'm so very sorry." The words ended with a wail.

Mercy's heart broke for her sister. "Ach, I'm sorry." Sorry for Joy, but not for herself. Overwhelming relief washed over her. Her parents wouldn't want her to marry Paul now, so she could still honor them while choosing Abner. If it wasn't too late.

But why was Paul's inheritance of the farm contingent on marriage to her? As the only sohn, Paul should be the one to get it nein matter what. Or was it because they saw him making foolish mistakes and wanted him married and settled? In that case, as far as Mercy knew, one Lapp dochter would do as well as the other. And if he loved Joy....

Tears burned Mercy's eyes. She'd been such a fool. Why hadn't she seen it years ago? Joy had always disappeared after Paul had left for the evening. Mercy had figured she'd gone to bed early or had left to visit her best friend, who lived next door. But now, in hindsight....

"*I wish you every happiness.*" Abner had said those exact words to her before he'd walked out last nacht. She handed the phone to Shanna.

Shanna brought the device to her ear and started talking to Joy, who would undoubtedly repeat the conversation if Shanna were to prod. Knowing Shanna, she would get the whole story—and more.

Numb, Mercy wiped Serena's hands and face, lifted her from the high chair, and set her on the floor.

Paul and Joy. Who knew? She'd been lied to all this time. Her grief, her loss, all a lie. The past year wasted grieving for a boy who'd never loved her. And Abner....

She needed to write Paul a letter, ending the relationship. Permanently.

And then find Abner.

She hoped it wasn't too late.

Abner struggled to wrap his mind around the news. Mercy's own sister had known that Paul was alive? He watched from the porch as Mose walked out of the buggy barn, carrying a plastic bag. The head of a white teddy bear poked out of the top of the sack.

Abner smiled as the man approached. He had purchased the bear for Mercy on Friday. He'd also purchased the plaque that had almost brought him to his knees.

"Be still, and know that I am God."

He accepted the bag Mose handed him, muted the ringtone on his cell phone so it wouldn't offend Ruthie, then slipped it into his pocket.

What now? He couldn't go to Mercy claiming Paul had lied. He had nein proof of it, only what Matthew had told him. Hearsay.

It was probably best to wait and see what happened next.

Even if Mercy still planned to marry Paul, they'd have to wait until November, after the harvest, and after they'd completed baptism classes. Neither one of them had joined the church. Still almost a year. Just over ten months, to be exact. A lot could happen in that time.

He could be patient.

"Buying yourself stuffed toys, bu?" Mose teased.

Abner glanced at the teddy bear and grinned. "It would appear so, jah."

"And gourmet chocolates, too, I see." Mose gestured at the bag.

His smile widened. He'd forgotten about the box of candy he'd bought for Mercy at the grocery store. He wouldn't be deprived of sweets, after all. "Jah. Chocolate, too." He winked at Mose and turned toward the haus.

"You had a phone call."

Abner paused, his hand on the door handle. Had he nein privacy? Did Mose need to know everything? But the fatherly concern somehow comforted him, in spite of his annoyance. "Jah. It was Matthew Yoder."

Silence. But not the type that meant he had nothing to say. It was an expectant type, inviting Abner to fill in the blanks.

He sighed, turned to Mose, and told him the gist of the message.

"So, what are you going to do?"

Abner shrugged. "I'm leaning toward waiting."

Mose nodded. "Wise. Still leaving?"

"Jah. Early morgen on Second Christmas. I called the bus station for departure times after I finished milking the cows."

"We'll miss you around these parts. Your folks did a fine job with both you and your twin."

"Danki. I'll tell them you said so." Abner shifted the plastic bag. "I'd better put these things in my room."

Mose glanced over his shoulder toward the barn, then nodded at the bag. "Might have a box that would fit them, if you want to deliver a surprise gift to...a certain someone."

Abner considered the idea. Mose had wise advice. But he shook his head. "Nein. Right now, I'm just going to wait."

At least until he had clear direction to do otherwise.

❧

"You need to tell Abner. Now." Shanna reached for her cell phone. "I have his number."

Now? "Nein. I can't. I'll tell him when it's official. After I tell Paul. I need to write him a letter."

Besides, she didn't know what to say to Abner. "I broke up with Paul, and I want you back"? What made her think he'd still want her? But then, he'd said he loved her. Said that they'd survive this. They'd prayed together.

Shanna frowned and set the phone on the table. "It's better to tell Paul in person, but Kristi is supposed to kum by today for a post-birth checkup, and I don't have time to take you to the Grabers'. Really can't give directions, either. Roads are unmarked in some parts, and it gets confusing, especially if you're new to the area. I guess you should write a letter."

Shanna walked to the hutch, opened a drawer, and retrieved a notebook. She set it and a blue ink pen in front of Mercy.

"Danki." Mercy picked up the pen, frowned at it, then closed her eyes. *Gott, I don't know what to say. Except that we're over.*

And maybe that was where she should start.

Paul,

> *I talked with Joy. Found out the truth about your relationship with her—and with me. With that in mind, I release you from your promises to me, so you are free to marry the girl you love.*

And she was free to marry the man she loved. She smiled.

> *I wish you the best.*

> *Mercy Lapp*

214 Laura V. Hilton

She folded the letter and put it in the envelope as Shanna returned.

She set a slip of paper down in front of Mercy. "Here's the Grabers' address and a stamp."

"Danki, Shanna." Mercy sealed the letter and carried it through the falling snow to the mailbox, even though it wouldn't be picked up until tomorrow. Hadn't Natalie said it rarely snowed in southern Missouri? But the snow made her feel less homesick. It seemed more like Christmas.

She slipped the letter into the mailbox, put up the flag, and shut the door. Then she turned back toward the haus.

Shanna greeted her at the kitchen door, all smiles. "Matthew and I are going to dinner at my parents' haus tomorrow nacht. We're joining them for the Christmas program at the school. My youngest sister is reciting a poem she wrote. And Katie has invited you to join her family for dinner. We'll call a driver to take you."

Mercy blinked. "She did?" There was a burst of hope, but as Shanna grinned, Mercy remembered the results of Shanna's previous matchmaking attempts. She reined in her excitement. "You mean, you invited me to join them." *Oops.* That had bordered on disrespectful.

Shanna's eyes widened. "Me? Never. She called and told me that Abner bought a bus ticket north. He's leaving on Second Christmas. Mose told them about Joy's phone call."

Abner knew?

Mercy glanced toward the road, half hoping to see his horse and buggy coming in their direction. Maybe she wouldn't have to make the first move, after all.

"Nein, wait," Shanna said. "I mean, about the shelter's call. Joy hadn't called when Matthew left."

Mercy slumped. He didn't know, then. Or he knew just some of the story. Whatever Matthew had chosen to say. Or maybe Shanna told Katie about the phone conversation with Joy. So maybe Abner did know—or at least was finding out right now.

"Tomorrow nacht?" That felt like forever.

Shanna shrugged. "It takes less than a day for letters to travel from one haus to another in this area. Paul will get your message tomorrow, jah? If he's marrying you to inherit his daed's farm, then he'll kum here tomorrow evening and try to talk sense into you."

Mercy stared at her. He would. And he'd manage to manipulate her again, using the purple octopus, as he always did when he tried to get his way. She frowned.

"This way, you won't be home," Shanna reminded her. "You'll be with Abner. And, hopefully, Paul will have given up long before Abner brings you home."

It made sense.

Mercy studied the red candles encircled with pine boughs on the kitchen table. Christmas would be here in a week. And she still needed a gift for Abner. Something practical, yet something that conveyed her love.

She didn't have a clue what it might be.

Other than herself. And maybe a tinful of cookies for his sweet tooth.

A car pulled into the circle drive and parked.

Abner?

Nein. The man who climbed out of the backseat looked like Abner, but he was bearded.

Abram Hilty.

Chapter 30

Katie and Ruthie's whispered conversation ceased as soon as Abner walked into the kitchen on Monday morgen, and it resumed just as he left. Mose avoided him, or at least appeared to. Every time Abner entered an area where Mose worked, he walked out. Even Abram had disappeared. Abner hunted every inch of the farm for his twin, but he couldn't be found. The horses and buggies were there. None missing.

It was almost as if Abner were being shunned.

Was having a fancy ringtone a serious enough offense to cause the family to disassociate with him? Or was it something else? Maybe he shouldn't have agreed to stay longer.

With a sigh, Abner strode into the kitchen again. Conversation ceased, as before, but both Ruthie and Katie were hard at work, baking up a storm in preparation for Christmas. Cookies cooled on a wire rack, pies were lined up on the counter, cakes sat ready to be frosted, and a ham waited to be placed in the oven. The room smelled like heaven. His stomach rumbled. He eyed the two women, who appeared to be ignoring him, so he reached for a cookie.

A wooden spoon slapped down on his wrist with stinging force. "Ow. Ruthie, you're cruel." He returned the cookie. "Just one?"

"Nein. Now, scat."

Women. "Where's Abram?"

Katie and Ruthie exchanged glances. Then Ruthie shrugged. "Somewhere around. Perhaps he went to visit a neighbor."

Abner hitched a brow and fixed a stare on his sister-in-law. Katie met his gaze and blushed. She bit her lip and looked away.

Aha. The whole family had something up their sleeves that they were keeping from him.

And, based on Katie's blush, it was a gut thing, not a shunning over his ringtone.

He grinned, grabbed a cookie faster than Ruthie could deliver another blow, and walked out.

A Christmas surprise. He loved it.

It couldn't be more perfect, unless....

His smile widened.

⟨∽⟩

Mercy opened the door to let Abram in. He stomped the snow off his boots on the porch, then stepped inside.

"Would you like some koffee?" Shanna asked, moving to the stove.

Abram shook his head. "Nein, danki. Sounds gut, but I can't stay long. The driver's waiting. I just came to talk to Mercy for a minute." He shut the door and stood there, surveying her. He looked so much like Abner—or how he would look as a married man—it made her heart hurt.

Mercy furrowed her brow. "Talk to me? What about?"

"Abner. Paul. What are you going to do? You broke up with Abner to marry Paul. Mose, my father-in-law, told me about the recent phone call."

"I wrote Paul a letter...breaking things off."

Abram frowned. "Gut. But not gut enough. You need to talk to him in person and make sure he gets the message."

Mercy shifted and looked away. She'd hurt Abner so needlessly. "I...I can't. Shanna has a...an appointment, and she can't miss it. She couldn't give me directions to Micah's haus."

Abram glanced at Shanna, then returned his gaze to Mercy. He tugged at his beard. "And Abner. Did you break up?"

"Jah. But I want to un-break up, if he'll have me. I...I love him." Her voice cracked.

"I'll take you to Paul now, if it's okay." He looked at Shanna again.

Mercy bit her lip, not sure if she had the strength to face Paul. To stand up to his manipulation.

Shanna nodded. "I'll be fine. Besides, Kristi will be here, and she'll probably stay for lunch. And in a car.... You'll be back before then."

"But what about all the work we need to do?" Mercy asked.

Shanna shrugged. "Laundry will wait. And we're celebrating Christmas at my brother's next week, so all we need to bring are a couple pies. We can make them later." She grinned. "Go. And give him what for."

Mercy blinked. "What?"

Abram opened the door. "She means, let him have it. If you're worthy of Abner, you'll need to. Bundle up, and let's go."

Mercy pulled in a deep breath, mustering her courage. She put on her coat, as well as the black bonnet, and tugged on her boots. She and Abram climbed into the car, and then, long before she was mentally prepared, the driver parked the car outside the Grabers' haus.

"I'll be with you for emotional support, but you need to do the talking," Abram said as he opened the car door.

Paul stepped out on the porch as Mercy came around the outside of the car. He looked from her to Abram. "What brings you by?"

Abram glanced at her. The glint in his eye nudged her forward.

Mercy swallowed hard and tried to dredge up every bit of courage she owned. "I know about Joy. I know why you want to marry me. I want to be released."

Paul's lips curled. "I don't think so. Kum on, Mercy. We've been together forever. Joy is your kid sister. Stop being foolish. You need to quit letting that fuzzy purple one-eyed octopus control your remaining brain cells."

Abram hitched a brow. Mercy watched his hand slowly curve into a fist. Just like Abner's had.

Mercy garnered courage from his movements. "Don't talk to me like that, Paul. The octopus has nothing to do with my intelligence level. My fiancé went missing and was presumed dead for twelve months. Spent one month at a homeless shelter. How many months did he spend with my sister? Even a one-eyed purple octopus knows the answer is eleven…and that's eleven too many for this future bride to accept. We. Are. Finished. I don't know why your daed said you had to marry me to get the farm, but whatever the reason, I don't care. Joy will work just as well. Or some other girl. You can marry whom you choose. And so can I."

Abram's eyes widened, and he stared at her. "Bravo!"

Mercy turned away and headed back around the car.

"Kum on, Mercy," Paul pleaded. "Don't be stupid. You can't throw away what we have."

Breathing a silent prayer for help, Mercy turned and started toward Paul.

"That's my girl." He aimed a smirk at Abram.

Mercy looked him in the eye. "Nein? You didn't have any trouble throwing away what we had when you pretended to drown, pretended to lose your memory, and then spent time with Joy—for as long as you 'courted' me. You're a deceitful liar, and I'm finished."

Abram followed her around the car and opened the door for her. She slid in.

"Mercy." Paul came down the porch steps. "Please. I have to marry you. Daed says you're the...the...." He pulled in a ragged breath. "He told me you're the best of the bunch. That I'd be a fool to let you go. I can't let him down again."

Paul's daed had said that? Really? She couldn't keep from smiling.

"You aren't letting me go, Paul. I'm letting *you* go."

Abram shut the car door, said a few quiet words to Paul that she couldn't fully hear, then climbed in beside her.

As the driver pulled away, Abram leaned over. "That was pretty impressive."

Mercy pulled her coat over her face as the dam of stress ruptured and she burst into tears.

∬∿∬

The rest of the afternoon passed in quiet busyness. Abram said nothing to Abner about his disappearance. And the whispering and unwarranted almost-shunning continued. But it seemed as if his family was afraid to talk to him, lest they spoil the surprise.

And Abner was beginning to get excited, coming up with all kinds of possible scenarios in his head. All of them involving Mercy.

"Are you going to a school program to-nacht?" he asked Ruthie as she and Katie started dinner. If he were free from family obligations, maybe he would take the gifts over to Mercy after supper.

Ruthie gave him a startled look. "We planned to, but we've nein family with kinner in school, so, well, to-nacht promises to be more...uh...well.... Nein. We're not."

So close to spilling their secrets.

Ah, well. He'd try again later. He went upstairs to his room and retrieved the teddy bear and the yet-unopened box of chocolates. Maybe he'd make a mid-nacht run, instead, and leave the gifts for Mercy on the Yoders' front porch. Mose was right—she'd been under so much stress, she'd need a furry friend to cuddle, nein matter which man she chose.

He stepped off the porch as a vehicle turned into the drive. He paused, watching it approach. It stopped in front of him.

And there, in the backseat....

He caught his breath and pulled the bear closer to his side.

Mercy.

Chapter 31

*H*er heart in her throat, Mercy opened the door and slid out of the car. She bunched her coat in her fists, scared to look at Abner. Her heart pounded.

He just stood there.

Silent.

Finally, she dared to peek up at his face. At his smile that reached his eyes. She opened her mouth to apologize, but the words froze on her lips. She'd never seen a man clutching a teddy bear to his heart while holding a candy box in his other hand. She stared at him, speechless. Dare she hope…?

"Ach, Mercy." Her name came out as a breath. "They're for you. Merry Christmas." He stepped forward, pressed the bear and the candy into her arms, and shut the car door. Then he reached into his pocket and pulled out his wallet.

The driver shook her head. "I've already been paid. Merry Christmas."

"Merry Christmas." He pocketed his wallet, then retrieved the gifts and set them on the porch. He reached for Mercy's hand and tugged her across the yard and into the shadowy interior of the barn as the car disappeared.

Inside her, excitement warred with worry. Did he want privacy for makeup kisses or for a complete, final breakup? "I'm so sorry," she said.

"Nein, Mercy. Just tell me. Are you and—"

"I broke up with him. Abram went with me, and—"

"That's all I need to know." He cupped her cheeks in his hands, and his blue eyes looked deep into hers. "Marry me, Mercy. Ich liebe dich. Forever."

Danki, Gott, for directing me to Missouri and to Abner….

"Jah." She let the answer out on a breath of air, wrapping her arms around his neck.

He started to lean nearer, then hesitated.

"Do you want to marry—as Amish—in Shipshewana this fall?"

She closed her eyes, trying to imagine living alone next to his parents for eleven more months, without Abner, then standing before their families—maybe even Joy and Paul. That would be so awkward. *Gott, what should I do? Is what I want right?*

After a moment, she nodded.

"Then I'll marry you in November," he said quietly. She detected disappointment in his voice.

She didn't want to hurt him again. And, really, what she wanted wasn't to wait. "I want to go with you to Montana." She opened her eyes and looked at him.

He grinned. "Wunderbaar. I planned to leave on Second Christmas for a visit home, but I could stay here a few days longer. We could go to the courthouse." His gaze searched hers. "Ich liebe dich, Mercy. Whatever you want to do. Wait and marry, as Amish, or marry now, beforehand, and face the consequences of elopement together."

She pressed herself nearer to him. "I want to marry now." She'd never been surer of anything.

He slid one arm around her lower back and held her tight against him. The other hand cupped the back of her neck.

"Danki, Gott, for Mercy," he whispered against her lips before his mouth completely claimed hers.

Her arms went around his neck as she wholeheartedly agreed. *Danki, Gott, for Your mercy.*

$\mathcal{D}$ear reader,

I hope you enjoyed the story of Mercy and Abner. Some of the other couples featured in this book were the protagonists of past stories of mine. The courtship of Becky and Jacob Miller is featured in *Patchwork Dreams*, book one in the series The Amish of Seymour. The story of Shanna and Matthew Yoder is told in *A Harvest of Hearts*, book two in the series The Amish of Seymour. And you can read the story of Katie and Abram Hilty in *Awakened Love*, book three in the series The Amish of Webster County.

As always, thank you for joining me on this journey. I hope you'll follow me to Jamesport, Mississippi, for my next series, The Amish of Jamesport, opening with *The Snow Globe* (releasing in November 2015).

Remember, every Amish community is unique. Webster County, Missouri, comprises many different Amish communities, and most are very strict in their Ordnung. The districts featured in my books are fictitious and naturally differ from the actual districts there.

Again, thank you, and to God be the glory.

May you have a blessed Christmas as you worship Him.

—*Laura V. Hilton*

[from chapter 22]

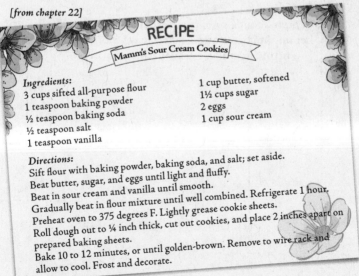

RECIPE

Mamm's Sour Cream Cookies

Ingredients:
3 cups sifted all-purpose flour
1 teaspoon baking powder
½ teaspoon baking soda
½ teaspoon salt
1 teaspoon vanilla
1 cup butter, softened
1½ cups sugar
2 eggs
1 cup sour cream

Directions:
Sift flour with baking powder, baking soda, and salt; set aside.
Beat butter, sugar, and eggs until light and fluffy.
Beat in sour cream and vanilla until smooth.
Gradually beat in flour mixture until well combined. Refrigerate 1 hour.
Preheat oven to 375 degrees F. Lightly grease cookie sheets.
Roll dough out to ¼ inch thick, cut out cookies, and place 2 inches apart on prepared baking sheets.
Bake 10 to 12 minutes, or until golden-brown. Remove to wire rack and allow to cool. Frost and decorate.

About the Author

A member of the American Christian Fiction Writers, Laura V. Hilton is a professional book reviewer for the Christian market, with more than a thousand reviews published on the Web.

Her first series with Whitaker House, The Amish of Seymour, comprises *Patchwork Dreams*, *A Harvest of Hearts*, and *Promised to Another*. In 2012, *A Harvest of Hearts* received a Laurel Award, placing first in the Amish Genre Clash of the Titles. Her latest series, The Amish of Webster County, includes *Healing Love*, *Surrendered Love*, and *Awakened Love*.

Previously, Laura published two novels with Treble Heart Books, *Hot Chocolate* and *Shadows of the Past*, as well as several devotionals. Laura and her husband, Steve, have five children, whom Laura homeschools. The family makes their home in Arkansas.

To learn more about Laura, read her reviews, and find out about her upcoming releases, readers may visit her blog at http://lighthouse-academy.blogspot.com/.